TANGLED
MARK

BECKY HARMON

Bella
BOOKS

2016

Dedication

For Sheri.
Thanks for being my example.

About the Author

Becky Harmon was born and raised just south of the Mason-Dixon Line. Though she considers herself to be a Northerner, she moved south in search of warmth. Becky calls many places home, but she is happiest with her partner, their daughter and the rest of their four-legged family. She can be contacted at beckyharmon2015@yahoo.com.

Acknowledgments

To my mom. My first reader and always my biggest supporter, no matter the endeavor.

To all of the wonderful authors who have paved the road in front of me. Your dedication and sacrifice has brought me many hours of enjoyment.

To Linda and Jessica Hill, thank you for helping Bella Books flourish and continue to grow. And for welcoming me into the family.

To my editor, Medora, thank you for turning my story into a real book.

To Judy Fellows, thank you for creating a cover that gives life to the Flagler building.

To the readers, thank you for taking a chance. I hope you enjoy it. I did my best to keep things real but it is fiction and I did take some liberties to make the book more enjoyable. I apologize for any errors.

CHAPTER ONE

"You have a go, Sierra One."

Nikki took a deep breath before responding into the headset microphone that rested along her cheek. "Roger," she said softly. Without moving the rest of her body, she switched the rifle's safety off with her thumb. Slowing her breathing, she made a final check on the wind direction before gently pulling the trigger. The rifle gave a small kick as her target exploded. Flipping the switch back to safe, Nikki silently rolled over and moved to a sitting position.

She had barely found her feet before she heard Mission Control say the words she hoped to never hear during a mission. "Your position has been compromised, Sierra One." She cradled the rifle to her chest and began running in the direction of her team. There wasn't time to wait on Brad to secure her weapon. She listened to multiple voices in her headset as the team ran through its evacuation protocol.

"Move, move, move," Brad demanded as she searched the trees in front of her, willing him to appear. "Come on, Nikki. Get here. Now."

A flash of light to her right warned her of the upcoming explosion and she veered to the left, trying to avoid it. The impact pushed her forward and she struggled to remain standing. Her legs worked quickly to find their rhythm again. When she could no longer feel the heat from the fire on her back, she slowed to a steady jog and smiled. She was going to have a talk with Josh when she returned to base. She was sure he was responsible for the location of that explosion. She was thankful there was enough of the morning sun showing in the sky to keep her vision from being hindered by the burst of light.

"It's about time." Brad fell into step alongside her, unzipping the rifle case in his arms.

"It's not like I was out for a stroll." She passed her rifle to him, and he secured it before swinging the carrying strap across his shoulders.

There was a lot of things Nikki liked about Brad, but this was one of the best sides of him. Brad didn't carry her weapon to be chivalrous. He carried it because it made sense. His six-foot-two frame could handle the four-foot-long rifle better than hers could, especially on the run. For her and Brad, efficiency was not something they debated.

He bumped her shoulder. "That explosion looked really close to you."

"It was."

Brad laughed, but before he could comment a burst of heat and fire blocked their path. "Well, shit!" he exclaimed. "Let's pick up the pace." He took off through the trees and around the fire.

Nikki ducked her head, using her arms to protect her face as they skirted the flames. Clearing the heat, she watched Brad check their direction on his GPS wristband. When it came to directions outside of urban terrain, Brad was a genius. Nikki knew if their GPS should fail, Brad was equally efficient with a map and compass. She would follow him anywhere. She'd had several partners since she first joined Flagler Security, but she and Brad had been inseparable for the last five years. She considered him the brother she never had.

"Big jump coming up," Brad called over his shoulder.

Nikki watched him take a flying leap, bending his knees to take the impact of his landing. She lost sight of him when she launched herself over the ledge behind him. She pulled her legs in close to her chest, allowing her body to roll when her feet met the ground. Thankful there wasn't a tree in her path, she let the momentum from her jump carry her back to her feet as she cursed Brad under her breath. The fifty-pound pack they each carried on their backs didn't seem to faze him, but on her 160-pound frame, it was unbalancing. She tightened the straps on the pack and grasped her P90 with both hands. One of the advantages to the personal defense weapon everyone on the team carried was its hands-free capability. Nikki could clip it to any piece of equipment and let it dangle until she needed it again.

"ETA." The gravelly voice of Tyler, their team leader, sounded in her ear.

"Not more than ten," Brad responded.

Nikki sighed and wiped the sweat from her face. Based on the information Brad had relayed, they must have a little over a mile left to cover. It appeared they were past the explosions, but Nikki still watched the tree line closely. After a while, she allowed the sound of their boots on the damp earth to soothe her and she replayed the mission. This was only a practice run. When they returned to base, Josh would give them their final briefing and then they would catch their flight. Practice would be over.

CHAPTER TWO

Forty-eight hours later

Nikki fought the urge to lift her head from the scope of her rifle. She listened to the nocturnal sounds of the forest surrounding her, checking them all off as normal. The gruff grunts and hoots of night monkeys broke the silence repeatedly as they defended their territory from her and Brad. Nearly thirty minutes had passed since Brad had finished his reconnaissance on the villagers and moved out of her line of sight. She calculated the distance to the village below as barely within the effective one-mile range of her M82 sniper rifle. It shouldn't take Brad longer than twenty minutes to cover that distance, but she knew he would avoid a direct path back to their position. She listened for any sound identifying his return.

Nikki flexed her muscles to keep the circulation moving throughout her body. The seasons south of the equator were the reverse of those in Florida, so it was summer here. But now, in the early hours before daybreak, the ground was cold and hard beneath her body, and there was a pebble under her stomach that sometime in the last hour had morphed into a boulder. Taking a deep breath, she blinked her eyes several times, shifting her cheek against the cold steel of the rifle. She peered through the thermal imaging scope mounted on it and scanned the valley below, returning to rest on a group of people gathered around a campfire on the eastern edge of the village. A quick count confirmed that no one had moved out of her line of sight in the few seconds her eyes had been off them.

The display inside her scope was set to Zulu time, the universal basis for all time zones. Flagler preferred this for reports and operational briefings to avoid confusion. After years of working within multiple time zones, Nikki could quickly make the conversion from civilian time, the twenty-four-hour military time or Zulu time with barely a second thought. She mentally calculated local time. Argentina was three hours behind Zulu time and she knew from the mission briefing, sunrise was barely three hours away. She hoped instructions would come through soon so she and Brad would be able to complete this mission under the cover of darkness.

Listening intently, she heard a soft crunch of leaves and gave an involuntary shiver at what could be moving in the darkness around her. She again fought the urge to pull her eye away from the scope, not wanting to lose a visual on the target area until Brad returned. There was another rustle of leaves, and she heard Brad's voice whisper softly through the trees, "Hot dog." She smiled, resisting the urge to shake her head. Brad took great pleasure in creating the passwords they would use on each mission. On this mission it was all about hot dogs and their condiments.

Nikki relaxed slightly as she felt Brad slowly lower himself onto the ground beside her.

"I count fifteen people in the village," he said softly. "All men. No women. Houses are empty and everyone is around the fire. I sent a secure text to Josh before I started back." He shifted his position, trying to find a comfortable spot before continuing. "I'm back on the team frequency. Any word from Mission Control yet?"

"Nothing," she whispered. She couldn't help wondering if instructions from Josh would make things any clearer. "So we continue with the initial mission directive."

"Watch the village and stand by for fire support." Brad sighed. "Yeah, I got that part."

Nikki could hear the usual frustration at lack of information in his voice. "Don't forget to say 'only if needed.' Fire support only..." she paused for dramatic effect "...if needed."

"Right. Clear and concise, as usual."

Nikki knew he was smiling now. She liked to lighten his mood. She knew she was better at the follow-instructions-without-question attitude that Flagler expected. Missions were operated on a need-to-know basis and she understood that she didn't need to know. Josh would consolidate incoming information from all sources and send them new data when necessary. Brad wanted more details and instructions faster. He would wait with the rest of team, of course, just not very patiently.

Brad softly broke the silence. "The buzz I heard before we left was that it was political."

"They don't look very political to me."

"Political or not, they're having one hell of a party." Brad shifted his position again. "I wonder if they do this every night or if it's a special occasion."

"So all of the houses were empty?" Nikki confirmed.

"Yep, everyone is around the fire."

"No nonparticipants already in bed?"

"A complete village party."

"Well, all right then." Nikki sighed. "Settle in. I have visual."

Several hours passed as Nikki watched the sky through the trees as it lightened with the coming of the new day. Brad lay beside her with his spotter scope and they watched the villagers below pass the bottle. The details given during their flight didn't elaborate on the identities of the villagers. Based on their appearance and the lack of women, Nikki assumed this was a farming camp. They had been told the area was sparsely populated and lacked roads capable of being traveled during the wet season. Which told her farming was the main occupation and that their families probably didn't live nearby. Though this was the wet season and they had packed for rain, it looked like they might make it out before it came. The majority of individuals around the fire appeared to have passed out, but a handful were still talking and drinking. She couldn't imagine that this behavior was a nightly ritual. Even fraternity boys couldn't drink all night and function properly the next day. It did seem odd to her that no one was returning to his residence but instead choosing a spot to sleep around the fire. To her the night seemed chilly so maybe they preferred the warmth of the fire to the huts with open windows.

Nikki didn't like to think she was targeting farmers with her rifle. Over the years, she had learned to compartmentalize the more difficult issues of her job. She trusted Flagler and the integrity of their directives for each mission. If they told her to fire, then she obeyed. Her training officer had taught her early on that hesitation could get her and her team killed. She wondered if additional instructions would follow today or if they would only be told to return, as they had on the last couple of missions. Reconnaissance and nothing more. The missions seemed insignificant to her, but apparently the information they were gathering was important.

She and Brad were considered veterans and usually worked alone. Mostly they were assigned protective details for US dignitaries traveling abroad. On those missions they were briefed thoroughly before leaving the United States and they always knew what was expected of them. Unlike this mission, where they were operating as part of a six-man team and seemed to always be in standby mode, being fed small morsels of information at a time. As part of a team, she and Brad normally worked with Tyler, the team leader, who was always accompanied by his number two man and technical genius, Shawn. The other two members had changed several times in the last two years, but Mike and Jewels had been with them for almost six months now. Mike was also a sharpshooter; Jewels was his scout. Nikki had worked a training mission once with

Jewels and she had been surprised at her stealth. She was five-foot-eight, just over two hundred pounds of solid muscle, and could move like a feather, barely rustling a leaf or brushing a tree branch. Brad was equally talented even though he was at least twenty pounds heavier than Jewels. Nikki often wished she had their abilities, but somehow Flagler had managed to match each team member with their own greatest skills.

The majority of missions Flagler Security agents were sent on were shrouded in secrecy, and Nikki had discovered quickly that she liked this lifestyle. Over the years she had settled into the position and found it was easier to avoid having friends outside of Flagler rather than having to create lies to explain her absences. As for family, all she had was the foster mom and dad who had taken her in when she was ten after her parents had been killed in a car accident. Their death had taught her two things: that things she loved could be taken away and that loss was easier if she wasn't emotionally attached. Her relationship with Brad had melted some of that coldness, but she still insisted she had the ability to control whether to love someone—or not.

The vibration on her headset signaled an incoming update. She felt Brad shift slightly and key the mic to acknowledge they were ready to receive their next directive.

A digital voice, neither male nor female, came through her headset. "Alpha One. Mission follows."

Nikki listened closely as the message relayed from the operations center in Pensacola was disseminated to the rest of her team. Though the voice of Mission Control was digital, Nikki knew Josh Houston, the on-site leader for this mission, was giving the instructions. She didn't necessarily need to know where the team would be headed once they all linked back up, but if anything occurred during the linkup, she would have to find the extraction point on her own. So she stored the details in the back of her mind. Beside her, Brad typed the coordinates into their GPS, in case they did need them. She heard Shawn acknowledge receipt of the mission.

Then it was her and Brad's turn for instructions.

"Sierra One. Mission follows," said the mechanical voice. "Lay silent support for Charlie Ten. Black Jeep approaching from the west."

Nikki took a deep breath and let it out slowly. Designator Charlie meant CIA agents were involved and, unfortunately, that meant even less information than normal.

The mechanical voice continued, "Charlie Ten will approach village for package exchange. If mission is a success, you will receive two flashes of the vehicle's headlights as it exits from the village. Return to the rendezvous point. If the flashes are not given, hold your position for further instructions. End message."

She felt Brad's hand move slowly to the mic on his shoulder and double-click it to acknowledge that the mission had been received.

Releasing a soft breath, Brad whispered, "So, all we have to do is 'watch.'"

"Yeah," she whispered back. "Easy enough." She was relieved there was more to this mission than there had been to the last couple. "Watching someone do something" was a step up from reconnaissance. It meant the possibility of needing to pull the trigger, and there was nothing she took more seriously.

She slowly scanned the entire area below them again, taking a quick inventory of all fifteen bodies, each dressed in jeans or coveralls, still around the campfire. None of them looked like soldiers, but she knew from past experience that what might seem insubstantial, like men drinking and chatting, could quickly turn into a fight for her life. She hoped all of these farmers were as they appeared and that she wouldn't have to fire upon them. She slid her finger back and forth along the trigger housing, remembering another occasion she and Brad had been on a mission to provide fire support only. A sheepherder, along with his flock, had stumbled upon their mark. He had looked harmless enough until the group of insurgents traveling with him emerged from the shadows. Luckily she had been able to take down enough of them for their mark to retreat.

The thermal imaging of her scope didn't allow her to identify faces or expressions and she was thankful for that. Her first kills had occurred under the cover of darkness, but the cover didn't follow her home. Despite her intensive training, after the first one she had become withdrawn and sullen, remembering the loss of her parents. Flagler had forced her to a therapist who helped her learn to separate the two situations. Now she could identify the people she saw through her scope as targets or marks. She was sorry for her part in their demise, but her trust in Flagler outweighed her regrets. She studied the few men that were still awake by the fire, trying to identify which mark would pass the package. None seemed inclined to move, but when they did, Nikki would be watching and ready to act.

It wasn't long before she could hear the faint rumble of a vehicle in the distance.

"There he comes," Brad said.

She didn't respond but blinked her eyes several times to clear them. Readjusting her position to get a more secure grip, she flipped her safety off and rested her index finger along the side of the trigger housing.

"Moving," Brad said to let her know he was not spotting for her. Less than five hundred feet in front of them, a Jeep rumbled along on the barely broken trail. Brad used the cover of the noise to pull a gel pack from his rucksack. He bit the top off and spit it back into his pack.

"Open."

Keeping her eye in the scope, she opened her mouth and Brad poured the entire container of energy gel into her mouth. She held the thick goo in her mouth, letting it blend with her saliva, before swallowing the strawberry sugar mix.

She heard him take out another gel pack for himself as a flash of color moved inside her scope. "I got movement," she said softly, alerting Brad.

Brad stuffed the empty container into his pack and grabbed his scope, settling in beside her again.

"Red shirt. Right side," Nikki whispered.

"Got him," Brad mumbled around the gel still soaking in his mouth.

They watched the man withdraw from the group around the fire and move into one of the surrounding huts.

"Damn," Brad whispered. "I wish we had eyes down there. How are we supposed to know what he is doing inside that building?"

They continued to watch in silence as their thermal imaging scopes tracked his movements. After a few moments he returned with a manila envelope tucked tight against his side. He walked toward the edge of the village and the approaching vehicle. When he emerged from behind the last hut, Nikki could see him silhouetted by the lights of Charlie Ten's Jeep. It was clear by the positioning of the vehicle that Charlie Ten was aware of the location of his fire support. He'd angled it to give them a clear view of the exchange.

Nikki watched Red Shirt through her scope, scanning as much of the area around him and the CIA agent as she could see. She counted on Brad to watch a broader area and to let her know if she needed to shift her focus. Red Shirt approached the window and passed the envelope to the hand that emerged. The inside of the vehicle was dark, despite the lightening sky, and Nikki was unable to see anything more than the silhouette of the agent. The conversation was brief and within seconds the agent had turned the Jeep around and was headed back down the firebreak flashing his lights twice. They temporarily held their position and Nikki watched Red Shirt return to the fire to take a swig from the bottle that was passed to him. As soon as the Jeep was out of earshot, Brad got quietly to his feet, securing his spotter's scope in his pack, and then turned to assist her. Switching the safety back on, she allowed him to steady her rifle on the ground while she moved into a sitting position and the circulation slowly returned to her muscles. Brad detached the bipod and ammunition magazine from her rifle, and with one hand dropped them into his pack.

Standing, Nikki slung her rucksack onto her back and took the rifle inside its protected carrying case from Brad. Pulling the strap over her head, she attached the Velcro strips of the long case to her rucksack, compensating for the awkwardness of its length by carrying it at a forty-five-degree angle. If they came under fire, Brad would take the rifle, allowing them both to run faster, but otherwise his objective was to clear their path with his machete, as quickly and as quietly as possible.

She quickly ran her hands over the tactical load-carrying vest she wore, conducting an inventory of all her equipment and checking that all straps were secure. The Five-seveN pistol strapped to her waist weighed less than two pounds and the pound of ammunition she carried worked for both it and the P90 dangling at her side. When she completed her check, she cradled her P90 in her arms and looked at Brad. His black and green tactical clothing and camouflage-painted face hid him in the shadows of the trees—until he smiled and his teeth gave off an eerie white glow. Knowing she looked much the same, she smiled back and gave him a nod to move out when he was ready. Punching buttons to pull up the coordinates on the GPS, he took off at a trot with her on his heels.

Thirty-five minutes later, Brad slowed, allowing her to move beside him. He pointed into the tree line and she strained to see what he saw. Apparently the return trip in the daylight had been faster than their outbound trek, which had been more cautious and after dark. Brad led the approach and, as they neared a clump of trees, they heard a faint "Halt" followed by "Pickle." Nikki recognized Tyler's voice and gave a little sigh of relief.

"Relish," Brad whispered in response as the two of them entered the perimeter.

She heard Tyler chuckle before he stood and led them into the circle of camouflaged bodies. "Move out." Tyler motioned for Mike and Jewels to take the lead while he and Shawn followed. Brad and Nikki brought up the rear. With packs on their backs, the six of them formed a staggered line and headed toward the extraction point.

When they reached the coordinates that they had been given, Nikki waited for Tyler to direct each of them to a security position around the perimeter of the landing zone. Nikki's number within the group was five and she would board in that order, the same as she had exited when they arrived the previous day. She took cover in the spot Tyler directed her to and scanned the area in front of her. She couldn't see him behind her, but she knew he would be dropping chemical sticks to mark the landing zone before taking his position in the perimeter.

Several minutes later, she could hear the wop-wop of the helicopter's blades growing louder and then the wind began to whip as it lowered to the ground. Nikki counted in her head, allowing fifteen seconds for each team member to board in front of her before pulling her focus from her assigned area. She moved when her counting reached sixty. Jogging backward her first couple of steps, she gave a final scan of the area before turning toward the waiting helicopter. She grabbed the hand that reached down to her and allowed herself to be pulled into the helicopter, taking a seat on the narrow bench behind the pilot. She swung her pack around her body to rest in her lap, the rifle filling the space in front of her, as Brad slid onto the bench beside her. The helicopter's engine roared and she felt them leave the ground, gaining altitude quickly. With the whipping of the wind in the open doorway, there was no possibility of talking, so Nikki relaxed against Brad and dropped her head onto her pack. She dozed until they landed at the airfield.

CHAPTER THREE

Nikki awoke as the helicopter began its descent and she nudged Brad awake. In the tight space, she maneuvered her gear around her body, sliding her arms back into the straps. Through the open door, she could see the small commercial airfield they had arrived at almost twenty-four hours earlier. Nikki followed Brad out the door as the helicopter landed in front of the blue hangar that contained their travel boxes and provided a place where they would exchange the gear they wore for their travel clothes. Nikki dreaded the commercial flight they would return home on, but she was thankful that Flagler always handled their weapons and other gear.

Nikki and Brad waited while the rest of the team ducked under the rotors and jogged over to join them outside the hangar. When the noise of the retreating helicopter began to fade, Tyler handed each of them a boarding pass. Before he could begin his briefing on the details of their return travel, though, the hangar door opened and two men in black tactical clothing emerged. They gave a nod to Tyler and walked toward the opposite side of the hangar, disappearing around the corner.

Tyler was speaking quickly to disseminate the relevant information when the rumble of an approaching vehicle drew everyone's attention. On the road circling the inside of the airfield, a black Jeep came into view.

Brad nudged Nikki. "Isn't that the Jeep from this morning?"

She nodded but didn't say anything as the entire team watched it draw closer.

"Is that who we were babysitting?" Jewels whispered.

Brad nodded. "I think so."

The two men in black tactical gear came back around the building and met the Jeep as it pulled to a stop in front of the hangar.

Tyler resumed his briefing, but Nikki noticed everyone on the team was still watching the Jeep. When the driver exited the vehicle and turned toward them, Nikki's brows shot up. *Female.* Brad nudged her again and she gave him a crooked smile. Tyler stopped talking as the three CIA agents approached the hangar entrance.

Nikki appraised the woman as they got closer. Her shoulder-length, chestnut-brown hair was wavy and fell across her face as she moved. She was slightly taller than Nikki's five-foot-seven, and her broad shoulders stretched the black T-shirt across her chest. Her right arm was bent to hold the tactical jacket she had slung arrogantly over one shoulder. Her gaze briefly flickered over the team and slowed as it crossed Nikki's face. She seemed to find humor in being the center of attention. The three agents nodded to Tyler before disappearing into the hangar and letting the door slam behind them.

"Asses," Mike whispered under his breath.

Tyler gave him a hard stare.

"Well, they are," Mike declared.

"Maybe," Tyler agreed. "But we still have to work with them." He resumed his briefing again. "Normal protocols are in place. No contact once we leave the hangar. See you in Florida." He pulled open the hangar door and entered with Shawn on his heels.

Mike shrugged. "They didn't even acknowledge us and you know they know who we are."

"It's like we're below them and only here to serve," Jewels added.

"My lady," Brad said, pulling the hangar door open in front of her and bowing slightly at the waist.

Jewels strutted toward the door and crooned over her shoulder as she stepped inside, "Now that's what I'm talking about."

Nikki followed Jewels, pausing inside the door until her eyes adjusted to the dark interior. Under the muted glow of the fluorescent lights, she quickly located her lockbox in the far corner where she had left it. She scanned the room for the CIA agents, but didn't see them. A ray of light escaped from under the door of the small office in the opposite corner, and she imagined they must be inside behind the closed window blinds. She stopped at the team lockbox and secured her personal weapons with the straps designed to hold them in place before stowing her rifle in the bottom of the box. Crossing to her own lockbox, she dropped her remaining gear inside and grabbed her clean clothing before heading to the bathroom.

The shower was refreshing, but Nikki didn't linger. She scrubbed her face and neck to remove the camouflage paint and quickly ran the washcloth over the rest of her body before washing her hair. Jewels came in as she was finishing and they passed at the shower entrance.

"Perfect timing." Nikki smiled at her.

"So I've been told."

Nikki laughed as she crossed to the bench where she had left her clean clothing. Jewels was very flirty, even with the guys, so Nikki wasn't sure which team she preferred. If she was honest, she liked not knowing. There wasn't any tension or discomfort between them. She pulled on jeans and a cotton T-shirt, and quickly dried her short hair with a towel. She was lucky that her hair hung straight. Jewels would be another twenty minutes just fixing her hair.

She grabbed her travel mirror to check for remaining camouflage paint on her face but was caught by her own reflection. She ran her fingers through her light brown hair, pushing it back out of her face. Almost time for another haircut.

She had never been obsessed with her looks, but she knew keeping it short was key to avoiding styling time in the field. She studied her face. The bags under her eyes annoyed her. They made her look older and more tired than she felt. The rest of her body had adapted to the crazy hours Flagler required. Why hadn't her eyes? Shrugging, she pulled a wipe from her bag, scrubbed at the few missed spots of paint on her chin, grabbed her carry-on and exited the bathroom.

After stowing her towel inside a plastic pouch, she placed it and her tactical clothing inside another bag before securing them inside the lockbox. She knew from experience the sweaty clothing would be unbearable by the time they were unpacked in Florida. She dropped her muddy boots into a separate container and placed them beside her clothing. She pulled on a light Windbreaker and slung a backpack containing her iPad and cell phone over her shoulder before moving her lockbox closer to the door. It would be shipped back to Florida with their weapons and any other gear they had left behind. Tyler was still in the shower room, so she gave Brad a wave to let him know she was headed out. The commercial hangar was about a half mile across the airfield and she followed the dirt road leading to it.

Ticket in hand, she approached the security checkpoint inside the small airport. Her stomach gave a light tug as the agent closely inspected her passport and airline ticket. On a protective detail, she carried her real passport and traveled as an employee of Flagler Security, but on the dark missions, she could be anyone. For Nikki the thrill of using different identities would never get old, as her name was rotated with each mission. It was standard for the team to travel with no contact between them so it wasn't necessary for them to identify each other by name. She had been briefed on every overseas mission to remain calm if detained and Flagler would provide whatever documents or representation were necessary to get her released from custody. She had never had any problems, nor had she heard of any agents who had. Flagler took their agents' security and safety very seriously by producing professional government-issued documents. She gave the agent her best innocent look, and it must have worked, because he handed her ticket and passport back with few questions. She bought a bottle of water and moved to her departure gate to wait.

She took a seat by the window with her back to the wall and within minutes she saw Mike take a seat in the gate area too. She made eye contact with him and then returned her gaze to her iPad. Unlike other male team members, Mike wore his hair a bit shaggy. He didn't match the typical military profile. He, also, liked to wear baggy clothing that didn't show off his physique.

Out of the corner of her eye, she watched each of the other team members enter and take seats. Brad wore a brightly colored Hawaiian shirt and she knew she would harass him later about it. Probably a Father's Day gift from his kids. Tyler and Shawn both wore skinny jeans with sweatshirts and running shoes. Of course Jewels was last to arrive with her hair perfectly styled. She also wore jeans and her favorite black Chuck Taylors, as did most of the under-twenty kids at the airport. Nikki was only a couple years older than she was, but she liked to tease Jewels about her ability to blend in with the average teenager. To the casual observer, all six of them looked like typical weary travelers. Neither she nor Jewels was a high-heels, dress-wearing kind of woman, but she liked that they didn't look like soldiers ready for a fight either. Appearances can be deceiving, she thought with a grin. Either one of them could take anyone in the gate area to the ground in seconds, if needed.

When the gate attendant called their flight, Nikki placed earbuds in each ear to avoid conversation with fellow travelers. She kept the music low and sometimes she didn't even turn it on, but it discouraged unnecessary small talk. Her seat was in the rear of the plane so she was one of the last people to board. She was happy to see her window seat but unhappy to see the large man in the seat beside her. She really hated flying coach. She pretended to sleep and was thankful for the short flight to the international airport where she boarded a much larger plane for the return trip to the United States.

CHAPTER FOUR

Mel sighed heavily again. This was getting ridiculous.

"It was a clean pass," she said for the third time.

"The target didn't say the proper words," Joey, the dark-haired man in black tactical clothing, responded.

She closed her eyes and took a deep breath. "He was very nervous. I would say it was his first exchange. I should have prompted him, but at the time it seemed smarter to take the package and leave the area. Besides, the mission wasn't the package, it was to evaluate the team from Flagler, right?"

"She's right," the second man agreed. "Let's just get the details down and get out of here."

"Okay, but I'm putting it in my report, Melissa."

Mel rolled her eyes at the use of her full name before responding. "We all will."

* * *

Mel finished her report and emailed it to the US office before returning to the hotel with the guys to change and pack. She was relieved the company's private jet was refueling and would be ready to depart for Washington, D.C., as soon as they returned. Traveling commercial meant long lines, tight seating and restricted conversation, none of which they would face on their flight. The agency had made it clear this mission was important and no cost was too great.

Mel wasn't assigned to the D.C. office and she didn't think Liam or Joey were either. They had met there for a quick meeting before departing for this mission and now would return for debriefings. She had not worked with them before, but that was typical for her job. They discouraged relationship-building in her department, opting instead for secrecy and silence.

Once settled on the plane, Mel allowed her mind to wander. The team of six from Flagler had looked and acted efficiently. She had noticed two women on the team when she passed them outside the airport hangar. Her gaze had barely flicked over the guys, all looking the same in tactical gear and camouflage paint, but women always stood out to her. One had been bulky and muscular with medium-length copper hair. She appeared to be Mel's height. The other was a bit shorter with straight brown hair plastered to her head by sweat and a knit ski cap she had held in her hand. Her face had been hidden by the dark camouflage paint, but her blue eyes stood out, and Mel had been surprised to feel a flutter of attraction. She was always willing to admire a woman from a distance, but she never hooked up with anyone she found intriguing. She knew that kind of interest could lead to something more and she wasn't ready or willing to settle down.

Relaxing into sleep, her mind traveled to places she wouldn't have allowed if she were conscious. There was something about the woman's confident stance and the arrogant expression on her face that made Mel restless and haunted her thoughts. As her mind drifted in and out of sleep, she heard a voice talking near her.

"Melissa?" Joey said again.

Mel opened her eyes and found Joey and Liam sitting across from her. She rubbed her face to clear the lingering images of the piercing blue eyes. "What?" she growled, unhappy at where her mind had wandered more than with the fact she had been roused from her pleasant dreams.

Liam spoke first. "There's been a change in plans."

She sat up straighter, her mind alert as she glanced between the two men.

"We're going straight to Pensacola," Liam continued. "We need to dig deeper."

"Why? What happened?"

"Our contact has been killed," Joey said quietly.

"What?" She searched their faces for some understanding of what they were telling her. When neither spoke fast enough, she prompted them. "Details, please."

Again, Liam was the first to offer information, his voice deep and masculine as he spoke, explaining the message they had just received. "About an hour ago, our in-country operative attempted to locate the contact to get his take on the exchange. In case we needed him in the future." He shrugged. "You never know."

Liam paused and Joey continued. "Our operative went to his hut, expecting him to be passed out from the party, and found him with a bullet in his head."

"Well, crap." Mel rubbed her face again.

Liam handed her a bottle of water. "Things are going to get more intrusive for the Flagler team, I'm afraid."

"Yes," Joey agreed.

"How long until we land?" Mel glanced around as if she would be able to identify their location from a cloud outside the airplane window. "And where are we?"

Liam followed her gaze out the window. "We just crossed into US territory, but we'll have to stop and refuel before Pensacola, so at least six hours."

Joey retrieved his briefcase. "I brought some case files for us to go over, but since things have changed, we need to get more specific with our plan. A team is being put together in

Pensacola right now, and we will join them tonight after we start surveillance." He turned to Mel. "Don't take offense, but I want you to focus on one of the women. I think if we stick with our own gender, it will allow us to follow closer. At least while we are doing our surveillance out in the open." He paused as if waiting for her to object, and when she didn't, he continued. "For now, it doesn't matter which one." He handed her two files and she glanced at the top one. Julie Marie Singleton. She opened the folder to the employment photo and appraised the copper hair and round face before handing it back to Joey.

She held up the second folder. "I'll take this one." She only needed to see the faces to know which woman she wanted to follow.

Liam made a selection from the male team members and handed the other files back to Joey. They each returned to their original seats, leaving Mel alone with her folder. If there was one thing she did better than anyone else, it was tracking and investigating marks. She had a knack for knowing exactly how to get inside someone's head and get the answers that were needed. As she studied the face staring back at her from the inside cover, however, the plans she had worked out in her head began to fall apart. Deep blue eyes seemed to question her intentions, and for the first time she felt guilty for doing the job she had been assigned. She was about to intrude on every aspect of this woman's life and it bothered her, though she had no desire at the moment to analyze why. Turning the picture over, she eagerly began to read. She needed to know everything about Nicole Elizabeth Mitchell.

CHAPTER FIVE

Nikki woke up only to stumble through two more flight changes before they finally touched down in Pensacola. Their brief instructions after the mission included the final rendezvous point, a white Buick SUV parked in long-term parking. Once the team all arrived, Tyler drove them back to the office with a quick detour for fast food, which they ate on the road. After twelve hours of travel, everyone was ready to wrap things up and get home. Including the preparation days in Pensacola before leaving for the mission, they had been activated for almost a week.

Nikki glanced at her watch without lifting her head from where it rested against the seat. It was almost nine p.m. She needed to text Barbara, her dog-sitter, and let her know she would pick up the dogs tomorrow. The debriefing would take at least another hour, and she needed to pick up groceries before going home. One of the things she always did when she got a mission notification was throw out all perishables. Even short missions normally lasted at least four or five days, and she hated returning home to the smell of rotting fruits and vegetables.

Brad elbowed her. "Pick a straw." He held five straws in his hand with only the tops exposed. Within the mix would be a short one. The lucky person who drew it would go last for debriefing.

"That's okay. I'll go last." She really didn't mind waiting. Tyler, as team leader, would go first, and Brad had a wife and kids waiting at home. She wasn't sure about Shawn, Mike or Jewels, but it didn't matter. She had nothing but an empty bed waiting for her at home and there was no reason to rush. The guys fought over the remaining straws before Mike drew the short one.

Tyler showed his badge at the security office to get them inside Flagler's compound and then parked the Buick in fleet parking. Once inside, Nikki went straight to her desk and quickly typed out her after-action review. Brad was slated to be the second one to debrief and Nikki had just finished when he slid his chair beside hers. He was a slow typist on a good day, but when he was tired and anxious to get home, his one-finger pecking could take hours. He dictated his report and Nikki typed.

Flagler had a strict policy that mandated no discussion about mission details until after everyone was debriefed, but they only enforced it if weapons were discharged or things went bad during a mission. Nikki was always careful to remain silent and never offer opinions or suggestions. She typed exactly what Brad dictated without discussion.

Brad rushed out the door when they finished, and Nikki collapsed on the couch in the lounge. She pulled out her cell phone and texted a message to Barbara before turning the television to a baseball game. She was looking forward to her three days off. On day four, her team would return to the office for a normal workday. They would clean and prepare their equipment, fire weapons and practice drills until called for the next mission.

Nikki glanced up when she saw movement in the hallway. Mike was the last to debrief and he would let her know when it was her turn. She was surprised to see the three CIA agents pass the open door to the lounge. They had changed into civilian clothes, but Nikki instantly recognized the wavy chestnut hair. She got up off the couch and stepped into the hall in time to see them disappear into the debriefing room. Within seconds, Mike appeared in the hallway.

"What are they doing here?" she asked him.

"I sure as hell don't know."

She followed Mike back into the lounge. "Are you finished debriefing?"

"Nope. I was politely asked to leave after they barged in without knocking." Mike poured himself a cup of coffee and set it on the coffee table before flopping onto the couch.

"Seriously?" Nikki sat down beside him.

"Even Lewis seemed surprised to see them." Mike was referring to Byron Lewis, their director of operations who conducted debriefings, along with the OSL or on-site leader. The on-site leader changed with each mission, but Josh Houston had been running the majority of Nikki's missions during the past year.

"Did Josh say anything to them?" Nikki asked.

"No, but he seemed to recognize them."

"I can't recall ever seeing CIA agents here."

"Me either," Mike said, taking a sip of his coffee.

Ten minutes passed before Josh stepped into the lounge and motioned for Mike to follow him.

Nikki jumped to her feet. "What's going on?"

Josh put his hand up to hold off her questions and left the room. Mike shrugged and followed him.

Nikki collapsed back on the couch and tried to keep her focus on the ball game. Her eyes kept straying to the hallway, but it remained empty. Finally Mike came back and told her Josh was ready. She wasn't sure how much time had passed; it had seemed like hours. She couldn't stop herself from looking into each classroom as she walked down the hall. Unable to catch sight of the CIA agents, she prepared herself for them to be in the debriefing room and was surprised when she found the room empty except for Josh and Lewis. She was curious about their presence in the Flagler building and wondered if they had left by a back exit to avoid further scrutiny.

"Close the door, Nikki," Josh said when she entered the room.

Nikki took a seat at the table across from the men. "What's the CIA doing here?" She looked from Josh to Lewis. Both were still typing notes into their laptops, but neither seemed eager to answer her question.

Lewis finished first and sat back in his chair, his gaze on Nikki as he spoke. "Are you ready, Josh?"

Josh looked up from his laptop and nodded. "Take it from the top, Nikki."

Nikki glanced at Josh and then back at Lewis. The situation was unusual and their avoidance was putting her on edge. "Why did they follow us back? Is something wrong?"

"Just give us the details from the mission, Nikki." Josh poised his fingers over the keyboard ready to type when she began talking.

Nikki looked down at the table and shook her head. *Weird.* She didn't want to be disrespectful and it was clear they weren't going to offer an explanation, so she began her debriefing. It took her about ten minutes to run through the highlights and when she finished both men typed in silence.

Lewis again was the first to look up. "Did anything about the exchange seem off to you?"

Nikki hesitated while her mind replayed the details. "No."

"Nothing at all?" Josh added, looking up.

Nikki looked back and forth between them before pinning her focus on Josh. "What is going on?"

Josh glanced at Lewis and then back at Nikki before offering a brief explanation. "We think they screwed something up."

"Like what?" Nikki asked, confused. "We watched a successful exchange, right?"

"Our intel says their contact has been killed."

Nikki's eyes widened. "Oh, that's not good." She shook her head. "He returned to the party as if nothing was wrong. It looked like a good pass to us."

Josh stood. "Go home and get some rest. We can talk about all of this when everyone returns next week."

Lewis's focus had returned to his laptop, and he did not acknowledge her departure. He wasn't the friendliest supervisor at Flagler, but this was curter than usual for him. It was clear the uninvited guests were making everyone nervous. Nikki nodded at Josh and left the room, lost in her own thoughts. The whole situation was strange. The CIA had never shown up at Flagler after a mission, at least not one she was involved in, but there had never been an unexplained death either. Not a death, but a murder, she mentally corrected herself. Her mind reeled at the repercussions for the agents involved, as well as for the contact's family. As she passed the lounge, she caught a glimpse of a group of people gathered around the coffeepot. Nikki halted and took two steps back to glance into the room. She made eye contact with the chestnut-haired woman and nodded. She got a slight nod in return, but before Nikki could consider saying anything, she looked up to see a former team member coming down the hall.

"Hey, Turtle," Nikki addressed the short, blond-haired woman approaching her.

"What's up, Nikki? I hear you guys brought souvenirs back with you on this trip." Turtle laughed at her own joke.

Nikki nodded toward the lounge and dropped her voice to a whisper. "We didn't bring them. They followed us."

Turtle frowned at the potential meaning of that information. "Weird, isn't it?" She punched Nikki on the arm, returning to her carefree attitude. "Well, you can't keep them even though they followed you home."

Nikki shook her head and laughed. "No chance of that!"

"I better go. Wheels up in ten."

"Be safe," Nikki called to her as they parted. She headed for the locker room where her personal belongings were stored. She was going home and not a moment too soon.

* * *

"Isn't that your mark?" Liam elbowed Mel.

"Yep."

"Why don't you go ahead and go," Joey suggested. "We'll finish the follow-up with Lewis and fill you in later."

Mel started out the door but quickly stepped back into the lounge as soon as she saw Nicole still standing in the hallway. She could barely hear the conversation taking place in hushed tones. She and her team were definitely already making waves. It would be interesting to see what might be revealed when the water settled.

* * *

Nikki grabbed her keys from her locker and went straight to her car. She'd bought the dark blue Ford Edge barely a month earlier and still hadn't learned how to use any of the technical gadgets. She wasn't even sure why anyone would need a car that parallel parked itself. Gas mileage was comparable for an SUV, though, and the rear seats laid down to make room for her golden retrievers. That was what mattered. She was happy with her purchase, especially since she'd been able to get it in her favorite color.

There were four grocery stores she could go to on the way home, depending on which route she chose. She decided on the one with the best fresh vegetable selections and easily found a parking space there. Crossing the empty lot, she was happy to see there wouldn't be a lot of shoppers at this hour. She grabbed a cart inside the door and began filling it. Twenty minutes later she was headed for the checkout line when she caught a glimpse of someone with chestnut hair entering an empty aisle to her left. *Surely it wasn't.* Nikki circled down the next aisle and then doubled back behind the woman. The woman stopped halfway down the aisle, sensing someone behind her, and turned as Nikki approached.

Nikki hoped her mouth wasn't hanging open in surprise as she felt herself hesitate before pushing past with a quick nod. The seconds it took her to regain her composure annoyed her.

She wasn't easily caught off guard but this unexpected encounter had jolted her.

Nikki hit the first open checkout line and tossed her items onto the belt. Her earlier curiosity was now tainted with this invasion into her personal life. She wanted out of this store and away from that woman so badly she had been tempted to leave without her groceries. Realizing how irrational that would be, she forced herself to wait calmly while her groceries were bagged. Her mind, on the other hand, was not calm. It was racing through possible scenarios. Maybe this woman lived nearby. Or was staying at a hotel nearby. Nikki remembered passing several on this street alone. As she walked across the parking lot, Nikki's eyes searched around her, trying to locate the woman—who now seemed to have vanished. She loaded her car quickly and slid behind the wheel. Watching her mirrors closely all the way home, she pulled into her garage and hit the remote to close it behind her.

As she turned her engine off and sat in the dark garage, it crossed her mind that she should advise someone of the situation. She could imagine Brad's laughter as she described the meeting, which might be entirely coincidental. Neither Josh nor Lewis had seemed interested in talking about the CIA agents, and the next level was Vincent Flagler, owner of the company. Nikki had never spoken to him, but he had attended several predeployment briefings over the years. He was well-respected, and though it sometimes sounded weird in her head, he was always addressed and even thought of as Mr. Flagler, never called by his first or last name. Tyler had told her once that Mr. Flagler knew exactly what each team was doing at all times. He was a hands-on owner and every mission went through his office before being accepted, but it certainly wouldn't be appropriate to jump the chain of command to contact him.

Besides, if she called any of them what would she say? "I saw a CIA agent at the grocery store." Hearing the words spoken aloud, she laughed at herself. These things happened when large agencies worked in the same town. There was bound to be some accidental interaction outside the office. Clearly there was a CIA office somewhere in town, and the agents probably had come by Flagler simply to get their hands on the written after-action reports concerning their surveillance. This wasn't really a situation anyway. *Was it?* Still, she decided if she saw the agent again outside of work, she would call Brad and discuss it with him.

She sighed as she climbed out of her car and carried her groceries inside. When everything was stored, she turned out all the lights and headed upstairs. After a long shower, she fell into bed exhausted, sparing only a fleeting thought for the cocky CIA agent who might or might not be following her.

CHAPTER SIX

Mel turned off her GPS as she coasted to a stop outside the two-story house. There was only one light on inside, but she was confident Nicole had come straight home with her trunkful of groceries. Nicole was good at her job, but she was better. She'd watched her load her groceries from the darkness inside her own SUV, Nicole's curvy silhouette and facial features barely visible in the shadows from the parking lot lights. Mel was surprised at the twinge of desire she felt as she remembered the way Nicole's hair had fallen around her face as she leaned into the cart for each bag. Her face had been set and determined as she glanced around her at the parked cars, each time returning to her task with a false sense of security. When they left the parking lot, Mel had kept her distance. She wasn't ready for Nicole to catch her following her. Tonight she wanted to keep her curious. Tomorrow she would gradually increase her appearances until Nicole felt she had nowhere to turn. Mel had no doubt she would be able to manipulate Nicole into trusting her and when she did, the answers would flow—exactly the way they had with every other mark Mel had worked.

Sitting now in the dark in front of Nicole's house, Mel replayed the information in the file she had read on the plane. Nicole had been approached by a representative from Flagler during her sophomore year at the University of Florida. At that time she was hired for basic security work only and initially they had used her on protective details assigned to dignitaries only in the United States. Though she qualified expert with a pistol her first time on the range, her black belt in tae kwon do is what initially attracted Flagler. Nicole had ranked number one internationally for two years in a row. Mel had also held that rank, but she wasn't surprised their paths had never crossed at competitions. She was already in her second year with the army when Nicole earned her first title.

When Nicole graduated with her degree in criminal justice, she had expanded into the international area of operation. Mel was surprised when she reviewed Nicole's training records. Flagler had not only sent her to their basic operative training but had thrown in sniper school and two jump schools within a two-year period. She was qualified to parachute from a plane or rappel down a rope from a helicopter, cliff or building. Her sniper training was extended twice to familiarize her with environments around the world. There were no qualification badges with a sniper rifle, but Mel had reviewed all the details that were provided for each mission Nicole operated as the main sniper on and she was impressed with her dedication. She was clearly on the path to becoming a top agent.

Nicole's records didn't list any confirmed kills, but that was standard for Flagler. They had their own set of rules. Details were kept purposefully vague and targets were listed as extinguished, meaning they were moved, injured, fled or possibly killed. Mel knew from her time in the military that there were plenty of rules to be followed when operating in a foreign country. She had also come to appreciate the fact that Flagler didn't allow politics to stand in the way of mission completion. She had viewed some of Flagler's top agents in action over the years and her trust in their integrity never wavered. Not until recently, that is.

Since Brad was connected to Nicole, Mel had reviewed his file as well. He had all of the qualifications she did. His ability to move through the woods quietly and cover long distances perfectly complemented Nicole's sniper ability. Both had been employed by Flagler Security for more than ten years and they had been trained well. Neither had any black marks in their files other than an occasional disregard for protocol, but that had always been in response to the safety of their team, never a matter of showboating or seeking individual advancement.

Mel couldn't see how someone with Nicole's dedication or even Brad's, for that matter, could be the rat they were looking for. If she was honest, she didn't want it to be Nicole. She was intrigued by her background, though, and was going to enjoy getting a rise out of her. Her training would keep her from reacting like a normal mark, and Mel was excited to see the outcome. This woman had definitely stimulated Mel's interest.

Mel watched the light go out inside the two-story house before calling Joey.

"I got lights out here."

"Yeah, me too. Liam called about ten minutes ago with the same." Joey sighed. "I'd like to be in bed too."

"You can say that again. What's the plan now?"

"Let's meet at the office on Parker Street in twenty minutes. Mrs. Bowden is doing a briefing for the others assigned with us so we can catch them before they all disperse."

"See you there." Mel hung up without hearing Joey's reply. She had just enough time to grab a good cup of coffee before heading to the office. She glanced at the dark second-story window one more time before pulling out. She couldn't help but think about Nicole resting peacefully in her own bed. It wasn't the first time Mel had been attracted to a mark: it would not affect her ability to do her job. She was always in complete control of her emotions. She found it hard to believe that Nicole was the bad seed, but until she knew for sure, she would treat her as one. Clearly someone in the Pensacola office was on the take, and to make her life easier, Mel had to assume everyone was guilty until she found evidence that proved otherwise.

* * *

Mel stopped in front of the roll-up door at the Parker Street office and punched in her code on the mounted keypad. She pulled slowly forward as the door rumbled up. Securing the first open space inside, she grabbed her coffee cup and climbed the stairs to the second-floor office. Liam and Joey were already sitting in the back of the briefing room when Mel slid into the chair beside Liam. Mel counted nine bodies listening attentively to Bowden ramble about protocols. Liam rolled his eyes and then closed them to mimic sleep. She nodded, taking a sip of her coffee. Liam looked longingly at her cup and she gave him a glare.

"I see that our first agents on the ground have arrived, so I will let them take the floor to give us an update." Bowden moved to the side of the room and Mel led Liam and Joey to the front. Mel covered the highlights of the mission they had observed, and then each of them gave a brief overview of what their marks had done after leaving Flagler.

Bowden addressed the group. "Okay, let's get the rest of the team under surveillance. From now on we will operate on a twenty-four-hour rotation. Get with your counterparts and firm up the schedule. Twelve hours on. Twelve hours off. We will meet back here at ten hundred hours on Tuesday. Check in regularly and call if you see anything that needs a follow-up."

CHAPTER SEVEN

Nikki awoke with the first rays of light the next morning. Confident Barbara wouldn't be up for at least another hour, she enjoyed a leisurely breakfast at her favorite diner before driving to Barbara's two-story brick home. Located on a five-acre lot at the end of a cul-de-sac, the majority of the property was behind the house and enclosed in a privacy fence. Barbara had two golden retrievers of her own, and Nikki's dogs spent enough time there it was like a second home to them. Nikki pulled her Edge into the driveway and Barbara met her at the front door.

"Kids are in the backyard. Would you like to join them? I have coffee."

Nikki smiled. She and Barbara were not really friends, but they had the dogs in common. The few times they had sat and chatted, the conversation had always been about the dogs. "Thanks for the offer, but I want to get to the beach before it gets crowded."

Barbara nodded. Nikki always took the girls for a beach run on the first day she returned. "I'll call them." She left Nikki standing in the foyer and disappeared toward the rear of the house. Seconds later, Nikki heard the jingle of dog tags as the dogs excitedly flew around the corner and into her sight, their golden-furred ears flapping as they ran. She waved to Barbara and pushed open the door, stepping onto the porch. After a lot of whimpered greetings and a few licks, the golden retrievers crossed the yard and jumped into the open back door of Nikki's SUV. Riley stood on the console between the front seats, demanding to be petted. As she drove, Nikki ran her hand through the curly fur at her neck. Though they were littermates, Bailey's fur was straighter and she had more of a lion's mane around her neck. Their previous owners had dumped them at the shelter because they only wanted purebreds to sell. Nikki had adopted them immediately, pleased there was some poodle in their mix. Since neither of the girls shed, they had to be trimmed every couple of months. She had met Barbara at the groomers and they had begun chatting. Barbara volunteered to keep them whenever Nikki was out of town, and it became their regular schedule.

She drove to a secluded beach on the west side of Pensacola. Happy to see no other vehicles when they pulled into the parking lot, she turned the dogs loose and followed them down the beach at a moderate jog. An hour later, she slowed to a walk and turned back toward the car. The dogs continued to chase birds up and down the beach, but returned to check on her often. She liked them to stay close in case they ran into anyone else and she needed to put their leashes on, but, luckily, today they were alone.

Her mind relaxed as she enjoyed the heat from the Florida sun beating down on her back. The morning had been cool, but she had removed her long-sleeved T-shirt early in her run. She used it now to mop up the sweat dripping down her face from her hair. Normally, after a run, her mind was clear and she felt focused, but today her thoughts were muddled, jumping from one thing to another. She tried not to think about the possibility that the CIA might be following her. She was used to keeping secrets on the job. She knew that any leak regarding where she was going or who she was traveling with would be a breach of security and put the dignitary she was protecting at risk. She hadn't known about the dark ops missions when she signed her confidentiality agreement, but learning about them hadn't changed her mind. She liked her job and the people she worked with, and she liked doing the right thing for a company with integrity. Her pulse still quickened each time she received a mission text, and she always reported for duty well within the allotted three hours.

She had to admit that the CIA agent had quickened her pulse too. Under very different circumstances, she might have pursued her, but she didn't play with anyone she worked with. She had made that rule with herself after her first mission with Flagler. She liked the job too much to risk it for a little bit of fun.

On the other hand, the job had never crossed into her personal life like this before. She found herself wondering at every turn if she was being watched. Did she need to be more guarded away from the office? There had been a dark SUV on her street when she had left the house this morning. She had watched closely, though, and she didn't believe it had followed her.

She shook her head, trying to clear it. Over the years, she had become a master at maintaining a calm manner that kept anyone around her from asking for details. That was probably the best tack to take now. She decided to continue to monitor the situation and keep quiet about her suspicions until she knew something for certain.

When they returned home, she headed to the couch for some much-needed rest, the dogs returning happily to their favorite spots beside it. After a long nap and a late lunch, she turned on some jazz music, taped her hands and began punching on the body bag hanging in her spare bedroom. Her mind was still spinning and she longed for the peace that normally followed her workouts.

Giving in to the ramblings of her mind, she replayed her run-in with the CIA agent at the grocery store and the dark

SUV she'd found parked outside her house again when she returned from the beach. The angle had prevented her from telling if there was anyone inside, but she had been tempted to walk over and check. No matter how hard she tried, she couldn't convince herself that the CIA agent lived nearby or that the SUV belonged on her street. She wasn't normally paranoid, but this was starting to weigh on her. Maybe she should run it by Brad. He didn't overreact to anything and could help put it all in some kind of order.

After an hour of punching and kicking, she collapsed onto the floor, her body aching. Sweat dripped down her face as she again talked herself out of contacting Brad. She wasn't being threatened, so it could wait until they returned to the office in two days.

She pulled herself from the floor and took a long, cold shower before turning on her computer. She checked her email, deleting the spam, and then sent her foster parents an email to let them know she was back home. She didn't provide travel details; over the years they had learned not to ask questions. She opened an Internet browser and paid a few bills before surfing around a bit. She had too much nervous energy to sit still, and neither the run nor the workout had helped. Maybe she would go out tonight. It had been a month or more since she had looked for female companionship, let alone explored the soft skin of a woman. She wasn't interested in the complicated situations a relationship involved, and she didn't think she ever would be. She never brought anyone back to her place. It made life simpler to follow them home; she was always back in her bed before dawn. She preferred it that way. She wasn't lonely or in need of someone to share her life.

While her chicken cooked on the grill, Nikki played with the dogs in the backyard and then gave them a bath. Both were certified for patient assistance and tomorrow they would visit the local hospital. While they recovered from the trauma of being bathed, she stir-fried some vegetables to go with the chicken. She stood at the counter to eat. There was no need to set the table when she was by herself. Deciding that a bath would be more relaxing than a trip to the bar, she placed her dish in the sink and, after filling the large tub in her master bathroom, she took her glass of merlot and settled into the bubbles. She closed her eyes and leaned her head against the back of the tub, moving only to take an occasional sip of wine. She hoped the wine and bath would settle her mind enough to allow her to sleep. She should have brought a book in with her or turned on some music. Her mind drifted again. She did have a few friends—well, acquaintances—at the bar. Maybe the release her body was craving would be best satisfied by a female companion. When she climbed out of the tub and saw the time on her watch, she laughed. Her long, relaxing soak had lasted for barely ten minutes.

Toweling off, she headed to the bedroom and put on her favorite black jeans. Normally she would have chosen her faded 501 button-fly Levi's for a trip to the bar, but she felt like dressing up. She wasn't completely sure what she was looking for tonight, but it was always easier to say no if she attracted the wrong woman rather than to attract no one at all. The black jeans were Levi's too but a different style, and molded to the curve of her butt. The tightness showed off her muscles when she walked. She took a couple of steps in front of the mirror to confirm that.

She chose a black bra and pulled a black tank top over it. She knew the white button-down shirt would be a little see-through, but she liked the way it looked under the lights in the bar. She selected her black low-cut boots with the buckles on the side rather than the plain ones she normally wore with her suits for work. Hesitating at the dresser, she considered changing the earrings she wore but quickly changed her mind. She liked the small white gold hoops that she wore when she wasn't working. They had been a gift from a previous girlfriend, the best gift Nikki had received from her. She grabbed her Fitbit and buckled it on her wrist as she went down the stairs. Knowing she was headed out, the girls waited patiently on their beds for goodbye treats. She gave them each a special stomach rub before handing out the treats.

It was too early to show up at the bar, so she headed for a nearby coffee shop. She drove in circles on the way, partly to kill time and partly to see if she was being followed. She sat at a table by the window and sipped her coffee, watching the traffic on the street. Okay, so maybe she was being a little paranoid. She didn't see any vehicles that caught her eye. If someone was out there, they were staying out of sight. She glanced around the coffee shop. It was filled with the usual crowd of yuppies drinking expensive coffee and intently typing on various electronic devices. No one seemed particularly interested in her.

Her stomach churned. She was good at waiting when she was on a mission, but she had no reason to be patient here at home. She tossed the rest of her coffee into the trash can, strode to her car and drove to The Phase, hoping to find someone there who *was* particularly interested in her—or in her body at least.

When she arrived there were still spaces in the parking lot, but the music was already booming. Something by Demi Lovato if she had to guess. The bouncer gave her a nod and waved her through without looking at her ID. There was only a handful of people on the dance floor and even fewer at the bar and tables around the dance floor. Nikki walked to the far side and took a seat at the bar, putting her back to the wall so she could watch the entrance.

CHAPTER EIGHT

Mel stared at the door her mark had just entered. Though she was pretty sure she was sitting outside a lesbian bar, the quick search she'd done on her cell phone confirmed her suspicions. The parking lot was large, but there were only about twenty vehicles here this early. On a Friday night, it wouldn't be long until the lot was filled.

Mel had chosen Nicole as her mark because she was interested in her, but she hadn't thought about the possibility of watching her hook up with someone. She pondered her next move. She could wait for Nicole to come back out, or she could go inside and apply pressure by allowing her to spot her. She should have done that at the beach this morning, but Nicole had looked so peaceful as she ran that Mel couldn't bring herself to follow orders and try to unsettle her. It wasn't like her to be solicitous of someone she was tailing, especially this early in the mission. She really needed to find a way to distance herself from this woman.

As if displeased with Mel's thoughts, her phone rang. Mel looked at the caller ID, took a long breath and connected the call.

"Mel?" The caller didn't wait for her to speak first.

"Yes, Mrs. Bowden."

"What's your status?"

"I'm sitting outside a bar."

"Your mark is inside?"

"She is."

"Okay," her supervisor said, slowly drawing out each syllable. "And why aren't you inside?"

Good question, Mel thought. "I was going to check in first." She grimaced at the lie.

"Is she getting nervous?"

"I haven't pressured her since last night. She's been inside most of the day," Mel said, lying again. "So I've just been sitting on the street."

"Well, get inside that bar then."

Mel hesitated before responding. "Okay."

Bowden was silent for a second. "Is there a problem, Mel?"

"No. No problem." *What is my damn problem?* "I'm headed inside now."

"Sounds good. We need to put them on the defensive and see what that stirs up. Keep on her."

Mel sighed. Normally she had no problem being aggressive when they were asked to pursue or investigate. She really wasn't going to admit defeat just because Nicole was a beautiful woman. She sighed and slid out of the car, slamming the door hard behind her.

* * *

Nikki turned her gaze to the door again as it opened and watched as the now-familiar chestnut-haired woman crossed to the bar. Fueled by the liquor that was coursing through her body, she stared directly at her. After the bartender set a glass of amber liquid in front of her shadow, she finally made eye contact with Nikki. Nikki raised her glass and offered her a silent salute, which she returned before knocking back the drink and turning back to the bartender for a refill. Downing the last of her beer, Nikki cruised the growing number of single women now in the bar. There were none who got her attention quite like the agent across from her. She really was cramping her style, letting all the air out of the ball of pent-up energy that had brought her to the bar in the first place.

Resigning herself to striking out tonight, Nikki slid off the barstool and headed for the bathroom. She resisted the urge to look back and see if she was still being watched. The woman seemed very comfortable with her surroundings; this clearly wasn't her first time in a lesbian bar. Nikki supposed she should be thankful that her nemesis was easy to look at. The cocky bad-girl image looked good on her. Very good. She did wonder if the black leather jacket hid a weapon since she didn't remove it when she came inside. The thought intrigued her.

Nikki was zipping up her jeans when she heard the bathroom door open and close. She had a feeling she knew who had entered. She opened the door slowly, prepared to see the agent, and she was not disappointed. She leaned against the frame of the stall and raised an eyebrow at the woman resting against the sink across from her.

"I seem to be seeing a lot of you lately," Nikki stated, receiving only a nod in response. She crossed to the sink, choosing the one the agent leaned against rather than any of the other three.

Nikki's arms lightly brushed the taller woman's body as she rubbed her hands under the water. She was surprised at the thrill that rippled through her at this small amount of contact. She turned off the water and stepped right, stretching around the woman to reach the towel dispenser. Quick hands grasped her waist and spun her into the wall, making her head swim. Unwilling to resist, she suppressed the urge to deliver an elbow strike and responded instead to the lips trying to take control of her own. Opening her mouth to the touch of the agent's tongue and her legs, as a muscled thigh pressed hard into her crotch. Warm hands slid under Nikki's shirt, grazing her stomach before cupping her breasts, and her body gyrated reflexively against the leg locked between her own. Nikki's fingers twisted through the thick hair, holding their heads tight together. Their kiss deepened as their bodies began to scream for release.

The door squeaked open behind them and they broke apart quickly. Without a word, Nikki walked out of the bathroom. She went straight to her car and dropped into her seat before inhaling deeply. Her body tingled all over, and between her legs wetness still flowed. She banged her head on the steering wheel. *What the hell just happened?*

* * *

Nicole's fast exit spun Mel's back into the wall, where she remained struggling to catch her breath. She placed her hands on her knees and leaned forward. The woman whose arrival had precipitated Nicole's departure gave her a curious glance before popping into the empty stall.

Holy shit. She couldn't remember ever becoming aroused so quickly. She took a deep breath and pushed through the bathroom door. After a quick look to see if Nicole had returned to the bar, she stepped outside in time to see the Ford tear out of the parking lot. Climbing into her SUV, Mel followed at a distance, not ready for another encounter. She was pretty sure Nicole was heading home, but she hung with her to make sure. She pulled to a stop outside Nicole's house as a closing garage door hid the Edge from view.

Mel refused to allow herself to replay the kiss: she had crossed a line and she knew it. She was disappointed with her lack of control. She'd intended to apply pressure on Nicole when she followed her into the bathroom—she had used sexual energy to harry marks before. But the way Nicole responded had led her to take it further than she had meant to go.

She took a deep breath and dialed Joey. Bowden was too intuitive. If she called her, she would read more into the situation than Mel was ready to admit.

"Hey, Joey," she said when he grunted hello. "I need to make a switch."

"What?"

She hesitated, realizing she had awakened him. "I need to switch to the other woman. Do you see a problem with that?"

"Well, yeah. The agents involved will have to be debriefed and reassigned. What's going on, Melissa?"

Mel wasn't going to give him any information. He wasn't in her usual chain of command, and she would have to put her feelings into words for him to understand the situation. She wasn't prepared to do that or to ruin her image. "Nothing is going on. I just thought it would make more sense."

"Well, you should have mentioned it last night. Why do you want to make the change now?"

Headlights shone into Mel's rearview mirror. *Fuck it. I can handle this.* "Never mind, Joey. Forget I called." Mel hung up the phone as a dark body approached the passenger side of the car and opened the door, dropping into the seat beside her.

"She in for the night?" Angela asked.

"Yeah, I guess so."

Angela's frown was barely visible in the dim light. "What happened?"

"Nothing." Mel felt bad for being short with Angela. She liked her and hated sounding like an ass.

Angela shrugged. "Okay then. Anything to pass on?"

"No, it was a quiet day until this evening when she spent about an hour at a local bar. She came home about ten minutes ago. My guess is she's in for the night."

"Okay. See you in the morning." Angela slid out of the car and quietly closed the door behind her.

Mel pulled onto the street and drove straight to her hotel. Taking the four flights of stairs instead of the elevator did nothing to calm her still-racing pulse. She threw her jacket onto the bed and grabbed several small bottles from the minibar. Stepping through the sliding glass door, she rested her arms on the metal railing surrounding her and downed the first bottle. She was disappointed in her own behavior tonight. She was coming extremely close to losing her perspective on this assignment. She downed another bottle of liquor, the scotch burning her throat but covering the taste of the tequila from the first bottle.

She needed to get a grip on her emotions. Tonight had been nothing but a normal response to a very attractive woman; she would not allow it to jeopardize her career. She was good at her job and too experienced to lose her professionalism over a kiss. No matter how good it felt. A soft breeze lifted her hair off her neck, and she shivered, remembering Nicole's hands in her hair. She opened the third bottle without looking at it. It didn't matter what was in it. She hung her head and held the cool bottle against her face. Taking a deep breath, she downed the amber liquid, hoping it held the secret to forgetting how her body had betrayed her.

* * *

Nikki turned off all the lights and pulled the bedroom curtain back, watching her silhouette as a woman returned to her car and then the SUV pulled away. Now she knew she was being watched. There was nothing paranoid about this.

What did the CIA want with her? And what the hell had happened in the bar bathroom? Nikki couldn't erase the memory of heat she had seen in the woman's eyes before she stormed out of the bathroom. Normally, she would have been eager for a temporary fling, especially given how aroused she had been. Thank goodness they had been interrupted, because she knew she would not have stopped on her own. Even though she suspected the woman was following her, she might have willingly stayed or even followed her home.

It had been a long time since a woman had that kind of immediate effect on her. Her body still roaring with arousal, she let the curtain fall before heading downstairs. In the kitchen, she filled the coffeepot and set it to brew before popping a frozen apple pastry in the microwave. She leaned against the counter, considering what to do next, then nodded, pleased with her plan to get some answers. When the coffeemaker beeped, she wrapped the hot pastry in a napkin and poured coffee into a travel mug. Taking her own cup, the travel mug and the pastry, she left the house and crossed to the parked car.

* * *

Angela dialed Mel and laid the phone between the seats as Nicole approached. "Someone is not asleep," she whispered into the dark.

Nicole slid into the seat next to her, handing her the travel mug and pastry.

"Thanks." Angela tossed the pastry on the dash and took a sip of the coffee.

"Black okay?" Nicole asked.

"Yes."

The silence stretched between them and Angela smiled. She could wait. She was here all night.

Nicole leaned her head against the back of the seat and sighed. "So." She paused dramatically. "Are you enjoying your night?"

Angela laughed. She was impressed with Nicole's cool demeanor. "Yes, it's a lovely night."

Several more minutes of silence passed as they drank their coffee.

"How about you tell me why you are sitting outside my house?"

Angela grinned, openly appraising Nicole in the glow from the streetlight. "Because I was told to."

"And you were told to because?" Nicole raised an eyebrow.

Angela shook her head and took another sip of coffee.

Again the silence stretched into minutes until Nicole finally shrugged. "I'll leave you to your surveillance." She opened the car door and slid out. "I'm headed to bed if you want to catch a nap too." She closed the door on Angela's laughter.

* * *

Mel downed the remaining bottle of liquor from her minibar while holding the phone to her ear. The exchange between Nicole and Angela had stretched into several minutes of silence. She was relieved for the break actually, finding the sound of Nicole's voice to be more than a little disconcerting. She couldn't stop thinking about how it felt to press her body hard against Nicole's or the way her nipples had tightened under Mel's touch. The alcohol was playing havoc with her body, and she stifled a groan. She heard Angela's laughter and the slam of a car door.

"That was interesting." Mel could hear the smile in Angela's voice.

"Yeah, she's going to be a challenge."

Angela was silent and Mel hoped if she had heard the slight hitch in her voice that she would grant her a reprieve tonight. Nicole *was* going to be a challenge, and Mel needed more time to process the events of tonight. She was relieved when Angela finally spoke.

"The lights are out again so I hope this time she really went to bed."

"Call me if you need help handling her," Mel said, meaning it more than she or probably even Angela realized.

Angela laughed. "I got this."

CHAPTER NINE

Nikki loaded the girls into the car before opening the garage door, and when she pulled onto the road, she didn't even glance at the dark SUV. The whole situation was ridiculous. The CIA had no reason to put her under surveillance. Besides, weren't there rules about them performing missions inside the US borders? She had decided last night she would just ignore them for her remaining days off. Josh would set everything right on Monday.

Her mind drifted back to the agent in the bar, as it had every time she tried to sleep last night. What she had seen of her body was impressive. What she had felt was what fantasies were made of, hard and strong where it had pressed against her, but soft in the places Nikki had touched. The memory was burned into her mind, and no matter what she did, she couldn't seem to forget.

Reaching the hospital, she pulled into the parking lot and began circling. She always parked in the last row, never taking a space near the hospital entrance. In her mind, those were reserved for the visiting families. She found a spot and slid out of her Edge, pocketing the keys. One at a time she called Riley and Bailey out of the car and secured them in their harnesses and bright red certification vests. With one on either side of her, she gave them a quick bathroom break before walking toward the five-story tan building. They had only gone a short distance when she spotted her tail, leaning casually against the wall beside the entrance. Nikki fumed as she walked toward the agent. Her resolve to ignore this unjustified stalking was shot to hell. She looked at the woman and anger washed over her in waves. She was ready to speak her mind.

Even though she didn't want to, she raked her eyes over the hard body. The agent's broad shoulders pulled a black button-down shirt taut across her chest and Nikki caught a glimpse of a white tank top tucked into black jeans. The jeans were stretched tight across her muscular thighs and narrowed to cover the tops of her black boots. Nikki's fingers twitched, aching to touch her.

* * *

Mel waited while Nicole secured the dogs. She had considered walking to meet her but even from a distance she could see the angry look cross Nicole's face when she spotted her. Mel smiled. Angry would work better than sexy. A flush swept over Nicole's face and Mel's body pulsed with arousal. *Crap!* The angry look was sexy too. Mel looked away in an attempt to focus her mind.

Her gaze swept the parking lot and then back to Nicole. She was surprised to see the look of anger fading as the heat from Nicole's eyes burned into her body. The normally closed face was open and the desire Mel was feeling was reflected back at her. Their eyes connected and a look of panic flashed across Nicole's face before being replaced by a stoic expression. Mel couldn't stop the grin that spread across her face as she read Nicole's thoughts.

"What the hell?" Nicole blurted, looking to Mel as if she knew she'd lost ground in the psychological battle they seemed to be engaged in.

Mel raised her eyebrows at Nicole's burst of emotion, but she didn't respond. The dogs, Mel noticed, had picked up on the tension, and their heads were lowered as they strained forward to sniff the air, trying to get a scent of Mel.

* * *

Irritated that the agent had again gotten a rise out of her, and knowing she'd get no explanation, Nikki walked past her as coolly as she could and through the sliding doors into the hospital. She gave a wave to the familiar security guard sitting at his desk and continued down the hall to a small waiting room. Relieved to find it empty, she took a seat in the corner and the dogs immediately relaxed at her feet. She dropped the leashes and buried her face in her hands. Being able to maintain an even demeanor was something she prided herself on. This woman had pushed her through so many emotions in the last twenty-four hours, she didn't even feel like herself anymore. The stalking she could handle, but her real discomfort came from the unshakable feeling of desire she felt every time she saw her. The burning need that she couldn't quench. Some people might have those feelings of uncontrolled lust, but she never had. She had accepted years ago that she never would. It was just the way she was built.

Soft footsteps approached from the doorway. "Nikki?"

Nikki looked up into the dark eyes of her favorite nurse. "Hey, Rachel." She smiled, hoping to clear her face of the previous anguish.

Rachel sat down next to her, giving both dogs a pet before laying her hand on Nikki's knee. "Did you already hear? I wanted to get to you first."

Nikki frowned. "Hear what?"

"I told Carl to call me as soon as you arrived." Rachel referred to the security guard at the front entrance.

"Rachel, what's going on?" Nikki fought to keep her emotions from bubbling to the surface again.

"Tiffany died on Friday," Rachel said softly.

Nikki dropped her head into her hands again.

"You didn't know? She went during the night while she slept. She looked very peaceful." Rachel gave her leg a comforting squeeze. "It's just the way it happens."

This was part of the risk when dealing with cancer patients. Even with all of the breakthroughs, there were some who didn't make it. Nikki rubbed her face. "How's Lisa doing?" Nikki asked about another patient who had been friends with Tiffany. Both children were fifteen years old and the oldest of the patients Nikki normally visited.

"Lisa is trying to stay positive, but she keeps asking when Riley and Bailey are coming to visit." Both dogs lifted their heads at the mention of their names. Rachel patted Nikki's leg and stood. "She'll be happy to see you."

Nikki rubbed her face and forced her mouth into a smile. "Let's go then."

Rachel touched her arm as they walked down the hallway. "You looked upset when I found you. Is everything okay?"

"Yeah, sure. Just work." Nikki gave her a reassuring smile.

Rachel frowned. "Sometimes I don't like your work much."

Nikki laughed. They both knew Rachel had no idea what Nikki did for a living. She knew only that it took Nikki away for days at a time and, occasionally, Nikki would return with an injury. Rachel was always willing to refresh a bandage or check a wound if Nikki didn't want to drive to Flagler on her days off. Rachel had learned quickly not to ask questions if she wanted to be allowed to help out.

CHAPTER TEN

Mel dropped back out of sight as the nurse and Nicole left the waiting room. She had heard enough of the conversation to know someone had died. She felt a twinge of sadness for Nicole. Mel watched the elevator light indicate a stop on the fifth floor and then punched the up button herself. As soon as the elevator doors opened on the fifth floor, she heard the sound of excited children, all talking at once. Halfway down the hallway, she paused in the doorway, taking in the confusion. Nicole sat on the floor with her back to the door, surrounded by children. One dog sat with Nicole and the other one lay on the bed beside a teenage girl. Every inch of the dog on the floor was being petted by small hands. Mel watched the teenage girl on the bed stroke the dog's head repeatedly with a look of contentment on her face. The dog appeared to be asleep with her head resting on the young girl's stomach.

Mel watched the interaction for a few minutes. She liked the way Nicole focused her attention on each kid as she or he spoke, addressing each of them by their name. When Nicole stood and approached the teenager on the bed, Mel drifted down the hall toward the elevators. There were times to apply pressure, and this was not one of them. She would let Nicole do her visiting without distracting her.

Mel relaxed casually against the wall, watching people and hospital staff come and go. After about twenty minutes, Nicole stepped outside the room and leaned against the doorframe. Her head fell back and she stared at the ceiling. The nurse Mel had seen with her earlier stepped out of the room and placed her hand on her arm. Their heads bent together as Nicole listened to the woman, who was clearly more than an acquaintance. A flash of jealousy hit Mel as she watched their intimate exchange. She wanted to look away, but she couldn't make her head turn. The nurse's eyes caught Mel's as she turned to reenter the room behind them. She whispered something to Nicole and kissed her cheek before walking away. Nicole looked directly at Mel, who was shocked at the anguish in her face. Several seconds passed as they stared at each other before Nicole turned and followed the nurse back into the room.

Mel couldn't erase from her memory the look of agony on Nicole's face. Wandering the halls of the hospital until she found the coffee shop, she purchased two cups of coffee and carried them outside to wait for her. It wasn't long before she and the dogs exited the sliding doors. Mel fell into step beside her and handed her a cup before taking one of the leashes from her hand. The dog stayed glued to Nicole's leg but walked easily between the two women. They veered toward a small pond beside the hospital. Once away from the hospital, Nicole unclipped the dogs, who immediately ran to the murky water for a drink before wading in for a swim.

Both women stood silently and watched the dogs, their red vests now soaked with water. When they emerged from the water, both shook themselves violently and then returned to Nicole before leading the way along the path. She turned and began following the dogs along the edge of the pond.

Mel followed, waiting until she caught up before breaking the silence. "They're beautiful dogs. What kind are they?"

"Retriever mix." Nicole's response was clipped.

"Well, they are beautiful and well-behaved."

The silence stretched between them as they walked, and Mel could feel the tension in Nicole's body starting to fade. Though her face still carried a hint of sadness, her shoulders were relaxed and her fingers aimlessly played with the leash in her hand. When she finally spoke again, Mel was surprised at the frustration in her voice. "I don't even know your name."

Mel glanced at her. "Do you need to?"

Nicole took a deep breath. "No, I guess not," she said bitterly.

Mel took a sip of her coffee, hiding her smile. It wasn't necessary to keep her name a secret, and she had been about to tell her before her words slipped out. Now sensing Nicole's frustration, she decided to hold out a little longer. There were no rules about getting to know her better though. "How long have you been making visits to the hospital?"

The silence stretched until Mel wasn't sure an answer was coming.

"About four years."

"Was that the oncology wing?"

"Yes."

"Do you visit the adults too?"

Nicole shrugged. "Not normally."

Mel remained silent, hoping Nicole would elaborate but when she didn't, she asked the question she had been avoiding. "Who died?"

Nicole rubbed her face. "A fifteen-year-old girl."

"Oh, that's tough."

"Tiffany was a sweet kid. Always happy and upbeat no matter what was happening to her. She was diagnosed the first time before her fifth birthday. I didn't know her then or even when they brought her back four years later." Nikki sighed. "I met her for the first time about two months ago. It had spread so fast there wasn't anything the doctors could do."

"How is that possible? Wasn't she being tested regularly?"

"She was." Nicole gave the standard response Rachel always gave her. "It's just the way it happens."

"Well, that's just shitty." Mel squeezed Nicole's arm before running her hand comfortingly across her back.

Nicole stopped and looked at her. The anguish on her face again tore at Mel and she longed to comfort her. Mel touched her cheek and Nicole tilted her head into Mel's hand. After several seconds, she took a deep breath and stepped back. Mel let her hand fall back to her side.

Nicole turned and tossed her coffee cup into the trash can before facing Mel again. The anguish was replaced with anger. "What the hell are you doing here?"

"I like you?"

"No! Why are you following me?" Nicole demanded.

"Because I was told to."

"That's what your partner said last night too. So, why is the CIA interested in me?"

Mel frowned and shook her head. Handing the leash back to Nicole, she turned and walked toward the parking lot. Nicole clipped the leashes back on the dogs and caught up to her. "You're not going to answer my question?"

Mel sighed. "I like you and sometimes my job sucks, but I still try to do what I'm told."

"That's convenient," Nicole fumed. "Oh, and evasive."

Mel shrugged. "Have you ever noticed anything out of the ordinary with your job?"

"My job is out of the ordinary."

"No, I mean something that wasn't the normal. Like a package you were sent to pick up, but then you were told not to bring it back."

Nicole walked toward her car and this time Mel hurried to catch up with her. "Or something that simply seemed off?"

Nicole continued walking. "I work for a secretive company. One of their rules is that I do not discuss my job with anyone! Even the CIA."

"But I work for—"

"No!" Nicole interrupted her. "I don't care who you work for. I'm not disclosing any information."

She opened the rear hatch and the dogs jumped in. She slammed it closed and turned to face Mel. "Something is really off here and I don't know what it is. Until I find out, you need to stay the hell away from me!"

Nicole climbed into her car and roared away. Mel returned to her car but didn't try to pursue her. She was sure Nicole was headed home, and she would catch up to her there. She picked up a drive-through meal and then parked down the street from her house. Before pulling her food from the bag, she walked to Nicole's garage and looked through its window to make sure her Edge was there. She returned to her SUV and unwrapped the cold hamburger. She thought about all the things she wished she could have said to Nicole to make her understand. Never in her life had she ever had a desire to make an explanation for her actions, but Nicole had touched her. She cared what Nicole thought, and it disturbed her to think she had caused Nicole any more pain than she had already experienced today. She opened the file on the seat beside her and stared at Nicole's phone number. The realization hit her hard. She was about to cross the line again. She dialed Angela.

"Hey, Angela. It's Mel." She took a deep breath. "I'm sorry to ask, but can you cover me early tonight?"

"Sure. Everything okay?"

"Yes, I'm feeling...I think I need a break."

"That's cool. I was going to call you shortly because I was thinking about asking Garrett to cover the early morning hours anyway. He isn't assigned a specific task and asked if he could help us out."

"That would be great. I'll meet up with him tomorrow morning then."

"Okay. I'll see you shortly."

"Thanks, Angela."

* * *

Nikki plugged her iPod into the speaker box and cranked the volume. Sitting on the floor, she wrapped cotton tape around her hands, taking her time with each layer. She slid her feet into the black boxing shoes and pulled the laces tight. At the first punch into the hanging bag, both dogs bolted out of the room. Nikki laughed as she spun into a back kick. She pounded her fists into the bag as she ducked and weaved around the makeshift arms she had sewn onto it. She moved her feet to the rhythm of the music, punching harder and faster. Soon the sweat covering her body was running into her eyes, and she stopped to wipe her face. Movement on the street outside her window caught her eye and she stopped to watch the woman disappear into the dark SUV.

* * *

"Anything I need to know?" Angela asked, sliding onto the seat beside Mel.

"Nope. She spent most of the day out with her dogs and returned about an hour ago. I haven't checked in today. Can you do it?"

"Sure. I'll take care of it. Get out of here." Angela opened the door and stood. "Well, isn't that a sight?"

Mel followed Angela's gaze looking toward Nicole's house and her breath caught. Standing on the front porch watching them was Nicole, dressed in shorts and a sports bra. The sweat dripped off her body and she stood with her arms crossed over her chest. Her gaze was glued to the woman behind the wheel. Angela leaned back into the car. "I think you've angered the beast. Better get out of here. I'll call you tomorrow afternoon."

Mel gunned the engine and pulled away from the curb. Angela gave Nicole a wave as she returned to her car.

* * *

After a few moments, Nikki returned to her workout. The agent outside her house was as attractive as the one that had just left, but Nikki didn't feel the same emotional connection. As she worked her body through a simple yoga routine, she concentrated on clearing her mind. Mission after mission flowed through her memory as she thought about which ones could be called odd. She knew her ability to follow instructions without asking questions could also allow someone to play her. Her problem was that she didn't know the big picture. What might be unusual to her could be normal when combined with a mission from another team. Who was she to second-guess her instructions? Trusting Josh and the other OSLs was how the organization functioned. She was really looking forward to returning to work and getting a better picture of what was going on. Maybe it was time to talk with someone else. She grabbed her cell phone and dialed Brad.

"Peanut butter."

"What?" Nikki frowned into the phone.

"I'm thinking cookies would make an excellent code."

"Oh." Nikki laughed relieved to enjoy a moment without stress. "Chocolate chip."

"Snickerdoodle."

Nikki laughed. "You can't say that fast enough to avoid getting shot."

"Snickerdoodle, snickerdoodle, snickerdoodle," Brad chanted.

"Hey, nimrod. I called for a reason."

"Oh, and I thought you had called to get a heads-up on the next code." Brad laughed at his own joke. When she remained silent, he stopped laughing and cleared his throat. "Let me guess. You have company."

Nikki hesitated for a second. "Yes, and I'm getting very annoyed."

"I imagine you are, but play nice for now. I called Josh earlier, but he hasn't called me back yet. I'll let you know if he says anything useful when he does."

Nikki sighed. "Do you think we're the only ones?"

"I'm not sure, but I'll ask when he calls me."

Nikki disconnected the phone and tossed it on the floor. She made a salad for dinner and added a grilled chicken breast to the top of it. Afterward she settled onto the couch with her dogs and tried to read a book. The character in the romance novel quickly became the chestnut-haired agent she couldn't seem to get out of her head. Eventually, she gave up and went to bed.

* * *

Mel drove straight from Nicole's to a local gym and bought a one-day membership. She changed clothes in the shower room and stretched quickly before locating an empty treadmill. She increased her speed and incline until her muscles screamed. Unfortunately, the fast pace and an hour of lifting weights afterward did nothing to erase Nicole from her mind as she had hoped.

She returned to her empty hotel room and took advantage of the hotel service that restocked her minibar each day. After draining the first bottle, she called room service and ordered a pasta dish. She only took a few bites before pushing it away. Food couldn't satisfy what her body craved, and as long as Nicole danced in her mind, she wouldn't be able to sleep. She sat on the balcony and watched the lights of the city below her. When the night air cooled her, she pulled the comforter from the bed and returned to her chair outside.

CHAPTER ELEVEN

For the second morning in a row, Nikki used the cover of the garage to load the dogs into the car before opening the garage door. When she reached the street, she purposely turned right, moving away from the dark SUV in front of her house. Accelerating fast and braking hard, she maneuvered around the first couple of turns as fast as her Ford Edge would allow. She hadn't heard back from Brad yet, and she couldn't decide if it was good or bad that he was being tailed too. She had planned to stay in today, but her foster mom had called and invited her to lunch. She refused to drag her family into this, whatever it was, so she needed to lose her tail before heading to their house. The CIA probably knew everything about them, but just in case, she wanted to keep this as far from them as she could.

After several turns, she pulled into a parking lot and watched traffic for about ten minutes. When the black SUV didn't pass, she pulled back into traffic and drove to the ranch house where she had spent her middle school and high school years. Her foster parents lived on a quiet street outside the city limits. They loved Bailey and Riley and had even fenced in their backyard so they could visit. Occasionally, they would doggie sit, but Nikki preferred to leave them with Barbara. Her parents were known for feeding the dogs table scraps, and after a rough case of pancreatitis, Riley was on a strict diet.

Bob and Sandra were sitting on the porch swing when Nikki arrived. She parked on the street, checking traffic before letting the dogs out.

Sandra stood as Nikki approached. "Hey, Mom." Nikki kissed her on the cheek.

"Iced tea?" Sandra asked, stepping into the house with the dogs on her heels.

"Yes, thank you. Please don't give them human food," Nikki called to her mother's disappearing back. She bent down and kissed her dad on the cheek. "How's retirement?"

He rolled his eyes. "How's your job?"

Nikki laughed. She was traveling so much in college that she told Bob and Sandra she worked as a flight attendant. That lie had stuck, and now it was easier than trying to explain a portion of the truth. "The job has been better."

"Well, retirement could be better too. Your mom doesn't want me in the house all day and, honestly, I don't have anywhere else to hide. I was thinking about building a workshop in the backyard."

"Sounds good." She smiled at him. "With a television, of course."

"Of course."

Sandra stepped onto the porch. "I put the dogs in the backyard with some bones." She handed Nikki a glass of iced tea. "The quiche needs about ten more minutes in the oven, but the salad is ready if you're starving."

"No, I can wait, if you guys are okay."

"We slept a little late today so it was almost eight when we had breakfast," Sandra explained.

"If you can even call it breakfast," Bob grumbled. "Half of a grapefruit and a piece of toast is not even a snack."

Sandra laughed. "I'm dieting and your father feels he is being punished."

"Why are you dieting, Mom?" Nikki looked at her mother closely. She was curvy, but Nikki would never refer to her as chunky.

"Oh, I don't know." She smiled shyly.

"Now, Sandy." Bob looked his wife and then at Nikki. "That Sheila Andrews across the street made a comment and now your mother thinks she's fat. It's just crazy." He shrugged. "Maybe you can talk some sense into her. She won't listen to me."

"Sheila Andrews has always been a little chunky, plus she's short. You are neither of those things." Nikki reinforced her father's argument.

"You are both very kind, but those jeans I bought last fall barely button now. It has nothing to do with Sheila." Sandra stood. "The quiche should be almost done now so let's go inside."

Bob shrugged and gave Nikki a quick hug as they stood to follow Sandra into the house. "We tried."

Nikki hugged his waist and then held the door open for him to enter first. Though she enjoyed the comfortable banter her parents shared, she still didn't believe that kind of happiness would ever be in her future. Her stomach gave a twinge as she thought of the walk yesterday with the no-name agent and how comfortable it had felt. Her reminiscing quickly turned ugly as she remembered the evasive answer she had received when she asked her name.

The sound of a car door slamming pulled Nikki's attention back to the street. "Unbelievable." She mumbled under her breath as she took in the form in the faded jeans and button-down shirt leaning against the dark SUV parked behind her Ford. Even at a distance, Nikki could feel the dark eyes boring into her. She stepped into the house, allowing the screen door to slam behind her.

"Please, don't let the screen door slam, Nikki," her mother called from the kitchen.

"Yes, Mom," Nikki automatically answered her mother as she stared across the street. She should have known she wouldn't be able to lose her that easy.

* * *

Mel climbed back into the vehicle to wait. She knew from the file on the seat beside her that this was the home of Nicole's foster parents, Bob and Sandra Tillman. Mel had read and reread every shred of information about Nicole, but there was no explanation on why she had never been adopted. She had lived with Bob and Sandra from age ten until she left for college.

The blinking GPS tracker on Mel's phone caught her eye and she turned the application off. Thank goodness for the technology that allowed her to track people via their cell phones. She could have called into the office at Parker Street and had the GPS device on Nicole's car tracked, but her ego hated asking for assistance. Just calling in status checks annoyed Mel, and she felt bad for dumping that detail on Angela yesterday. The guilty feeling pushed at her until she dialed the phone.

"Mel?"

"Yes, I'm just checking in."

"It's been a while since we heard from you," Bowden said, stating the obvious.

"Nothing to report."

"And where is she now."

Mel felt a moment of protectiveness toward Nicole's personal life and hesitated before answering. "At her foster parents' house."

"Okay. I understand Garrett covered the night shift last night."

"Yes." She hoped Angela had cleared that before bringing Garrett in.

"Make sure he comes in with you tomorrow for the debriefing."

"Will the surveillance continue after that?" Mel asked.

"I'm not sure. Nothing has stirred up yet." She paused for several seconds and Mel could hear her typing in the background. "That's the problem with marks being agents, they don't throw out the red flag for every event. When they all return to the office tomorrow and start talking, we'll see what happens."

"Okay. See you in the morning."

* * *

Sitting at the stoplight, Nikki studied the agent's features in the rearview mirror. Unfortunately, she was exactly what Nikki looked for in a woman. Tall, dark and disturbingly handsome. Nikki couldn't help but wonder if things would play out the same way if she went back to the bar again. She couldn't stop herself from wanting to kiss her again. Her heart raced with the possibility.

Nikki dialed Brad. "Can I stop by?" she asked as soon as he answered.

"Sure."

"Meet me outside. I have the dogs in the car."

"You can bring them in."

"I'm not staying. I just need to run something by you."

"Okay, but pull in the driveway. My tail is still on the street."

"See you in ten."

Brad was waiting when she pulled into his driveway, and he handed her a can of soda when she climbed out. "So what's up?"

Nikki took her time opening the can. Now that she was here, she wasn't sure she wanted to ask his opinion. She knew what he would say. She was making this personal and neither of them had any idea who this woman was.

"Nikki?"

"I talked with her yesterday." Nikki took a sip of the cold soda.

Brad frowned. "Your tail?"

"Yep."

"And?"

Nikki looked at the two dark SUVs parked across the street and then back at Brad. She leaned against the car, turning her back to the agents. "She implied someone in our organization is dirty."

"That doesn't explain why they're the ones investigating it or us."

"No, but they showed up at Flagler before I left Thursday night. Josh said their snitch was killed after we left the party."

Brad turned his back to the agents and leaned against the car beside her. "Wow. Interesting."

"She asked me if things were off on any missions."

Brad frowned again. "What did you tell her?"

"Nothing. Have you made contact with your tail?"

"I wave at him as I come in and out."

Nikki laughed. "Does he wave back?"

"No, just the customary CIA asshole nod." Brad imitated the stone-faced head bob before he continued. "What I don't understand is the blatant in-your-face surveillance."

"Unless it's not really us they are trying to put pressure on."

Brad nodded. "Josh?"

"Maybe."

"He hasn't returned my call, by the way." Brad looked back at the surveillance vehicles. "Wait a minute." He turned completely around, staring directly at them. "Is that the same woman we saw at the airfield?"

Nikki grinned. "The one and only."

"Damn. She was hot."

"Yes, I felt the same way when she was sticking her tongue down my throat the other night."

Brad laughed and then his face grew serious as he stared at her. "You're not kidding?"

"No." Nikki took another drink of her soda. "She followed me to the bar Friday night."

"Holy crap! That's above and beyond the call of duty."

Nikki laughed.

"Don't hold back. Tell all."

"I came home and she sat outside in her car. End of story." *Well, not completely*, she thought.

"But you made out with her at the bar?"

Nikki shrugged. "It wasn't my idea. It happened really fast and then we were interrupted. I left before anything else could happen."

"So she was trying to seduce you?"

"Yes…no." Nikki laughed. "It's not like I resisted."

"And you would do it again?"

"In a heartbeat." Nikki turned to stare at the vehicle behind them and sighed. "Which is why I am going home now."

"Good idea." Brad smiled. "We'll hash this all out tomorrow with the team."

Nikki smiled back at him before climbing into her car. Brad always had a way of making her feel better.

CHAPTER TWELVE

Mel arrived outside Nicole's house on Monday morning while it was still dark. Garrett had no information to pass on so she sent him home to sleep for a couple hours before the debriefing. She used the quiet morning hours to type her notes for the last couple of days into the laptop. She entered only the facts, leaving out any specific personal details. After wrapping up her notes, she drove to the nearby coffee shop. She picked up two large cups of black coffee before returning to her spot outside Nicole's house.

She picked up her cell phone and punched in the number her fingers had been itching to dial.

"Mitchell," Mel said seductively, using Nicole's last name when she answered.

Nicole's breath caught and Mel wasn't sure if she was shocked or pleased to hear from her. "Now what?" Nicole asked arrogantly.

"What kind of reception is that?" Mel asked with a hint of laughter in her voice. "I have coffee. Want to let me in?"

"No," Nicole said too quickly.

Now Mel laughed openly. "I thought we were becoming friends, Mitchell."

"Friends? Really?" Nicole couldn't help but laugh too. "I'll be out in five. Keep my coffee warm."

Not for the first time, Mel wished she had met Nicole in a different situation. She liked the sound of her laughter and longed to hear it again.

A few minutes later the garage door opened and Nicole's SUV backed out. She didn't stop at the end of her driveway, but backed into the street and lined up her driver's window with Mel's window.

Mel passed a cup through the window. "We could be friends," Mel said with a smile.

Nicole tilted her head, as if in thought. "No, I think I know all of my friends' names." She smiled as Mel laughed. "Thanks for the coffee."

"To the office now?" Mel asked.

Nicole laughed. "I'm not going to make your job easier." Nicole dropped the SUV into gear and hit the button to close the window. "Try to keep up."

Mel spun the SUV into a U-turn and gunned the engine. At the first intersection, she went right instead of left to follow Nicole. She had enough time to enjoy breakfast before her meeting at Parker Street.

* * *

Nikki saw the dark SUV turn right instead of left and frowned. For the next several blocks she scanned the vehicles behind her to see if she had a new tail. Traffic thinned as she approached the dead-end road to Flagler and she was confident there was no one following her.

She pulled to a stop at the security gate, and the uniformed officer gave her a wave as she swiped her access badge. The gate arm lifted, allowing her to enter the secure facility. She circled in front of the Flagler building before choosing a parking spot in the first row. Flagler was a popular name in Florida, dating back for centuries. When she first came to work here, she was told that the building had been used by soldiers in the 1800s. As she approached the stucco wall that surrounded the one-story building made of the same material, she glanced through the archway into the courtyard. With its arched windows and clay-tile roof, she always felt the Spanish-style building held as much history as the name Flagler.

At the heavy wooden front door, she swiped her badge again and was walking the empty halls before her shift started. She smiled to herself as she refilled her empty coffee cup in the break room. The coffee had been a pleasant surprise this morning, but now it reminded her again of her irritation at not knowing this woman's name. She looked at the hard plastic coffee cup with the local store's logo on it and then at her watch. She quickly dumped her fresh coffee into a Styrofoam cup and bolted from the room. Five minutes later, she exited the lab and jogged down the hall to the receiving department to join her team in unpacking their container from the last mission. The lab would have fingerprint results for her by noon; she couldn't help smiling again.

"Nice of you to join us, Mitchell." Mike harassed her as soon as she opened the door.

"Did you have trouble losing your tail?" Brad asked.

Nikki frowned. "I don't think she followed me this morning. If she did, I didn't see her."

Jewels put down her rucksack and looked at Nikki. "Are you being followed too?"

"I think we all are." Tyler jumped to his feet to address the group. "I've already talked with Josh this morning and he said he would be in shortly. When we finish here, I want everyone to write this up. Something is not right and we need to have it all documented."

"The CIA has never intruded into Flagler like this before, have they?" Nikki asked.

Tyler shrugged. "Not that I'm aware of. That's why I want to make sure we keep a record of everything."

Everyone nodded and then went back to unpacking. Josh arrived about an hour later.

"Okay, here's what I know," Josh began as soon as he entered the room. "The individual that made the package exchange was killed about an hour after we cleared the scene. Our only guess is the CIA thinks we were involved."

Josh held up his hand to silence the mass grumbling and continued. "We have produced all of our voice transmissions and flight paperwork to prove we were out of the area before it went down. Lewis and I compiled all of your after-action reviews and have already briefed Mr. Flagler. He has all the details and I am confident he will make this—and them—go away."

"It sounds to me like the CIA has a leak," Mike said.

Josh nodded his agreement. "I think so too." He waved his arm around the equipment-strewn room. "Finish up here and then go to lunch. Be in the conference room at thirteen hundred hours."

Everyone nodded and went back to work. Nikki listened to the conversations around her as everyone complained and told their stories of being followed. She gave Brad a look to let him know she didn't intend to share. She carefully cleaned and repaired her personal equipment so it would be ready for the next mission or practice exercise, whichever came first. She completely agreed with Flagler that the way they trained would be how they would perform in the field. There were no shortcuts.

All equipment was cleaned and stored with an hour and a half to spare until they needed to be in the conference room. The team gathered around their personal lockers.

Brad slammed his locker shut and looked at Nikki. "Mexican?"

"Sure." She nodded but lowered her voice. "I need to make a stop first."

Brad raised his eyebrows. "I'll follow." Turning to the rest of the team, he said, "We'll meet you at the restaurant."

Nikki headed for the lab with Brad giving her questioning looks. The analysis technician handed her a printout when she walked into the room. She quickly folded it and stuffed it in her pocket.

"What's that?" Brad asked.

"I'll tell you when we get in the car."

Nikki had barely slid into the seat when Brad turned to her. "Spill it."

"Just drive and I'll tell you on the way."

She waited until Brad put the car in gear before she pulled the paper from her pocket. Brad watched her and the road while she read.

Nikki absorbed the information. *Melissa Jean Carter. Height 5'9." Weight 165. Hair brown. Eyes brown. University of Tennessee Bachelor of Science, Criminal Justice. US Army Military Intelligence, current employment classified.*

Nikki waved the piece of paper at Brad. "She brought me coffee this morning and I had the cup printed."

"What?" Brad laughed.

"I have talked with her several times over the last couple of days, and every time I asked her name she would avoid the question. I was starting to get annoyed. I wanted to know who she was." Nikki stared at the black-and-white photo on the sheet in her hands.

"So, what's it say?" Brad asked.

"Absolutely nothing on her employment. Classified. But at least now I know her name."

Nikki folded the paper and stuck it back into her pocket as they crossed the parking lot to the restaurant. She couldn't wait to see Melissa again. She wondered if her friends called her "Mitzy" or maybe "Jean." She wasn't sure either name fit. "Carter," though, that stuck in Nikki's mind. She repeated it over and over in her head until Brad nudged her to follow the rest of the team to their table.

* * *

Mel arrived at Parker Street with a full stomach and her second cup of coffee. She squeezed her SUV into a corner space and took the elevator to the briefing room.

"Hello, Melissa." Joey motioned to the chair beside him.

Mel smiled. For once his use of her full name didn't bother her. "Hello, Joseph." Mel earned herself a frown from Joey as she took a seat beside him.

"Hey, Mel." Liam leaned around Joey to see her.

"Hey." Mel acknowledged him. "Have I missed anything?"

Liam shook his head and all three turned to look at Bowden in the front of the room talking with a group of agents. The agents dispersed and Bowden addressed the room.

"Take twenty minutes to compile your data for each tail and one person from each group can brief." She turned and left the room.

Mel looked around spotting Angela and Garrett seated near the front and she moved to join them.

Angela spoke first. "I got nothing. She was in her house for all of the time I was watching her." She grinned. "Except when she visited me in the car."

Mel laughed. "She is very bold."

"She spoke to you?" Garrett asked curiously.

"She did," Angela stated. "Walked right out to the car and climbed in beside me. Oh, and brought me coffee and a pastry."

Garrett laughed with them. "I bet she had questions."

"She did, but when I wouldn't answer she went back inside."

Garrett looked at Mel. "Did you talk with her too?"

Heat coursed through Mel's veins and she felt her skin burn as she remembered the feel of Nicole when she pressed her against the wall in the bar and the appreciative look she had given as she appraised Mel's body outside the hospital. She took a sip of coffee and regained some of her composure before answering Garrett. "Yes, a few times."

Garrett looked surprised.

Mel shrugged. "We were told to stay visible. No one said to avoid contact."

"It would be hard to avoid contact when you are putting yourself right in front of her," Angela agreed.

Garrett nodded. "I guess so. Just not our normal mission. So, what did she say?"

"She thinks we're CIA." Mel took another sip of her coffee. "Which is understandable since we used call sign Charlie on the mission."

"Bowden said we did that to throw them off. What if they attempt to confirm it now that we are tailing them?" Angela asked.

"Mr. Flagler will take care of any inquiries," Mel explained. She looked at Garrett. "Nothing for you to report?"

"Nope, inside sleeping is my guess. There weren't any lights on."

"Okay, I'll brief then." Mel stood. "I need to grab a refill." She noticed Angela studying her face before she walked away. She knew she should fill Angela in on everything that had transpired, and she knew the fact that she wasn't doing so spelled trouble. She promised herself that she would talk with her, but right now she needed to compile her briefing before standing in front of the entire team.

Mel struggled to stay focused as each team's briefing sounded the same as hers. Some small talk had been exchanged, which wasn't surprising since their goal was to be observed. Clearly, the Flagler team was used to unusual situations, but they weren't used to being tailed at home, and that made them curious. No one had any late-night visitors or clandestine meetings to report.

Bowden and a technician with a stack of papers in his hands approached the front of the room. "We have reviewed every cell and landline call for each of the team members and there is nothing out of the ordinary."

From the back of the room a voice called out. "Maybe we should drop out of sight for our surveillance now."

Bowden looked up. "No, our intent was to put pressure on them. We weren't convinced the leak was at the team level, but it was a place to start. The results of the pressure we have applied will ricochet up the ladder. No change of tactics, at least for now." She looked at Mel. "Take five others with you and head to Flagler. You are going to train with them for the next couple of days. Talk to them, make friends and see what you can dig up."

Mel stood up and asked for volunteers. A lot of eager hands rose and she chose four guys and another woman to join her.

CHAPTER THIRTEEN

Nikki and Brad selected seats in the back of the room to continue their conversation from the car.

"So can you think of anything?" Nikki whispered softly without looking at him.

"Nothing jumps out at me." Brad glanced at her. "Can you?"

Nikki frowned. "Maybe."

"Which mission?"

"Well, I was just thinking that this wasn't the first time we watched a package exchange hands and then returned."

"That's our job, Nikki." Brad stood and placed his hands on his hips in the traditional Superman pose. "We are here to serve and protect."

Nikki laughed and pulled him back down into his seat. "Will you help me go through some files tonight?"

"My wife will not be happy with either of us but I will if…" He pointed a finger at her chest. "You buy the pizza and beer."

"You got it."

Josh entered the room and everyone grew silent. He approached Tyler and spoke quietly for several minutes then he addressed the group. "Nikki and Mike, head to the range for the afternoon. Everyone else is with Tyler."

The conference room door opened as Josh finished speaking and a group of six entered the room with Lewis. Nikki was shocked to see Carter leading the group and watched with great interest as the CIA agents took seats across the room. They were dressed the same as Nikki and her team in black long-sleeved T-shirts, black tactical pants and boots. Josh and Lewis spoke in hushed tones before Lewis left the room. Josh turned to the new group. "I need two of you to be spotters on the range and the rest can go with Tyler." Josh pointed to Tyler and he nodded his head in acknowledgment. Nikki's eyes were glued to Carter.

"I'll spot." Carter stood, giving Nikki a cocky smile before focusing her attention on Josh. "Me too," a deep voice echoed from within Carter's group.

"Great." Josh turned to Tyler. "Go ahead and take off. Call if you need anything."

Tyler nodded and motioned his group to follow. Carter and a tall, dark-haired man approached Josh.

Brad whispered as he stood. "See you in the office later?"

"Yes, I'll type your surveillance report before we head home."

Brad wiggled his eyebrows and looked at the two agents in the front of the room. "Have fun." He followed Tyler out of the room.

Nikki slowly approached the remaining group in the front of the room. She appraised the two agents as they spoke with Mike. Things just kept getting weirder and weirder. Whatever Lewis had said to Josh was enough for Josh to allow the CIA team to integrate themselves in today's training. She looked at Josh and he motioned her forward. "Nikki, this is Mel. She'll be spotting for you this afternoon."

Mel held out her hand and Nikki took it tentatively. "Nikki," Mel said softly.

Nikki dropped her hand and headed for the door. Over her shoulder she called back to Mel. "Let's go, Carter."

Mel hesitated for a second as the use of her last name registered, and then she followed Nikki out the door. She lengthened her stride and quickly caught up with her. "So, you checked me out?"

"I ran your prints from the coffee cup."

Mel laughed. "And now you prefer Carter to Mel?"

"I think it's my choice since I did the work." She liked the sound of Mel's laughter. "Have you ever spotted before?"

"Yes, when I first started with Fla..." She let the final word drift away before continuing. "Then I realized I was better at tracking."

"And now you just stalk people."

Mel laughed again. "Your file should have said smart-ass under your name."

Nikki rolled her eyes and led the way into the arms room where she checked out her rifle and a spotter scope for Mel. Nikki handed Mel ear protection and inserted one disposable ear plug into her own ear as they exited the building. Nikki did her best to block out Mel's presence as they followed a narrow gravel trail that ended at a patch of trees. She turned left onto the two-mile rifle range and waited until they were cleared to enter. On the range, Nikki selected a lane and lay down on the ground, doing a couple of breathing exercises. She waited to see if Mel would lay on her left side to avoid the ejection port of her rifle and was pleased when she did. Within a few minutes the range alarm sounded to signal an active range and an announcement was made to remove anyone downrange.

The first green fatigue-dressed silhouette target popped up and Nikki took a breath before shooting it. The targets began appearing randomly at varying distances, all less than one thousand meters, and Nikki took out each one with one shot. When the range alarm signaled the round was over, Nikki switched her safety on and removed her ear plug.

Mel removed her ear protection and rolled on her side to look at Nikki. "Impressive."

Nikki shrugged. "Don't you want the best when you're a sitting duck on foreign soil?"

"You were watching my back last week?"

"Yep. Me and Brad."

Mel searched Nikki's face. "You've been thinking about what I asked you, haven't you?"

"Maybe." Nikki loaded a full magazine into her rifle and chambered a round.

"And you thought of something that wasn't right?"

"I'm not sure." Nikki wanted to confide in her, but she was CIA, after all. She couldn't disclose anything from Flagler to someone on the outside, even if it seemed like Mel had full access. She would look into the files tonight with Brad, and if they found something, they would decide who to trust with the information.

"What did you think of?" Mel pushed.

Nikki shook her head. The firing range alarm sounded again. Nikki replaced her ear plug, closed her eyes and focused on her breathing. For this round, the targets were in motion. She would have thirty seconds to sight and fire on each target. Mel was quick to supply the wind direction for each one, and target adjusts for the few times Nikki missed on the first shot. With her aid, Nikki was able to take out all of the targets within the allotted time.

When the firing range alarm sounded to end the round, Mel was talking almost before they had removed their ear protection. "Just give me a scenario. You don't have to say anything specific."

Nikki looked hard at her. "I am not going to discuss classified Flagler missions with the CIA."

Mel sighed. "What if I don't work for the CIA?"

Nikki loaded another full magazine and chambered the round before glancing at Mel. "This conversation is over. I don't care who you work for. I am not going to have this discussion with you."

They finished the last two firing rounds in silence. Mel and her team member talked softly in a far corner while Nikki and Mike cleaned their rifles before turning them back into the arms room. Then all four of them signed out Five-seveN pistols with multiple clips. They returned to the same path, turning right onto the small arms range. Along with traditional cubes for target practice, the pistol range had a qualification course. It was all stationary targets, but the shooter was required to move to each position. They would fire right and left from behind barricades and from standing and kneeling positions. Each clip was only loaded with five rounds to force the participant into changing clips multiple times.

Mel looked over at her. "If I can match you or beat you, you owe me lunch."

Nikki smiled. "Okay, but if I beat you, I want dinner instead of lunch. For the record, I prefer Italian."

Mel laughed as the firing range alarm sounded indicating an active range. The range attendant confirmed they were each ready and then blew his whistle for them to begin the course.

Nikki could see Mel out of the corner of her eye and knew they were maneuvering the course at the same speed. She couldn't tell if she was hitting her targets though. When they cleared the last target, they both holstered their pistols and walked back to the starting point. Together they walked first Mel's course and then Nikki's.

Nikki groaned. "I cannot believe you hit bull's-eye on every target."

Mel shrugged. "I run this course almost every week, and you only missed a perfect run by two."

"Yes, but I'm a sniper." Nikki laughed. "What is it you do for a living?"

"I stalk people." Mel turned toward the building.

Nikki shook her head and followed Mel back to the arms room. The workday was almost over and she needed to file her report as Tyler had requested. Weapons were cleaned in silence and the four went their separate ways. Nikki went straight to her desk and began typing her report. She was surprised when Mel slid a chair over beside her.

Nikki clicked a button on her keyboard, returning her monitor to the home screen to cover her report. She looked at Mel. "Can I help you, Carter?"

Mel laughed. "When are you buying my lunch?"

"How about tomorrow? Are you going to be here? Or am I not the only person you are stalking right now?"

"You are currently the only woman in my life." Surprised flashed across Mel's face as she quickly stood and headed for the door. "I'll see you tomorrow."

"Hey, wait," Nikki called, and Mel turned around. "No stalking tonight?"

"I'm not sure. I'm going to find out right now." The cocky grin was back as Mel strolled away. "Try not to miss me if I don't see you tonight."

Nikki returned to her report. She knew she should enter everything that happened into the records, but she didn't think Flagler needed to know she had made out in the bathroom with a CIA agent. She thought to herself how unprofessional it was of both of them. She had spent the day with Mel, and she didn't get the feeling that Mel would disregard her mission like that. *What if her mission was to seduce me?* Nikki frowned. Things were becoming a little bit clearer now, and she wasn't sure if she liked what she was seeing.

Nikki quickly finished her report and emailed it to Tyler. When Brad returned, she typed his report while he dictated and then they both headed home. They would meet back at Nikki's after Brad took his boys to karate practice.

* * *

Nikki took a sip of coffee and looked at Brad. They both had had a beer with dinner but had switched to coffee as the evening progressed. Nikki had downloaded their mission reports for the last year onto data sticks and each of them now sat in front of a laptop clicking through files. Nikki rubbed her face and then looked at her watch.

"Geez, it's almost midnight." She groaned, clicking on the last file on her drive.

"Yeah, we should call it a night." Brad yawned.

Nikki stared at the screen. "Here's another one." She skimmed the report giving Brad the highlights. "Remember about a year ago when we were sent to Tehran? It was supposed to be a package pick up at the airport."

"Yeah, Josh was the OSL on that mission too. I remember because he called us himself after we received the package and told us not to return with it as had originally been instructed."

"We took it to a bus depot and left it in locker…" Nikki continued to skim the report. "Eighty-two. It was locker eighty-two."

"Right and we had to run to make our return flight."

Nikki looked up at Brad. "Remember how nervous the guy was when he gave us the package."

"Yeah, we laughed about it containing a bomb." Brad's eyes widened. "You don't think?"

Nikki closed the file she was looking at and opened a search engine. She typed in Tehran and bomb. It only took a minute for her to locate an article the day after they had returned from the mission. She turned her computer for Brad to read too. He stared at her when he finished. "It doesn't mean our package contained a bomb, Nikki."

"I know, but…"

Brad's phone chirped with an incoming text message and Nikki's did the same a second later. Brad stood. "I need to get home and tell Marianne we're leaving again."

Nikki nodded.

"We'll talk about this when we get back from this mission, okay?" Brad asked her.

She nodded again as she walked him to the door. "I'll see you in a couple of hours." She watched Brad get in his car and drive down the street out of sight. Her gaze traveled over all the cars sitting on the curb up and down her street. Tonight there was no dark SUV and she felt a little alone.

Stepping back into the house, she dialed Barbara. After apologizing for waking her up, she explained she would drop the dogs off within the hour. Then she searched through her call log on her cell phone until she located the incoming call from that morning.

"Carter," Nikki said as soon as Mel answered.

"Mitchell?"

"Meet me at the coffee shop by my house in thirty minutes."

Mel hesitated for a second. "Okay."

Nikki hung up without saying goodbye. She cleaned her kitchen and refrigerator of all potential rotting hazards before taking a shower and loading the dogs. She stopped at Barbara's and punched in the gate code to the backyard. Both dogs ran through the doggie door and into the house. Nikki heard Barbara's dog bark a greeting, so she locked the gate behind her and returned to her car.

CHAPTER FOURTEEN

Nikki pulled into the empty lot in front of the coffee shop and turned off her engine. Traffic had been light and she had arrived faster than she expected. She sat in her car as her mind raced through all the possible answers to the questions she planned to ask. If Mel was CIA, then the conversation would be over and their meeting would have been for nothing. *Well, not for nothing*, Nikki thought with regret. She would have a chance to talk with her one last time before she severed their relationship. When the dark SUV entered the parking lot, she climbed out of her car and crossed the lot to meet Mel at the door of the shop. Mel was still in her black battle fatigues and her hair was disheveled as if she had repeatedly run her fingers through it. Nikki wondered where she had been since they parted hours earlier.

"Coffee?" Nikki asked, holding the door open for her.

Mel nodded and approached the counter. Nikki glanced around. The shop was empty, not surprising at this hour. Noticing that the wall to her right was covered with mirrors in an attempt to make the small shop look larger, she took advantage of them to get a clearer view of Mel. Her dark clothing was a contrast to her own light blue T-shirt and faded jeans. She had specifically chosen these jeans for their comfort, but she had known that she would be seeing Mel too. She glanced up at Mel's face, wondering if she appreciated the way her jeans sat low on her hips accentuating her hips and butt. She got her answer when Mel's eyes lifted to meet her own.

Knowing she had been caught, Mel gave her a cocky grin. Nikki wasn't surprised that Mel was without shame or embarrassment. She didn't strike her as someone who would backpedal or have regrets. Her actions were confident and without concern for the approval of others.

Nikki smiled her thanks when Mel turned and handed her a mug of coffee. She followed her across the shop where Mel selected a table in the corner, giving them both a view of the front door. Nikki met Mel's eyes again as she sat down across from her. The look of desire that had flashed across her face had sent a shiver through her body. Now, however, her face was inquisitive. Nikki took a deep breath, searching for the professional distance she needed in order to ask her questions.

"Who do you work for?"

"What did you and Brad find?" Mel countered.

"No one was on the street tonight. How did you know I was with Brad?"

Mel smiled but didn't answer.

Nikki leaned closer across the table. "I need to know who you work for."

Mel pulled a badge case from her pocket and flipped it open on the table. "I work for Flagler, Internal Investigation Division."

Nikki sat back and frowned. "I didn't know Flagler had an Internal Investigation Division."

"You didn't need to know. We work out of the Tallahassee office, but we go wherever Mr. Flagler needs us to. And we do whatever he asks of us." Mel touched her hand. "What did you and Brad find?"

"Mr. Flagler knows there is an internal problem?" Nikki continued to stare at the badge on the table, trying to work through what Mel was telling her.

"Yes. He's been trying to figure out who is behind it for almost a year. What did you discover tonight?" Mel asked again, putting her badge back in her pocket.

Nikki sighed, rubbing her hand across her face. "Several missions that seemed to change midstream and Josh Houston was the OSL on all of them."

Mel nodded.

"You already knew this?"

"We were pretty sure. That's why your team has been getting the most scrutiny. We needed to make sure it wasn't at team level before moving up the line to focus on Josh."

Nikki looked at her watch. "I don't have time to go over what we found, but I'll call you when I get back." She didn't want to say it out loud, but she also wanted time to process what Mel had told her.

Mel frowned. "You have a mission?"

Nikki nodded.

"You can't go on a regular mission now. You know too much."

"No one knows what we know except for you."

Mel shook her head. "I don't like it." Before she could say more, her phone buzzed with an incoming text message. She dug it out of her pocket and looked up at Nikki. "Looks like we might see each other sooner than you expected."

Nikki raised her eyebrows. "Let's go then."

They stopped at the counter and had their cups refilled before leaving the building. They crossed the parking lot together, stopping at Nikki's Ford.

"Be safe," Mel whispered as she held the door open for Nikki.

"You too." Nikki slid behind the wheel. Mel pushed her door closed and walked toward her vehicle. She stopped before sliding into it and looked back at Nikki, giving her a cocky smile. Nikki took a deep breath and started the engine. She didn't know exactly when Mel had gotten under her skin, but there was no doubt in her mind that she was there now.

CHAPTER FIFTEEN

Nikki was well within the required three-hour window when she arrived at Flagler. After parking, she secured her personal bag and went straight to the conference room. The room was empty except for Brad and Josh. Nikki slid into a chair beside Brad and gave him a subdued smile. He wrinkled his nose in return.

"Okay. Let's get started." Josh closed the folder he was holding and looked up at them. "Easy mission. Senator Jan Wyatt will be traveling to Tel Aviv, along with two other senators. She's been the recipient of recent death threats so, in addition to her normal US Secret Service agents, she has specifically asked for two of our agents as well. There is a suite at the Sheraton reserved already." He tossed a folder in front of each of them. "Check-in details and your flight arrangements are inside, along with a background on Senator Wyatt. I also had tech include some details on the Child Soldier Prevention Act, which is why they're meeting in Tel Aviv."

Josh paced the floor in front of them as he continued. "You're only responsible for her time in Tel Aviv. She'll arrive on Thursday and depart on Friday. The meeting is currently scheduled for Thursday afternoon. The earliest commercial flight I could arrange for you to return was Friday evening."

He headed for the door. "I'll be in the operations room if you have any questions." He looked at his watch. "The jumper flight to New Orleans leaves in an hour."

Nikki watched Josh leave the room before turning to Brad. "I spoke with Carter this morning."

"Carter?"

"Mel Carter. My tail."

Brad raised his eyebrows.

"She's with Flagler."

"Well, how about that? Go pack. I can hear the whole story when we get on the road."

Nikki folded two gabardine suits into her carry-on bag along with jeans and several shirts. Hygiene items were placed on top for easy access. Their pistols and other gear would travel separately and be sent to the embassy for them to pick up when they arrived in Tel Aviv.

Brad was leaning against the car when Nikki joined him. She tossed her overnight bag in the backseat and slid behind the wheel. One of the things she liked best about Brad was his relaxed attitude. There were very few things that created an issue for him and driving was not one of them. Over the years they had developed a natural flow and they were comfortable with each other. During the twenty-minute drive to the airport, Brad read from the documents they had been provided. She started to tell him about her meeting with Mel, but he shook his head and put his hand to his ear to demonstrate someone might be listening. Nikki wrinkled her face to let him know she didn't like that thought, but she remained silent. Once they were out of the car, she recapped her early morning meeting with Mel.

"So she got a mission text too?"

"Yep. Since Josh is the OSL, they'll probably be following our mission."

"Interesting. Flagler has an internal investigative branch. I guess that doesn't surprise me."

"Yeah, me either after I thought about it. Part of me is glad Carter's team is Flagler and the other part is pissed off about being tailed by family."

"And being lied to about it."

Nikki nodded. They cleared security quickly and walked in silence to their gate. Since this was a protection detail, they would sit together on the plane to their destination.

Nikki relaxed into her seat and opened the briefing folder. She looked over their itinerary first, inwardly converting the times noted there from Central Standard to Zulu and then to Israel Daylight Time. She would switch her watch to Zulu time once they took off from D.C.

"We're going to arrive in Tel Aviv tonight at our midnight." She leaned across the aisle closer to Brad.

"That's brutal."

"It will also be zero eight hundred hours Israel Daylight Time, which means we'll be starting our day when we land."

Brad groaned. "No need to even try sleeping yet. This flight is only about thirty minutes." He stretched his legs into the aisle and closed his eyes anyway.

Nikki continued to look over their itinerary, memorizing flight numbers and departure times. As Brad had said, they had barely taken off when the captain announced they were about to land. Nikki looked around at the three others on the flight. All were dressed in business suits, and she guessed that they made this flight every day for work.

Nikki tucked the itinerary away, her mind making idle calculations. Mel lived in Tallahassee—almost three hours east of Pensacola. Practically the same distance from Pensacola as New Orleans was to the west. Would either of them be willing to travel that distance every day? *What the...?* She sat up straight, shocked at her thoughts. She was tired. That was the only reason she could think of to be contemplating something so crazy. Nothing had happened between them to insinuate they might have a future together. Even if both of them were willing, they each traveled too much to even consider anything permanent.

Nikki struggled to focus on their assignment. There would be plenty of time to explore thoughts of this sort when the mission was over. She felt a smile tug at the corners of her mouth. She had never been interested in a woman as intriguing as Mel. She squeezed her eyes shut to block the sexy image that had appeared in her mind of wavy hair and deep brown eyes. And that damn cocky smile.

Nikki's eyes flew open as the plane lurched to a stop. Brad was stretched across the aisle, staring into her face, his eyes full of amusement. "What were you thinking about?"

"Nothing, nimrod," Nikki mumbled. She stood, pulled her bag from the overhead compartment and exited the plane without looking back at him. She knew he was behind her because she could hear his laughter.

"We only have an hour before our flight departs so grab your food on the run," she reminded him when he pulled alongside her in the concourse.

"There's good." Brad pointed to a coffee and bagel stand. Nikki stuffed their food into her backpack and grabbed a cup of coffee. They arrived at the gate as the last people were boarding and were able to walk straight onto the plane. Nikki took the window seat and held their coffee while Brad stowed their bags overhead.

They ate their breakfast as the plane taxied, and Brad was asleep before they reached cruising altitude. As soon as it was allowed, Nikki dropped the meal tray and opened the briefing folder again, reviewing the background information on Senator Wyatt. She was surprised to see that she had graduated from Harvard Medical School before pursuing a career in politics. Nikki had met her once before and she remembered her outspoken tendencies. It was not surprising that she was receiving death threats considering all the time she spent in front of the media. She was always the spokesperson for every committee she sat on.

Nikki stared at the photograph attached to the folder. Senator Wyatt was forty-seven years old with the body of the marathon runner that she was, in addition to being a powerhouse politician. In the file photo, a studio shot, she was wearing a power suit and heels. There was a small amount of cleavage exposed between the creases of the silk button-down shirt.

Button-down shirt. Nikki's eyes closed, and for the first time in days, she allowed herself to think freely about her encounter with Mel in the bathroom at the bar. Mel, who had been her enemy, holding her against the wall with her hard body while her mouth devoured Nikki. Now that she knew they were on the same team, Nikki didn't have to fight the memories of that moment. Instantly transported back in time, she could feel the wetness growing between her legs again.

"Did you just moan?" Brad's voice broke into her dream state.

She opened her eyes and frowned at him. "What?"

"You just moaned." Brad's face was sleepy but filled with laughter.

"Go back to sleep, Brad."

"Do you want to talk about it?"

"No!" But she did. She wanted to talk to Mel about it. They needed to discuss what had happened and to clear the air between them.

Brad leaned his head back against the seat with a smile still on his face. Nikki looked at him. He was a good-looking man... if you liked men. His six-foot-two frame was intimidating—if you didn't look too close at his little boy face. He had turned thirty-five on his last birthday but, even with a little splattering of stubble, his face displayed no sign of age. His jet-black hair was cut in typical military style. He ate like a garbage disposal but worked out on a regular basis and his body showed his dedication. He was never condescending like some of the guys and this wasn't the first time Nikki was thankful for having him as a teammate.

"Stop staring at me," Brad grumbled.

"Do you have holes in your eyelids?" Nikki laughed and went back to reading the file.

* * *

The flight transfer at Dulles International Airport in D.C. was fast with only an hour layover. Nikki managed to feed the beast traveling with her, and purchase a pillow for the flight to Paris. She planned to sleep for the duration and knew from experience that Brad's bony shoulder was not a good option.

They arrived at the Charles De Gaulle Airport in Paris Tuesday evening Central Standard Time, but Nikki knew it was already the early morning hours of Wednesday in Israel. Brad checked in with Josh as Nikki stared longingly out the window at Paris farmland. She had never been to Paris, other than passing through like this, and she hoped one day to visit as a tourist. She rubbed her face to clear the sleep from her eyes and inhaled the aroma of the dark roast coffee in her hand.

Brad flopped into the seat beside her and unrolled a napkin to reveal two buttery croissants. He handed one to Nikki and tore off a huge bite of the other, stuffing it into his mouth.

"Josh says everything is a go, but we'll check in again when we land in Israel," Brad managed to mumble around his croissant.

"Did our gear arrive?"

"Yeah, he said someone from the embassy will secure it, and we can get it from them when we sign out a car." Brad stood. "Do you want another croissant? I need a couple more."

Nikki shook her head. "More coffee would be great though."

"Okay. I'll be right back."

Brad returned as their flight was announced and Nikki stood to meet him, taking the coffee cup from his hand. "How many did you buy?" Nikki looked at the bag he carried.

"Six. It was cheaper to buy a bundled half-dozen than a couple individually wrapped."

Nikki laughed. "We're getting a real breakfast when we get to Israel."

"Don't you worry." Brad smiled. "I'll be ready to eat again."

The flight to Tel Aviv was quiet, and Nikki used the time to continue her review of the folder. The Child Soldier Prevention Act was just one of many causes Senator Wyatt was supporting.

Nikki was familiar with the Act but found the details that had been provided interesting. She sipped her coffee and did her best to keep her mind focused on the mission. Mel had seemed worried about it, but Nikki wasn't so sure. It seemed pretty basic, one that she and Brad had done a hundred times.

CHAPTER SIXTEEN

They landed in Tel Aviv on schedule and Brad sent an arrival text to Josh. His response was simple, "No change." They maneuvered through the Ben Gurion Airport to baggage claim, where they had been told they could find an ATM. They each withdrew the maximum of Israeli shekels allowed at one time, then they caught a cab and went directly to the US Embassy on HaYarkon Street.

Nikki studied the contrast of the gray concrete slab building to the white and light tan modern ones surrounding it. At first glance it appeared to lack any distinguishing characteristics, but then she noticed that engraved into the concrete was "Embassy of the United States of America." Directly above the words was the US coat of arms, the American bald eagle, devoid of any color, taking center stage with thirteen stripes. The olive branch and thirteen arrows were clutched tight in its claws.

The cab dropped them on the street and they crossed between the concrete pole barriers blocking the entrance. Brad showed his identification to the US Marine greeting visitors at the front desk. "Mr. Dayton is expecting us."

Nikki opened her ID case to display her photo card and badge as well. The sergeant took both IDs and picked up the phone, punching an extension. He waited several seconds before speaking. "Mr. Morton and Ms. Mitchell to see Mr. Dayton." After another pause, "Yes, ma'am."

Hanging up the phone, he returned their IDs and motioned to several chairs lining one wall. "Please take a seat. Mr. Dayton will be down in a minute."

Before they had a chance to sit, the elevator doors opened and a tall, thin man motioned them forward. He had a receding hairline that was closer to the back than to the front of his head. His dark suit gave him a distinguished appearance, and his closed face suggested he was not someone given to a lot of conversation. He stepped aside to allow them to enter the elevator. Pressing the G, for what Nikki assumed was garage, he allowed the doors to close before speaking.

"Ron Dayton." He held his hand out, shaking first Nikki's and then Brad's hands.

"Nikki Mitchell."

"Brad Morton."

Ron handed each of them a US Embassy ID card and a firearms permit. "I took the liberty of arranging these documents for you."

"Thank you for assisting us, Mr. Dayton," Nikki said, taking her documents and handing the others to Brad.

"Just Ron is fine. We're always thankful when private agencies can carry some of our load." Nikki and Brad nodded. "Senator Wyatt is a welcome visitor and we would not want anything to happen to her while she is here."

"We'll take care of her." Brad nodded. "Did our gear arrive?"

"Yes, yes. It's is in the trunk of the sedan in spot seventeen."

The elevator doors opened and Ron held the button to allow them to exit, remaining on the elevator himself. As the doors closed, he called out, "Keys are in the ignition."

Nikki raised her eyebrows. "Friendly enough, I guess."

"He came through and provided what we needed. I don't need him to be my buddy."

"Yeah, that's true." Nikki opened the door of the sedan in spot seventeen, sliding onto the leather seat. She pulled the keys from the ignition and tossed them to Brad.

Brad opened the trunk and then their combination lockbox. Taking out a mirror on a three-foot expandable handle, he began checking for foreign objects underneath their car. Nikki checked the pressure in each tire, then looked under the hood for fluid levels and foreign objects. Before closing the trunk, they each placed a shoulder holster under their jackets and secured their pistols in them.

Nikki pulled her iPad from her backpack and settled into the passenger seat. She logged onto the secure network from Flagler and downloaded Israeli street maps. Brad slid behind the wheel and started the car.

"Lead me, oh worthy one," Brad joked.

"Continue north on HaYarkon. The hotel is less than a quarter mile on the left."

"What if we left the car in the garage at the embassy? I could walk down and get it when we needed it," Brad suggested.

"We could, but there is an underground garage at the hotel too. In fact, let's check it out now. I'm starving and London's is within walking distance. They have a killer breakfast menu."

They parked at the Sheraton Hotel and walked a block toward the Mediterranean Sea before locating the London Resto-Cafe. It had a bar atmosphere and the tables were close together, but it sat on the boardwalk, or as the locals called it, the tayelet. The view looked out over the white sandy beach to the Mediterranean Sea and a bouquet of beach and salt water aromas drifted through occasionally. Nikki wasted no time ordering them both a traditional Israeli breakfast, and Brad's eyes grew huge as the waiter set plate after plate on their table, along with fresh juice and coffee. The eggs were made to order and came with a variety of hard and soft cheeses, olives and fresh baked bread. Another dish contained an Israeli salad made of finely chopped tomatoes, cucumbers and olive oil. They ate in silence until all of the plates were empty.

Nikki sat back in her chair and moaned. "It feels like it's been a week since I ate anything. That was delicious."

"We can't check into our room until this afternoon or I would suggest a nap." Brad covered his mouth as he yawned.

"Let's get familiar with the roads and then we can sightsee until time to check in."

Brad stood. "Sounds good to me."

When they stepped out of the café, Nikki took a moment to enjoy the midmorning sun that was starting to warm the day. "Let's walk back along the boardwalk," she suggested.

Brad shrugged. "A little more fresh air might help me wake up."

They joined the flow of tourists and locals as they walked south along the broad boardwalk. It was paved with pebbles and separated from the beach by a narrow strip of vegetation. At the end of the block, they crossed the street back to the parking garage in forced silence as bumper-to-bumper traffic raced past them.

Back in the car, they ran a few potential routes back and forth between the embassy, the hotel and the airport in preparation for escorting the senator.

"It's hard to tell we aren't in Pensacola, isn't it?" Nikki asked as she glanced out the window at the people dressed in shorts and the palm trees lining the median that separated the four-lane highway.

"Yeah, except for that." Brad pointed to the streetlight they were stopped at as it flipped from red to yellow and then to green.

"And the Hebrew and Arabic written on the street signs."

"At least there's English too."

Nikki held up her iPad. "I can't imagine going anywhere without GPS."

"How did we survive before it?"

"Map and compass," Nikki joked.

After a while they began randomly driving streets just to see where the streets would lead. Nikki tracked their movements on the iPad.

"I think we have a tail," Brad said.

Nikki looked up from her tablet and watched her mirror. "Cool. I was getting bored." She began sliding her finger around the touch screen. "Give me a minute and I'll find a dead-end street." After a few minutes, she glanced at him. "Turn right in two blocks and then make another right at the end of the block. I'll jump out as soon as you turn and wait for them to pass. The first alley on the right should be a dead end."

"Sounds good." Brad tightened his fingers on the steering wheel.

Staying in the right lane, Brad accelerated before making the turn and then slammed on the brakes. Nikki jumped out and dashed into a clothing store along the street. She watched through the window until the sedan tailing them had passed. She shielded her eyes to try to see the occupants, but the glare from the sun was too bright. As soon as it turned into the alley behind Brad, she sprinted to the corner. Pistol drawn, she crept into the alley. Brad was out of the car with his pistol pointed at the driver. Nikki moved to the rear of the car and, in a few quick steps, she wrenched open the passenger-side door.

"Well, shit!" Nikki exclaimed.

"Hola," Mel said in her best Spanish accent.

Nikki holstered her pistol and started walking back to their sedan.

"Hey," Mel yelled. "We need to talk."

"Fine." Nikki turned. "But not in a dead-end alley."

"Follow us." Mel closed her door and their car roared backward out of the alley.

Mel's vehicle turned into the underground garage at the Sheraton with Brad and Nikki on its bumper. They circled to a deserted section before parking. Mel exited the vehicle first, handling the introductions. "We checked in earlier so we can chat in our room if yours isn't ready yet."

Nikki looked at Brad. "It's almost check-in time so it should be ready. I'll go check if you want to unpack the car."

Brad nodded and began removing their gear from the car.

Nikki entered the brightly colored lobby and approached the front desk. The desk clerk, conferring with a guest by the elevators, was easily identified by his button-down shirt and name tag. The tie was overkill in a lobby filled with casually dressed tourists, but standard for the hotel. When he noticed

Nikki approaching the desk, he quickly ended his conversation and resumed his post. She handed him her passport and waited while he processed the paperwork to check them into the room. Expecting a Middle Eastern accent, Nikki was surprised to hear a French inflection instead. Though his English was understandable she was pleased at his delight when he discovered she spoke in French as well. As she signed the last piece of paperwork and turned with room keys in hand, Brad entered the lobby with their luggage. He stepped into the elevator and Nikki pressed the button for the nineteenth floor.

"Where did our friends go?" Nikki asked.

"To their room. Apparently they're right across the hall from us."

"How convenient."

"I told them we needed some downtime, but we would meet them for dinner," Brad explained. "We should be able to get in a three-hour power nap."

"That sounds good. I'm in desperate need of a shower too."

Nikki passed Brad the spare key and opened the room door with the other. The entranceway opened into a spacious living area with a full-sized couch, two chairs and large television. Nikki appraised the view of the Mediterranean Sea through the sliding glass doors across the Club Suite. She crossed to the doors and slid them open, stepping onto the balcony. It was windy and she could smell the salt air on the breeze. Brad stepped out to join her.

"There are only two bedrooms. Let's each take one and we'll just make sure they change the sheets before the senator arrives tomorrow."

Nikki smiled. "I like that plan better than sleeping in the same bed with you or on the couch."

Brad smiled too. "Once the senator arrives, we'll be taking turns sleeping anyway." His smile got bigger. "Unless...you want to sleep across the hall."

"I'm still pissed about them tailing us today."

"Let's wait and hear what they have to say," Brad suggested. "Maybe they've got a good reason."

"I doubt it. Did you see the smile on Carter's face when I whipped open the car door?"

"I did and she looked happy to see you." Brad gave her a playful punch on the arm before turning back into the suite. "I'm taking a shower and then a nap."

Nikki reluctantly turned from the view and followed Brad back into the room. She grabbed her bag and turned right into the second bedroom, closing the door behind her. A king-sized bed was centered between two wooden nightstands and took up most of the floor space. The headboard and nightstands were made of a blond wood that Nikki couldn't identify. She threw her bag onto the luggage rack and removed her suits, hanging both in the bathroom. She turned on the shower to let the steam penetrate the material. She stripped, putting all her dirty clothes into a laundry bag and stowing them in her carry-on. The water was warm, and at times, Nikki's eyes closed for longer than a normal blink. Calculating when she had last crawled into bed, she realized it had been almost thirty-six hours. She forced herself out of the shower and dried off quickly before climbing naked into the bed. As an afterthought, she opened her eyes long enough to set the alarm.

CHAPTER SEVENTEEN

"Aren't you sleepy too?" Liam asked.

"I slept on the flight over," Mel replied without looking up from her laptop.

"I couldn't get comfortable." Liam sighed. "It was nice of Mr. Flagler to give us a charter again. It sure makes a difference not having to change planes five times."

"Catch a catnap and I'll wake you in two hours."

"Thanks. That'd be great." Liam went straight into the bedroom and closed the door.

Mel focused on the photo she was working on. Flagler's technical department had pinpointed a phone call from the Pensacola office to a phone in Tel Aviv, and Liam had been able to pull this image from a traffic camera. She had enhanced the photo, adding some brightness to it, before running it through the US drivers' license database—with no success. She punched the buttons on the laptop to start the scan again using the Israeli drivers' license database.

She turned on the television and surfed the channels, her mind elsewhere. Nikki had looked really good storming into the alley earlier. And now she was asleep across the hall. Probably curled under the sheets with a small amount of clothing. Or maybe no clothing at all. Mel sighed. *Pull yourself together. This is a co-worker you're thinking about and you need to get your head in the job. This is not a game, and until we figure out what Josh is up to, no one knows where the next path is going to lead.*

* * *

Nikki's alarm woke her from a deep sleep, and she would have bet only five minutes had passed. She rolled out of bed and into the shower. Her first conscious thoughts were of food and the woman across the hall. She liked being on the same team as Mel and looked forward to working closely together with her while they were in Israel.

Time to find out what's going on. She pulled on clean jeans and a T-shirt. Securing her shoulder holster, she slid her pistol into place and pulled a light jacket over the top of them.

When she exited the bedroom, Brad was sitting on the couch with his eyes closed. His hair was still wet from a recent shower, and he looked refreshed even in sleep. Nikki touched his shoulder. "Are you really asleep?" she whispered.

He grunted.

Nikki gave him a shake. "Do you want food?"

Brad's eyes flew open. "Of course I want food."

Nikki opened the door into the hallway. "Well, come on then." She held the door, waiting for Brad to catch up, then stepped across the hall and knocked.

Mel's smile widened as she openly appraised Nikki before calling over her shoulder. "Let's go, Liam. Your date is here."

Nikki rolled her eyes and immediately began questioning Mel. "What are you doing here?"

Mel gave her cocky smile. "I'm here to protect you, of course."

Nikki rolled her eyes again and Brad laughed.

Liam joined them in the hallway and Brad headed toward the elevator. "Dinner?"

"Where are we going?" Liam asked. "Not that I care. Food is food."

"The restaurant downstairs is open for another four hours," Brad suggested.

"I checked out the menu earlier and it looked good," Mel added. "Mediterranean."

"The Olive Leaf it is then." Brad punched the down elevator button.

The restaurant had a panoramic view of the Mediterranean Sea and more of the blond-colored wood Nikki had admired in the room. The olive leaf motif ceramic tiles around the room paid homage to the name of the restaurant. They had hit a lull in the dinner rush and were seated immediately at a table in the corner. After a short discussion, Brad and Liam decided they needed appetizers and selected Frena bread with olives and nuts served with three dips and sliced marinated salmon served with crispy toasts.

For a main course Nikki stuck with items she could recognize, sautéed chicken slices with grilled pineapple. She traveled a lot, but she seldom ventured off the well-beaten path where food was concerned. She wrinkled her nose at the caviar that came with the salmon appetizer when Mel offered it to her.

Nikki bit her tongue, allowing the group to discuss food from other countries where they had traveled until their meals were delivered. Unable to contain her impatience any longer, she only took a couple of bites before leaning toward the center of the table. "Spill it." She looked back and forth between Mel and Liam, waiting to see who would answer first.

Liam broke the silence. "This mission was created by us, and we were sent to assist you in case Josh throws any kinks in your plans."

"So this is a setup?" Brad asked, surprised. "The mission isn't real?"

"Yes, this is a setup," Mel answered. "But unlike your last mission, this one is real. The senator has received quite a few threats lately, but we made it appear worse than it was and asked her to request assistance from Josh specifically. She had heard good things about him from a friend of a friend." Mel smiled.

"We weren't sure when the mission would come through, and we hadn't planned on letting you guys in on the situation, but that changed when you called me." She looked at Brad and then back at Nikki. "You guys had drawn the same conclusions that we had, and I convinced our boss that it would be beneficial to have you in on the details."

"So are we supposed to feed bad information to Josh?" Nikki asked.

"No," Liam said, looking at Mel.

Nikki watched the exchange of glances between Liam and Mel and she wondered what he didn't want to disclose.

When Mel nodded, he continued. "Just follow the plan Josh laid out for you. What were you told your mission was, specifically?"

Nikki glanced at Brad. Secrecy was ingrained in them too, and it still felt awkward to share details with another team. She wasn't sure who could be trusted and who couldn't, but she knew she had trusted Mel when they met at the coffee shop and she wanted to trust her now. She took a deep breath before speaking. "We were told to provide security for twenty-four hours to Senator Wyatt."

Mel nodded. "And that's what you'll do."

"Honestly," Liam added, "we aren't here to do anything more than see if we can get Josh to make a mistake or to show his hand."

"We've tracked quite a bit of communication from Flagler to a local resident." Mel paused while their empty plates were cleared and Nikki placed her dessert order. When the waiter left the table, Mel continued, "Flagler has plenty of agents working in Israel so there's always a chance the calls could be legitimate, but we haven't been able to tie them to an active case. We think that if it is Josh, he may ask you guys to make contact with someone here before you leave. Since applying pressure to Josh and letting him know that you guys are all being watched, he hasn't made any contact in the last week, so we're hoping he'll take advantage of the situation. Plus we dropped surveillance on the rest of your team."

Conversation paused again as the waiter returned with Nikki's dessert. Everyone watched as Nikki took a forkful of the chocolate cake with a wild berry sauce and roasted pistachios. "So what if he doesn't take advantage of the opportunity?" Nikki asked after she swallowed the first bite.

"We have other avenues we are exploring while we are here," Liam explained.

Mel sighed. "Speaking of working other avenues, I should get back to the room and check my scan."

Brad leaned in conspiratorially, "So what are you working on now, Agent Carter?"

Mel laughed, giving him a smile before picking up her fork. "Let's finish Nikki's dessert and I'll show you."

CHAPTER EIGHTEEN

Nikki glanced around Mel and Liam's room. Two laptops were sitting on the coffee table in front of the couch, one of the screens flipping through random faces. Mel took a seat in front of the active screen. "This software is running a facial recognition program to try to match a camera shot of the individual we believe was talking to Josh."

Liam opened the other laptop. "This program is recording all incoming and outgoing cell calls for the same individual."

Almost immediately Mel's laptop locked on a photo. "There he is." Mel began typing on the keyboard. "Daniel Abbott. I've got his home address. It's not far from here." She looked at Liam.

"I'm on it." Liam disappeared into the bedroom and returned wearing a jacket over his pistol.

"Want company?" Brad asked.

Liam looked at Mel and then shrugged. "Sure. I don't see why not."

"Don't make contact with him," Mel reminded him as she pulled a copy of the photo from the printer and handed it to

Brad. "Study and then shred. You don't want to have to explain it if you get caught."

Brad nodded.

"He won't even see us." Liam smirked as he turned and left the room with Brad on his heels.

Nikki crossed to the couch and sat down. "What are they going to do?"

"Probably just a little surveillance. Check out the area." Mel opened the minibar and held up a bottle of scotch.

Nikki shook her head. "Too much wine with dinner."

Mel returned to the couch with two cans of Coke. "If we had more time and more people, we'd try to do a twenty-four-hour surveillance, but with just two of us, we'll have to work faster."

Mel handed Nikki one of the cans before she pulled the other computer closer. Nikki cradled the cold can as she watched Mel work. She typed quickly, bringing up the voice mail recordings. "There have been four cell phone calls this evening." She hit play and they listened to two conversations of an unknown man talking to another man he called "brother." They made plans to meet that evening at a hotel bar on Gordon Street. She paused the third call as her cell phone rang.

Mel looked at the caller ID. "It's Liam." She hit speaker as the call connected.

"Can you look back through the call logs and get info on the delivery place he ordered from the other night?"

Mel's fingers flew across the keyboard as she maneuvered through multiple screens quickly. "China Court or The Pizza."

Nikki recognized the search window Mel opened but couldn't see what she was typing.

"Looks like The Pizza is closer to you. Two blocks to the east."

"Got it. Thanks." Liam disconnected.

Nikki was confused and she gave Mel a puzzled look. "Hungry again?"

Mel laughed. "He's probably going to pick up takeout and pretend to be a delivery man. It's the easiest way of approaching a door without drawing suspicion."

"No one refuses a pizza, right?"

"They'll at least answer the door, even if they didn't order it. It seems reasonable that the restaurant might make a mistake, especially if you're able to use a place they order from often."

Nikki was intrigued by this new side of Flagler. She had never conducted an operation in an urban city. The technology Mel had at her fingertips was fascinating, as well as Mel's ability and knowledge to make things happen. Nikki was pulled from her thoughts as Mel hit a button on the keyboard and the third phone call began to play.

Nikki laughed as the male voice ordered a pizza. Mel shrugged and started the fourth call. It was in Hebrew and Nikki looked at Mel for translation. "I recognized 'country' and 'friends' but I have no idea about the rest."

"It seems we both speak about the same amount of Hebrew." Mel hit a few more keys. "Gotta love technology." The conversation was replayed by the digital laptop voice in English.

Nikki bent her head in concentration as they listened to the phone call.

"Hello," said the male voice they could now recognize after several calls.

"Peace upon you! I hope you are well," an unknown male voice responded.

"Very well. You have news?"

"Our friends arrived in the country earlier today."

"What do you need from me?"

"Let's meet tomorrow and we can discuss it."

"Fine. Goodbye."

"Be well."

Nikki glanced up to find Mel with her eyes still closed. She stared silently at her as Mel's forehead wrinkled in concentration.

"Do you think we're the friends he referred to?" Nikki asked.

Mel opened her eyes. "I certainly think you might be."

"I don't recognize that voice."

"Me either."

Nikki took a sip of her Coke. "I'm pretty sure it's not Josh."

"I don't think so either, but I'll run it through voice recognition so we can confirm."

"Will that identify him if he used some type of voice-altering software?"

"It should. It picks up on tempo and pace too."

Nikki leaned closer to look over Mel's shoulder at the laptop. She resisted the temptation to lean into her shoulder and allow their bodies to touch. She caught a faint familiar scent and inhaled deeply, trying to hold onto the smell.

Mel stopped typing and sat still for several seconds before turning to look at Nikki. "I am trying really hard to concentrate here."

Nikki tilted her head and smiled. "I'm just watching."

Mel shook her head and turned her entire body to face Nikki, a faint smile on her face. "No, I think you just sniffed me."

Nikki's smile widened. "I might have."

Mel cupped Nikki's cheek, sliding her fingers through the soft strands of her hair as she grasped the back of her neck and pulled her close. "I'm getting tired of trying to resist you," she whispered. Nikki could feel Mel's breath as she spoke and the movement of her lips softly grazed her own. She leaned forward closing the inches that separated them and kissed her.

She struggled to keep her hands planted on the couch between them, knowing that if she gave in to her desire, she would not be able to stop. Mel's hands, still wrapped through her hair, massaged the back of her neck, leaving a trail of flame each time her fingers brushed skin. The kiss deepened as their tongues touched. Nikki was about to lose her struggle, when Mel's hands cradled the back of her head, stilling their movement.

Again Mel spoke with their lips inches apart, "Hmmm, no resistance there." She kissed her softly again before resting her forehead against Nikki's. "As wonderful as this is, we have work to do, but once Liam and Brad return..."

Nikki mumbled her agreement and buried her face in Mel's neck, memorizing the intoxicating fragrance. She breathed deeply, allowing the aroma to consume her body. It smelled clean and fresh, pushing the stress from her body and exciting her at the same time. She had not forgotten about Brad and Liam, but she had to admit Mel had taken possession of every part of her, including her mind. Sighing, Nikki pulled her body back so again only their foreheads were touching. "You take my breath away."

"And I have been losing any semblance of professionalism since almost the first moment that I met you."

Mel's cell phone interrupted their confessions. Sitting up, Mel placed a hand on Nikki's thigh.

Mel looked at the caller ID and connected the call. "Hey, what's up?"

Nikki smiled at the gravelly tone of Mel's voice. She had to admit she enjoyed the effect she had on Mel.

Liam's voice came through the speaker. "I've got Brad on a three-way call. I've started the party and he's watching for our friend."

Nikki's eyes widened as Mel leaned over and spoke into her ear. "Liam's in the guy's apartment."

"Anything good at the party?" Mel asked.

"No, just the usual. I sent you some selfies though." Liam paused.

"Liam?" Mel prompted with a frown.

"Brad, I need you to hang up for a second. Mel, take me off speaker." Liam spoke rapidly.

Nikki remained silent as Mel punched a button and put the phone to her ear. She could still see the screen on the laptop and she watched her scroll through several pictures stopping on the last one.

"What's wrong, Liam?" Mel asked with a quick glance at Nikki before focusing on the screen again. "I see it...Okay...I'm hanging up. Call back if you need anything." Mel disconnected and tossed her phone on the coffee table.

Nikki leaned back against the couch, pulling a leg up she turned to face Mel. "What just happened?"

"Brad was calling him. Might be the mark returning." Mel closed the laptop and sank back into the cushions with her Coke. "I really like you, you know?"

Nikki raised her eyebrows. She already missed the pressure of Mel's hand on her leg and the change of subject had instantly swelled the gulf between them.

"And the more I'm around you the more I like," Mel continued.

"I really don't think you know me," Nikki challenged her. "Tailing me isn't the same as spending time with me."

Mel tilted her can toward her. "I'll give you that. But," she paused, "I have read all of your file notes, as well as what others have written about you. I know that you have integrity and that you cover your friends no matter the personal cost."

Nikki was silent as she listened, her eyes searching Mel's face for a sign she was being played.

"I know that you have a good heart and," she dramatically rubbed her Coke can across her forehead, "you are incredibly hot."

Nikki couldn't help but smile. "So if I'm all those things, why won't you tell me what Liam found?"

Mel took a deep breath and Nikki could see she was struggling with sharing what she knew. Nikki extended her leg and gently pushed on Mel's thigh with her foot. "Tell me."

"The info Liam found puts a new slant on things, and I don't want that knowledge to jeopardize your safety."

"I get to make that decision. Not you."

"Fine." Mel opened the laptop and turned it toward Nikki. "Recognize any numbers?"

Nikki scanned the list. With a sharp intake of breath she looked at Mel. "That's Mr. Flagler's office number."

Mel raised her eyebrows. "Yep."

Nikki scanned the header on the phone bill. "Is it incoming or outgoing?" she asked.

"Incoming." Mel paused, leaning closer to the screen. "But that's not the number we've been monitoring. Daniel Abbott has a second phone."

"So it could be anyone that had access to Mr. Flagler's office," Nikki stated.

Mel's attention was still focused on the screen and a frown creased the corners of her mouth.

"Or it could still be Josh," Nikki continued.

"Right." Mel nodded and pulled the other computer closer again. "Let's see if the voice software has finished analyzing the phone call from earlier." She paused while she continued to type. "Yep, it's finished. It's not Josh."

"So what does that mean?"

Before Mel could respond, the card reader on the hotel room door beeped and Liam walked in followed by Brad carrying a pizza.

Nikki couldn't help but laugh. She knew Brad would never dispose of a perfectly good pizza.

Brad tossed the box on the coffee table, and flipping it open, he grabbed a slice. "Hey, I figured people don't pay attention to a man carrying a pizza, and if they do, they might confuse me with a delivery man."

Liam shrugged. "It was a sound plan so I didn't argue." He grabbed a slice of pizza and bit into it. "Besides, it smelled good."

Nikki helped herself to a slice and Mel pulled drinks from the refrigerator for Liam and Brad before grabbing a slice too.

"Thanks for the fun, Liam." Brad saluted with his Coke. "I'm going to turn in now." He grabbed another slice of pizza on his way out.

Liam sat down across from them as he downed the slice and pulled another one from the box.

"Did you see anything else in the apartment?" Mel asked.

Liam took a bite as his eyes slid to Nikki and then back to Mel.

Nikki remained silent, waiting to see if Mel would include her.

"I showed her," Mel stated.

Liam shrugged before answering Mel's question. "Not really. It looks like Daniel Abbott enjoys takeout food and porn. Trash was filled with empty food containers and all of the videos were well above an R rating." Liam chewed another bite and they waited for him to swallow. "There wasn't any personal stuff. No pictures or letters. The desk was filled with nothing but bills."

"Like that might not be his only residence?" Nikki asked.

"Yeah. That's what I was thinking," Liam concluded before glancing at Mel. "Did you notice that bill was not for the phone we're recording?"

"I did. I'll tap into it and start recording those calls as well."

Liam took a long drink from his can before standing. "I think I'll turn in too."

Mel turned back to her laptop. "I'm going to search a few of these other US numbers on the phone bills you photographed." Nikki wasn't sure what to say or do so she remained seated.

"Good night, ladies," Liam said, crossing the room and closing his bedroom door behind him.

CHAPTER NINETEEN

Mel gave Nikki her cocky smile.

Nikki shrugged. "I was going to say something about helping you, but everything I could think of sounded so lame and obvious."

Mel laughed. "He might make the connection in a day or so, but honestly I don't care. It's not like I'm in the closet."

"Me either. I don't advertise, but I don't hide either."

"I've never worked with Liam before this case, but I'm sure my file arrived before I did. Just like I received Liam's and Joey's before our package pickup last week."

Nikki frowned. "You said something at dinner about our last mission being a setup. I got sidetracked with chocolate cake, but was that true?"

"Yes and no." Mel crossed to the minibar and poured a small bottle of scotch into two glasses.

Nikki took the glass from her, shivering as Mel's fingertips purposely brushed across the back of her hand.

Mel sat back down on the couch. "We were the ones making the pickup and that's not normally who you support, but our contact getting shot was not part of the plan."

Nikki took a sip of the scotch, feeling it burn all the way down her throat. "Do you know what happened there?"

"We think we were getting close to finding out who is behind all of this. We had tracked phone calls from Josh to that village, so we paid a man to make that package exchange, thinking it would make Josh or whomever nervous. We specifically planned the exchange on your team's rotation so we could check out all of you too. We certainly didn't plan for our setup man to get killed though."

"He didn't even know anything, right?"

Mel shrugged and Nikki could hear the stress in her voice. "Not as far as we know."

Nikki kicked her shoes off, pulling her feet onto the couch. She stretched her arm across the back of the couch and gently massaged Mel's neck. Mel's head bent forward and Nikki shifted closer to her. Her fingers tangled in Mel's wavy hair as she scraped her fingernails softly across her scalp.

Nikki took another sip of the scotch. "If the caller from Mr. Flagler's office isn't Josh, it has to be someone else, right?" Nikki didn't want to even think about Mr. Flagler having someone killed to cover up his actions. He was a father figure to most everyone who worked for him. With his rugged features and quiet manner, he had earned his employees' respect rather than demanding it. Nikki had heard the stories of how he had built the company by running each mission himself in the beginning. His hands-on approach, even now, allowed employees to speak with him directly and he insisted on an open-door policy. His secretary would schedule anyone who asked for a meeting with him, but you better have followed chain of command first or have a good reason not to. Nikki had never had a reason to schedule a meeting with him, but she had heard him discuss missions and mission execution during training and briefings. He would just appear, hang out and then disappear.

"Who would you look at?" Mel asked, turning her back to give Nikki better access as she continued massaging her shoulders.

Nikki complied without breaking the conversation, though her fingers were now memorizing every inch of the hard muscles and soft skin they touched. "I don't know. How about anyone that had a meeting with him? Maybe his secretary let someone into his office before he arrived." She thought for a minute. "How about the cleaning crew?" She sighed. "Or Josh?"

"Those are good ideas, but whoever it is has contacts internationally." She frowned. "Probably not the cleaning crew."

Nikki dug her fingers into the knots on Mel's shoulders, causing her to moan. "Can we stop talking now?" Mel asked.

"Just one more question," Nikki said, sliding her hands down Mel's arms and interlocking their fingers. She pressed her chest tight to Mel's back. "What's all this about? What has Josh or whomever done? I mean before killing your contact. What started this investigation?"

Mel set her glass on the coffee table and leaned back into Nikki's embrace. "I wondered how long it would take you to ask." She sighed heavily. "About a year ago we found a posting on a US chat board disclosing details about an upcoming mission. The case came to the internal investigation office and fell on my desk. It was a basic mission, and, at first glance, I thought it was a new employee. It happens sometimes when people are new and can't contain their excitement." She pulled Nikki's arms tighter around her. "But then I tracked it back to the office in Pensacola, and there weren't any new employees there."

Mel paused as Nikki unbuttoned the first two buttons on her shirt and ran her hand across her chest, pushing the bra strap off her right shoulder. "Keep talking, Carter," she whispered into Mel's ear.

The vibration from Mel's moan rippled through Nikki's body as she switched hands and slid the bra strap off her left shoulder. "Then the leaks started getting bigger. We had to cancel missions for the safety of our clients and our teams.

Mr. Flagler's reputation was being attacked internationally. I started tracking all international calls from the Pensacola office and that led me to where we are today." Mel finished as Nikki unbuttoned the rest of the buttons on her shirt. "Can we please stop talking now?"

* * *

Mel's body was on fire. Her skin was seared where Nikki touched her and she didn't want to stop the inferno that was threatening to consume her. Ten minutes alone with this woman and she was already begging. She tried to slow her heartbeat, but Nikki's hands roamed everywhere. Across the front of her bra, pushing inside her pants on the outside of the thin cotton covering her wetness and then back inside her bra. Her nipples were hard and ached to be released from the material covering them.

Nikki's tongue stroked her earlobe, sucking it into her mouth. Each breath pushed Mel closer to the edge. She was so hot and ready. She pushed Nikki's hand down inside her pants, her body convulsing as Nikki's fingers slid across her clit.

"Bedroom now, Carter." Nikki's voice was deep with arousal and Mel didn't need to be told twice. She stood and pulled Nikki to her feet. Downing the last of the scotch in her glass, Nikki pulled Mel close and kissed her.

The alcohol burned Mel's tongue as she slid it deep inside Nikki's mouth. Holding the kiss, she walked Nikki backward into the bedroom, kicking the door shut behind her. She pulled Nikki's shirt from her pants and with shaking hands attempted to undo its buttons. Discovering that her mind and fingers were unwilling to cooperate, she broke the kiss long enough to pull the shirt over Nikki's head. She let her own open shirt fall to the floor and took a step forward until Nikki's knees made contact with the bed and she collapsed onto it. She unzipped Nikki's pants and pulled them off, dropping them unceremoniously onto the floor. Hers followed but caught on her boots nearly tripping her. She had to make herself slow down to get the laces untied.

Boots finally off, she stood and unclasped her bra, letting it fall to the floor in front of her. She looked at Nikki, naked except for her bra, and her breath caught in her throat. She was so beautiful. Mel's gaze traveled the length of her body before returning to her face. "Slide up," Mel whispered as she knelt between Nikki's legs. Her mouth watered in anticipation as she waited for Nikki to get comfortable. She needed to taste her, to savor the sweetness and saltiness in her mouth. She kissed the inside of her knee and traveled up, following the kisses with her tongue. Nikki's body arched as her mouth closed over the warmth, sucking gently before allowing her tongue to slide inside.

"Not yet," Nikki cried.

Mel didn't want it to be over yet either, but she couldn't stop herself. She increased the pace of her stroking, ignoring Nikki's request. Nikki's body convulsed as she gave in to Mel's single-mindedness.

Mel rested her head on Nikki's thigh while she waited for her breathing to return to normal. She inhaled deeply, memorizing the fragrance, and her heart raced with desire. She raised her head and looked at Nikki. Her eyes were squeezed shut, and her arms were raised above her head where both hands had a death grip on the headboard. At Mel's movement, Nikki pried her fingers loose and ran them through Mel's hair.

"Carter." Nikki opened her eyes and met Mel's. "Come up here. Now," she demanded.

Mel slid her body up Nikki's, rubbing her nipples across her hot flesh. Still roaring with arousal, she took Nikki's silk-covered nipple into her mouth. She supported her weight on one elbow and slid the other hand underneath Nikki and unhooked her bra. She pulled the straps off both shoulders and tossed the bra to the floor before helping herself to a sample of each nipple. Straddling Nikki's thigh, she balanced her weight on her knees as her hands cupped each breast and then alternately sucked each one into her mouth.

Nikki's body arched and Mel ran her hand down it until her fingers were immersed in Nikki's passion. Stroking gently, she watched Nikki's face as she slid one finger inside her. "Oh yes," Nikki mouthed, but the words barely came out. Mel slid a second finger inside as she covered Nikki's mouth with her own. Nikki clung to her and her fingers dug into Mel's shoulders. Their bodies found a matched rhythm as Mel pushed deeper into her.

Without thought Mel ground her hips into Nikki's already slick thigh with a frenzy that surprised her. The pressure caused her body to spasm and she broke the contact, trying to regain her control. Nikki's touch brought the tumultuous feeling back and Mel arched, breaking their kiss as their eyes met. Mel stared into Nikki's flushed face and she felt the heat on her own. Nikki's blue eyes were clouded, deepening their color, and she was lost in their depths. She pushed her body hard against Nikki's as they moved in sync. Faster. Together and then apart. The orgasm erupted from each of them but they continued to pulse against each other as their bodies searched for complete release. Unable to hold herself up any longer, Mel collapsed on top of Nikki.

"Unbelievable," Mel panted as she rolled off Nikki and lay spread-eagled beside her, gasping for air, her body covered with sweat.

Nikki turned on her side and ran a hand across Mel's stomach and over a hard nipple. "What is unbelievable?" She smiled.

Inhaling deeply, Mel pried her lids open and looked into Nikki's eyes. "It's unbelievable that you are even hotter than I first thought you were."

Nikki narrowed her eyes. "Don't play with me, Carter."

"But I like to play with you, Mitchell." Mel raised her arms above her head and arched into Nikki's touch.

The quiet was cut by a deafening continuous, ascending and descending tone.

"What the hell?" Nikki exclaimed as Mel jumped to her feet.

"It's the air-raid siren." Mel tossed clothes from the floor onto the bed, searching through them for items that belonged to her. "We have to go to the bunker."

"You have got to be kidding me!" Nikki grumbled as she joined the clothing search.

"Get up. Get up. Get up." Liam pounded on the bedroom door. "Ninety seconds to seek shelter. Get up!"

"Go in the bathroom." Mel waited until Nikki closed the door before opening the connecting door to the living room. She held her shirt closed with her hand and looked at Liam. His hair was askew and he wore only shorts with his boots. "Go without me, Liam. I'm not going like this."

Liam hesitated. She could tell he didn't want to leave her. "Just go. I'll be right behind you," Mel reassured him.

Liam crossed to the door and whipped it open. Brad stood in the hallway, his hand raised to knock. "Is Nikki still over here?"

Both men turned to Mel and she nodded. She couldn't deny Nikki's presence to Brad and leave him to worry about where she was. She felt Brad's eyes appraise her appearance and then he grinned. "Come on, Liam. Let's check out this bunker." As the door started to fall shut behind them, Brad's head came in the door again. "Hurry up, Carter. It could be a real attack." His eyes were filled with genuine concern and she nodded.

Mel ducked back into the room and pulled on her pants, sticking her feet into unlaced boots. She pulled open the bathroom door to find Nikki fully clothed sitting on the side of the tub.

"Is Liam gone?"

"You mean Liam and Brad? Yes, they went to the bunker without us."

"Brad too?"

"Yes, I had to tell him you were here. He would have panicked trying to find you otherwise." She pulled Nikki into a hug. "Besides, we're not hiding here. Right?"

Nikki smiled. "No. I just hadn't planned to put on a display."

"Let's go. I'm sure they won't harass us until the attack is over."

Mel took her hand as they left the room. There was a loud thud above them as they entered the stairwell.

Nikki looked up as if she could see what had caused the explosion through the roof of the hotel. "Was that the Iron Dome blocking a missile?"

Mel shrugged. "Maybe."

Seconds later they met hotel guests coming back up the stairs so they turned around and returned to the room.

"Stay with me tonight." Mel pulled her into her arms.

She felt Nikki's hesitation but it only lasted for a second and then she agreed. "I'll grab my bag and give Brad a minute to harass me. Then I'll be back."

Mel kissed her before opening her arms and releasing her.

CHAPTER TWENTY

Nikki crossed the hall and let herself into the empty room. She hung both of her suits in Brad's closet and carried her bag into the living room before sitting down on the couch to wait for him. Brad opened the door and looked surprised to see her sitting there.

"That was fun." He grabbed two bottled waters from the mini refrigerator, and tossed one to her. "You look dehydrated."

"Thanks." She smiled at him. "I'll be across the hall if you need anything."

He nodded. "Breakfast?"

"Sure. The senator's flight arrives at noon. Meet us at zero nine and we'll decide where to go."

She turned to leave. "Thanks, Brad."

He grinned. "I'll store it up for when we are both more awake. Try to get some sleep, please."

She left the room to his laughter. Brad had been easy. Now she had to face Liam.

She crossed the hall and knocked lightly on the door. Mel pulled it open and Nikki scanned the room. "Where's Liam?"

"I sent him to bed." Mel smiled. "I thought you might prefer it that way."

"Absolutely."

"How's Brad?"

Nikki rolled her eyes. "Oh, Brad is fine." She grasped Mel's hand and pulled her toward the bedroom. "Let's talk about us."

Mel walked to the full-length window and opened the curtains to reveal a view of the port lights and miles of deep blue sea.

Nikki tossed her bag on the floor and turned out all the lights before crossing to the window. She stepped behind Mel, running her hands across the broad shoulders, her fingers tracing the hard ridges covering the length of Mel's back. She had felt them earlier when Mel was on top of her, and she knew her fingers were touching healed scars. She slid her arms around Mel's waist to the buttons on the front of her shirt. She wanted to see what her fingers had touched.

Mel grasped her fingers, stilling their movement, and leaned back into Nikki's chest. "So, you want to talk about us?"

Nikki kissed her cheek. She was curious, but whatever had happened in Mel's past was not something she needed to know today. She rested her head on Mel's shoulder. "Are you okay?"

"I am better than okay." Mel turned in her arms and kissed her hard. "And you?"

"I've never felt this good." Nikki pulled her toward the bed. "Enough talk." She spun them around and pushed Mel down onto the bed. Illuminated by the glow of the moonlight streaming into the room, she slowly began stripping out of her clothes as Mel leaned back on her elbows to watch, desire growing in her eyes. Nikki wanted to drive her crazy and it looked like maybe it was already working. With agonizing slowness, she removed each piece of clothing until she stood naked in front of Mel. She straddled Mel's clothed body and unbuttoned her shirt, displaying full naked breasts. Nikki gasped as Mel sucked a breast into her mouth. Her control was destroyed as Mel released the first breast and sucked in the second one. Mel interlocked their fingers, holding Nikki in place while her tongue stroked the nipple hard and fast. Nikki couldn't stop her body from sliding across Mel's bare stomach, giving in to the ecstasy.

CHAPTER TWENTY-ONE

Mel lifted her head and looked at the clock on the nightstand. They had just over an hour before Brad would come knocking on the door for breakfast. She wondered if Liam was awake and had checked the phones they were monitoring. She was glad she hadn't been too distracted to get Abbott's second phone set to record while Nikki was talking with Brad.

Nikki. She tried to move and her body ached as if she had run a marathon, reminding her of the events of the previous hours. Her mouth and lips were dry, and she looked longingly at the bottle of water on the nightstand. Before she could convince her hand to pick it up, Nikki reached across her and grabbed it. She twisted the cap off and downed half the bottle before waving it in front of Mel. "Thirsty?"

"Extremely." Mel grabbed it and drank the rest, tossing the empty bottle toward the trash can across the room. It bounced off the dresser and came to a stop in the middle of the floor.

Nikki laughed. "What was that?"

"That was me refusing to get out of bed yet."

"Well," Nikki snuggled into her, putting an arm across her waist, "I don't think you have to."

"That's debatable, I guess." Mel sighed. "But you do have to. You stink and Brad will be here in less than an hour."

Nikki laughed. "I'm not going to touch the stink comment, but how long do you really think I need to get ready?"

"There's no safe way to answer that is there?"

"No, probably not. I'll save you the trauma and just get up. However," Nikki rolled to her feet, "since I have time to spare…" She grasped Mel's hand and gave it a tug. "I think I might need assistance."

Mel sprang off the bed with a burst of energy. "I can offer assistance."

"Wow, where'd that surge come from. After last night I certainly don't have that kind of zing. Besides, my body is still on Central Standard Time."

Mel tilted her head as she calculated. "Oh, it's midnight for you then. You were up for what? Forty hours? Commercial flying can be brutal."

Nikki glared at her. "How'd you get here?"

"On a Flagler jet, of course. I got plenty of sleep on the flight plus we arrived about ten hours before you guys. I am well rested and fully able to help your body wake up."

Nikki stepped closer and ran a hand down Mel's chest before circling her waist. Pulling her close, she kissed her gently. "I'll forgive you your life of luxury if you shower with me, but then I'll need to get as far away from you as I can so I can work today."

Mel laughed. "Absolutely. I guess I should get some work done today too."

* * *

Brad arrived right on time, and the four of them decided to walk to breakfast at London's. Brad and Nikki walked together making plans for their day. Liam and Mel followed behind them, carrying on their own hushed conversation.

"I can look for parking lots near his apartment, but maybe one of us should just circle until he moves," Mel said.

"I'm positive his building doesn't have parking." Liam tilted his head. "He probably parks on the street like we did last night. Can you check for a vehicle registered to him?"

"I think so. I'll run through all the data when we get back to the hotel."

"I hate that we don't have much, if any, information about him. We should try to figure out where he works."

"I'll bring the laptop while we're on surveillance." Mel smiled. "But for now, let's eat."

They stepped inside the restaurant and the aromas took over their conversations while they waited to be seated. Their orders were taken and food was served before Nikki mentioned the air raid from last night. "What did the bunker look like?"

Brad laughed. "Concrete."

"I bet you were packed in like sardines," Mel commented, taking a sip of her coffee.

"The bunker was huge since it was for the entire hotel, but yeah, it was still pretty tight," Liam continued. "I'm glad the soldier at the Home Front Command post decided to sound the alarm since, clearly, we heard a missile being destroyed by Iron Dome."

Nikki frowned. "I thought the air-raid sirens were automatic."

"Not in Tel Aviv," Liam explained. "Here a soldier evaluates the data and decides if the trajectory is headed for a populated location or not."

"True," Brad agreed. "But it does go off automatically near the Gaza Strip because they only have fifteen seconds or less to seek shelter."

"Right," Liam said. "Like last night. You guys had ninety seconds to get to the bunker, but even that wasn't enough time for you."

Brad laughed and the others joined in too.

"We were in the stairwell," Mel stated. "Well, almost in the stairwell when the Iron Dome intercepted the rocket."

"That's right." Nikki jumped to their defense too. "Stairwells are considered safe places too."

"Only if you can't get to a bunker," Brad argued.

"Fine," Nikki informed them. "Tonight we will all remain clothed, just in case the siren goes off."

"Actually, that's not such a bad idea," Brad agreed. "Especially since we'll be dealing with the senator too."

Everyone laughed.

"Speaking of the senator…What are we going to do if the sirens go off tonight? I don't feel very safe taking her into that crowded bunker," Brad stated.

"Good question," Nikki agreed. She looked across the table at Mel and Liam. "Can we count on you guys to help out if that happens? I know she has other security too, but I'd feel better with help from you guys than strangers."

"Sure," Mel answered. "If the siren goes off, just wait in the room for us and we'll all go together."

"Although," Liam added, "we'll be out for a while."

Mel nodded. "True." She smiled at Nikki. "I'll check in with you when we return."

"Sounds good," Nikki confirmed.

Brad looked at Liam. "So what are you guys up to today?"

Liam grinned. "A little surveillance, I'm guessing."

"Yep. We're just going to be sitting around, watching," Mel added.

"I think we should just head back to the hotel, Brad. They aren't going to tell us anything else." Nikki nudged him and they both stood. "You guys be careful today and stay in touch."

Liam and Mel nodded. "We will. You guys too. We'll get the check when we're ready to leave," Mel told them before they left.

As soon as they were out of hearing distance, Liam made a suggestion. "I was thinking, let's try to flush him by doing our surveillance in the open."

"It's worth a try. Right now we got nothing and we need him to do something soon. Our time is short."

CHAPTER TWENTY-TWO

Brad stowed the security gear in the trunk and slid into the driver's seat beside her as he unbuttoned his suit jacket. "Car's clean."

"The airport is only about fifteen miles from here," Nikki said as they pulled up to the security bar to exit the hotel parking garage. She had her iPad on her lap and had already mapped their course to the airport.

Out of the corner of her eye, Nikki saw Brad give a wave and she looked up. "Liam and Mel," Brad said in explanation as he nodded to the two of them walking toward the hotel. Nikki gave them a mock salute. Mel laughed and said something to Liam. They returned the salute as they strolled past their vehicle.

Nikki's eyes were glued to the back of Mel, hypnotized by the movement of her body as she walked. The confident stride stretched the black jeans tight across her butt and around the curve of her hip with each step she took. Nikki's mouth watered involuntarily as she thought about removing the burgundy shirt and touching the soft breasts beneath it. She tried not to think about how long it might be before she would be able to touch her again. Tonight she would be on duty with Brad, and tomorrow they would fly back to Florida. She realized Brad was still talking and forced herself to focus on the job.

"The drive shouldn't take us long, and we should be at the airport at least thirty minutes before the senator's flight lands."

"That's good. I want to try to get all the way to the gate. I'm not sure how difficult that might be, but I'll find out," Nikki said as she tracked their course on her iPad, constantly mapping alternative routes until they arrived at the first airport checkpoint. They showed their embassy-issued credentials and waited while the car was x-rayed, weighed and inspected. After clearing the checkpoints, Nikki pulled two communication sets from the glove box and handed one to Brad as he pulled the sedan to a stop. Each of them placed a listening device into an ear canal and attached voice-activated microphones to the lapels of their shirts.

After they tested them, Brad dropped Nikki at the arrival gate and she approached a security officer. She explained the situation and showed her credentials, along with the US Embassy-issued permits, and was taken to a small room behind the ticket agent's desk. Again, she explained the situation and showed all of her credentials to the supervisor before she was approved for unescorted travel through the airport. She exited the rear of the office, bypassing the checkpoints, and made her way to the arrival gate with five minutes to spare.

* * *

Senator Wyatt left the plane with an entourage that included one assistant and two Secret Service agents, who stood with the senator as Nikki approached her.

Offering her hand, the senator introduced herself. "Jan Wyatt."

"Nikki Mitchell. My partner, Brad Morton, is with the car."

"Thank you for meeting me at the plane. I wasn't sure you would be able to."

"The Israelis have been very cooperative with the credentials issued by our embassy," Nikki explained before turning to address the two Secret Service agents. Both were dressed in the customary Secret Service attire, black suits and white shirts, and both wore the traditional stoic expression.

Nikki smiled as she shook their hands and offered a quick introduction. She hated crossing into their territory, but neither Robin nor her partner, Wayne, seemed upset to be relinquishing the senator's personal security to Nikki and Brad. It appeared they had been briefed before their arrival, and both were willing to take secondary roles. Nikki was relieved there would be no egos to battle and assured them they would be involved with every detail. Handing them two communication devices, she waited while they put them in place and then introduced them verbally to Brad.

Nikki took a position to the senator's right side, keeping her firing hand free and swinging one of the senator's carry-ons over her left shoulder. One Secret Service agent took the lead and the other followed behind the group. The senator's aide carried the remaining two bags and walked to the senator's left.

The first stop for the group was the restroom. Nikki dropped the luggage she carried at Wayne's feet as he took up a position outside the restroom. She cleared two stalls for the senator and her aide before waiting patiently outside for them. The next stop was baggage claim. The senator's aide, Carrie, as Nikki had learned while the senator was in the restroom, loaded their luggage onto a cart for the walk to the curb.

Nikki spoke softly into her microphone. "Ready to exit."

"Stand by," Brad responded.

Nikki placed her hand on the senator's arm. "Hold on for just a second."

The senator said nothing but raised her eyebrows in concern.

"Everything's fine. Brad needs to have the car positioned directly in front of the doors before you exit," Nikki explained. "We don't want you standing on the curb waiting."

"Ready," Brad's voice said in her ear.

"Here we go." She nodded at the agent leading the group and they began to file through the exit.

Wayne held the car door open and Carrie climbed in first, followed by the senator and then Nikki. After closing their door, he placed the luggage in the trunk and headed for the taxicab stand. He would catch a ride to the US Embassy and secure a second vehicle before meeting them at the hotel. Robin climbed in the front seat beside Brad, and Nikki heard them exchange pleasantries.

Nikki flipped through multiple screens on her iPad, giving Brad directions through the microphone on her lapel. Out of the corner of her eye, she could see the senator watching her and the screen. At the first red light, she looked up to scan their surroundings, knowing Robin would be doing the same thing, and her glance passed over the senator's face.

"This is all normal," Nikki said to reassure her. "Nothing is out of the ordinary."

"You're scanning multiple routes?"

"That's just protocol so we aren't caught off guard if there's a traffic situation."

"And sitting still makes you nervous," the senator observed.

Nikki didn't feel a need to respond to the senator's statement. It was clear Senator Wyatt was not new to traveling abroad, but Nikki noticed Carrie glancing around nervously. "Is this your first time in Israel, Carrie?" Nikki asked, hoping to take her focus away from the crowded streets around them.

"What? Oh, yes," Carrie responded.

"Only her second time outside the United States," Senator Wyatt added with a wink at Nikki.

Carrie nodded but didn't speak as her gaze returned to the urban scenery outside her window.

"Israel is beautiful. I'm sure you'll enjoy it, even though your trip is a quick one. Where are you headed next, Senator?" Nikki asked, keeping the conversation going.

"Please, call me Jan." She met Brad's eyes in the mirror and nodded for him to do the same. "Next stop is central Africa in the city of N'Djamena. That's in Chad."

"Why there?" Brad asked, taking over the conversation so Nikki could focus on their routes again.

"In the last screening, Chad did not have any children in their national army so they're a success story we want to bring attention to. Over several years, they made a concrete action plan and followed through with it."

"That's surprising when you hear the statistics of child soldiers," Brad said, scanning his mirrors as he changed lanes on Nikki's request.

"Yes, the problem is most of the recruitment for child soldiers now comes from non-state armed groups. Hence these meetings where we attempt to find creative solutions to the problem and figure out how to integrate these children back into society."

"I think that's the part most people forget." Nikki rejoined the conversation. "These kids have been taught to kill, no matter the cost, and you can't just return them to their families."

"Like we do with our military soldiers," Robin said softly.

Jan glanced at the back of her head and then at Nikki before acknowledging Robin's statement. "Resources are being deployed to assist our troops too, Robin."

Robin turned in surprise, a light blush quickly covering her face. "I'm sorry, Senator. I didn't mean to offend you."

"No offense taken. When I'm not traveling abroad, I am working on US issues too, and we certainly have plenty of them."

Nikki looked at the senator. Her face had softened at the mention of US troops and Nikki remembered a background note she had read. "You have a son serving abroad, right?"

"I do."

"And he's doing well?" Nikki's eyes searched her face in the soft light allowed by the tinted windows of the sedan.

"Yes, when I spoke with him about two weeks ago."

Nikki hesitated before responding. "That's a long time to go between calls."

"It is," Jan answered softly, turning away from Nikki's gaze.

Feeling that a response was neither wanted nor welcome, Nikki returned her focus to security. "Robin, will you jump out here and bring a luggage cart to the parking garage?"

Brad pulled to a stop at the entrance to the garage and Robin quickly exited. Once in the garage, he selected a spot near the elevator and in direct sight of the security camera.

Nikki remained seated until Robin and Brad had loaded the luggage and then held the door for the senator and Carrie to exit. Brad and Nikki went in the first elevator with the senator while Robin, Carrie and the luggage swung through the lobby for additional room keys. At the room, Nikki waited with Jan while Brad cleared the room, and then Nikki did a quick check on a second room for Carrie as they arrived with the luggage.

Robin nodded to the room across from Carrie's before grabbing her and Wayne's bags from the luggage cart. "I'll be back in ten," she said, swiping her key to open the room door.

Nikki rolled her eyes at her. "We have forty-five minutes until we have to load back up again. Take a shower and refresh. Brad and I have things covered until then. Oh, and there are two Flagler agents in that room too." Nikki pointed at Mel and Liam's room. "They're here working a different case."

"Got it. Thanks for the info and the break." Robin smiled as she closed the door to their suite.

Nikki pushed the luggage cart with the remaining bags into the senator's suite. Hearing the shower running, she and Brad quickly unloaded the bags into the senator's room before closing her bedroom doors. Brad placed the luggage cart in the hallway and called room service for a fruit and cheese platter.

CHAPTER TWENTY-THREE

"Robin and I will stay with the cars while you and Wayne go inside with the senator." Brad rolled through their afternoon plans again.

"Okay. I'll let you know as soon as they pick somewhere for dinner so you can map the course."

"We should suggest somewhere within walking distance of the hotel," Brad said, opening a search window on his laptop. After typing for a minute he spoke, "Here's one. Raphaels. It's right down the street. Good reviews. Oh," he moaned. "They have a bread waiter whose only responsibility is serving warm bread."

"Stop, you're making me hungry," Nikki complained.

"Me too." Jan walked into the room with wet hair. "Do you think room service could bring us something before we have to leave?"

A knock sounded at the door, and Nikki pulled her pistol as she approached. Opening it slowly, she stepped back to allow the waiter to push the room service cart inside. He hurried away as soon as Brad tipped him, and she closed the door, holstering her weapon.

"Wow, you guys are great." Jan looked appreciatively at the food.

Thirty minutes later, Brad cleared Carrie and Robin to enter. Robin ate a few snacks and then moved to a position outside the hotel room door. She returned for more food when Wayne arrived and took it for him to eat after he showered.

Brad and Robin cleared the cars and picked everyone up at the lobby entrance twenty minutes before the meeting. It was a short drive to the US Embassy, where Robin and Brad dropped them at the front entrance. Nikki and Wayne followed, allowing the senator to lead the way once they were cleared by the US Marine at the entrance.

The meeting room was small, with room for about twenty-five people. Only eight men and women were involved in the discussion. The rest of the room was filled with security personnel and aides. Nikki stood around the perimeter of the room directly behind Senator Wyatt. Wayne stood to her right and on her left was the security detail for Senator Andrew Thompson. He and Senator Roberta Mulligan were also staying at the Sheraton and would be accompanying Senator Wyatt to dinner later that evening.

About an hour into the meeting, a scheduled break was called and fresh coffee was brought into the room. The attendees moved around the room, chatting and drinking coffee. Nikki saw a break in the line at the coffee urn and motioned to Wayne to hold his position. Moments later, she returned and handed him a steaming cup of coffee. "Black?"

He nodded and gave her an appreciative smile.

Nikki leaned against the wall beside him and surveyed the room. The line of security agents around the perimeter made her smile. It wasn't likely anything would occur inside the US Embassy, but each of the dignitaries, even the Israelis, seemed to have several security agents at their disposal. Terrorists did like to select the least likely times to wreak havoc on unsuspecting noncombatants.

After another hour, the attendees began discussing when they would meet again and Nikki could tell the meeting was winding down. She sent a text message to Brad and then heard him advise Robin through his microphone. Within minutes, everyone stood and began moving toward the exit. Nikki and Wayne moved to Senator Wyatt's side and stayed with her as they were herded toward the exit. Senator Wyatt stopped at the exit doors and allowed Nikki to take the lead. "Coming out now," Nikki said to Brad.

"We're ready. Come right when you exit."

"I see you." Nikki approached the sedan and held the door open for Senator Wyatt, sliding in behind her. Carrie and Wayne slid in with Robin and both cars pulled away from the curb.

At the hotel, everyone changed out of suits and into more comfortable clothing before walking to the restaurant. A private room in the rear of the restaurant had been reserved for the senators and their aides. Nikki remained outside the private room with Robin while Brad and Wayne waited outside on the sidewalk. The bread waiter came through after the group had placed their order and offered the remaining basket to Nikki and Robin. Normally Nikki would say no, but with the private room separating the senator from other restaurant attendees she gave in to the smell of the food. They each took a roll and then passed the basket around to the other security agents. Nikki leaned against the wall and chewed her roll slowly. Still warm from the oven, it made her realize breakfast had been her last actual meal. Breakfast with Mel. She was surprised she had been able to keep her focus throughout the day. She glanced at her watch and wondered if Mel and Liam were having dinner now.

CHAPTER TWENTY-FOUR

Mel yawned again.

"Geez, Mel. Just close your eyes and take a nap. I'll wake you when he moves."

She glanced at Liam and nodded. "Thanks." Her eyes burned and she felt instant relief when she closed them. She wondered how Nikki was doing today and debated for the hundredth time whether to text her. She shifted in her seat to ease the pressure that had been building between her legs all day. The only way she could describe her feelings were clingy and that disgusted her. She was a love 'em and leave 'em kind of woman. No one ever spent the night at her house, mostly because she was never home herself, but it had been years since she had allowed someone to even come into her hotel room. She went to them by choice. That way she could leave when she was finished.

She concentrated on her breathing and tried to relax her body into sleep. Thinking about Nikki was not helping, but she couldn't stop herself. This morning, lying in bed with her, she had tried to remember how long it had been since she had awakened with a woman curled around her body. Maybe during college when she was too drunk to return home after sex. She had felt nothing for the women she was with then or even now. She was not relationship material and yet waking up with Nikki was something she wanted to do again. She could still feel the warmth of Nikki's body and the softness of her skin where they touched. She finally gave into a restless sleep.

An hour later, Liam nudged her leg. "Hey, he's headed down the street, maybe to the coffee shop on the corner. I'm going to get close and remind him we're still here. Want another cup?"

Mel picked up her cold cup and wrinkled her nose. "Yes, please."

"Be right back." Liam slid out of the driver's seat and slammed the door behind him.

Mel rubbed her face, trying to push the haze from her mind. The last thing she remembered before falling asleep was thinking about Nikki yet again. She looked at the clock and her stomach rumbled as if to remind her it was dinnertime. They'd caught Daniel Abbott leaving his apartment when they'd first arrived and Liam had made an obvious U-turn directly in front of him to get his attention. At first Daniel appeared puzzled by them, and Mel thought he might even approach the car, but it didn't take long for him to realize they weren't his friends. Who he thought they were was anyone's guess, and at this point Liam and Mel didn't care. They just wanted to see what he would do when they pressured him. While they sat in the car watching him go in and out of multiple stores, Liam and Mel took turns following him. After a while they devised a plan. If Josh sent Nikki and Brad to any kind of meeting tomorrow, then Liam and Mel were going to grab the contact. If it turned out to be Daniel Abbott, which they believed it would, then they'd have one more advantage.

Liam jogged across the road and slid into the driver's seat. He pushed both cups of coffee at Mel. "I think he went out the back."

Mel dropped the cups into the center console and was out of the car before Liam could start the engine. "Pick me up around back," she called to him over her shoulder.

She entered the coffee shop and quickly scanned the customers. No sign of Daniel Abbott. The man behind the counter watched her closely and she looked at him just enough to make sure he wasn't Daniel. She located the hallway leading to the restrooms and crossed, heading straight for the one with the universal male symbol. Pushing her way inside, she ignored one male conducting his business. There were no stalls or doors inside so a quick glance told her Daniel was not hiding in here. She made a quick check of the women's restroom also before exiting out the rear door. Leaving the alley, she could see Liam waiting at the corner. She glanced up and down the street. She stared into the store closest to the coffee shop. It was a clothing store, and Mel could see Daniel taking cover behind a rack near the front window while he watched their car on the street.

She texted Liam and told him to pull in front of the shop. She observed as Daniel watched Liam stop in front of the store. He was agitated and she wondered if they had pushed him too far. The store clerk approached him, and he replied harshly in Hebrew before bolting from the store. The clerk turned and shrugged, returning to his other customers. Mel left the store and slid into the car beside Liam. "He's starting to act irrational."

Liam's eyes followed him hurrying down the street in front of them. "Just where we want him."

"I'm not sure, Liam." Nikki took a sip of her almost-forgotten coffee. "He had crazy eyes back there."

Liam laughed. "Crazy eyes?"

"Yeah, like he needed to watch every direction at once because the world is closing in on him. Maybe we should back off a little."

"We can't, Mel. We need something to turn now."

"Look. He's getting on the bus."

They pulled in behind the bus and began following. After twenty minutes of following the bus through multiple stops, Liam came up with an idea. "Check your laptop and see where the next stop will be. I'll pull ahead of the bus and drop you at the spot. If you get on maybe you can flush him out."

Mel nodded. She wasn't happy with the idea of pushing him farther, but like Liam, she couldn't see an alternative. She located the next stop and gave Liam directions.

He gunned the engine and pulled ahead of the bus. "Put your hands-free headset on and keep the cell phone connection." He glanced at her. "Just in case we get separated."

She connected her cell phone headset and dialed Liam's phone. He hit the connection button on his steering wheel as he swerved to a stop at the curb. "Can you hear me?" he asked.

She nodded. "Loud and clear." She climbed out of the car and Liam pulled into a parking space just up the road. The bus turned the corner, closing in on her stop. She made eye contact with the driver and waved to him to make sure he would stop for her. She paid her fare and smiled at Daniel before taking the first empty seat several rows behind him. "I'm good," she whispered into her microphone.

"Excellent," Liam said. "I'm behind you. Let me know if he makes a move."

Mel stared at the back of Daniel's head. His hair was dark and greasy, the result of too much hair gel or too little washing. His body shook as he bounced his leg up and down with nervous anxiety, and his head spun from side to side, as he watched the people around him. Mel settled into the seat with her back to the window so she could watch people behind her as well as Daniel and the people in front of her. Once Daniel spun all the way around and stared at her. She gave him her best "I'm your friend" smile, and he glared at her. When he finally turned to face the front again, she glanced around her to see what her fellow bus riders thought of his behavior. Everyone seemed afraid to make eye contact with him and, by association, with her either.

After riding around a while, Daniel made a phone call. Mel shifted closer to him to try to hear his end of the conversation. "He's making a cell call," she advised Liam.

"Damn. I wish we could track it."

"Yeah, I wish I would have brought the laptop with me."

"Oh well." Liam sighed. "We can listen to it later. Did someone answer?"

"Either that or he's leaving a message."

"The bus is finishing its route and will start over again. In about thirty-five minutes you will be back where you got on. Do you think he has a destination?"

"He's watching out the window, but he doesn't act like he has any intention of getting off. I could move closer and see if that pushes him."

"Give it a try, but be ready for him to bolt."

Mel stood and walked past Daniel, sliding into a seat two rows in front of him and across the aisle. She again placed her back against the window, angling her body to see in front of and behind her. She stared at Daniel, waiting for him to make eye contact with her, but his gaze was focused on something outside the window. Mel followed his line of sight but couldn't identify any landmarks to tell her their location.

"Two stops away from where you got on," Liam said into her ear.

Mel frowned. What was Daniel doing? He leaned forward in his seat rocking back and forth. "He's going to bolt."

"Copy," Liam answered.

When the bus pulled to a stop, Daniel jumped up and sprinted down the aisle.

"He's moving." Mel followed him up the aisle and off the bus. He turned into the alley on the right and Mel stayed on his heels. She knew Liam would be following her, so she gave him directions. "Alley on the right."

At the edge of the alley, before she moved into the darkness, Mel slowed her pace and pulled her pistol from its shoulder holster.

CHAPTER TWENTY-FIVE

Carrie set a large bag of food on the coffee table in Senator Wyatt's room and headed off to bed with an escort from Robin.

"I'm going to call my family and then call it a day." Senator Wyatt headed for her bedroom. "We brought that food for you guys." She pointed at the bag Carrie had set on the table.

Brad's eyes grew huge. "Seriously?" He grabbed the bag and began pulling food out. "This is awesome."

Nikki smiled at the senator. "Thank you very much."

"Thank you guys for keeping us safe. Good night." Jan closed the door to her bedroom.

Nikki flopped onto the couch beside Brad. "Have you heard from Liam?"

Brad shook his head. "You?"

"Nope. I thought about texting Mel, but I don't want to interrupt something."

Brad scooped food onto his plate. "What do you think that is?" He pointed at one of the dishes.

Nikki stuck her fork into the container and took a bite. "Hmmm. Lamb and couscous." She moaned. "Oh that's good."

"I wouldn't worry about Mel and Liam. They might be out all night." Brad nudged her. "Besides, you're sleeping with me tonight."

"Like that's ever going to happen, Bradley."

Brad laughed. "Do you want the first or second shift?"

"It doesn't matter." Nikki took another bite. "I can sleep or make coffee." She yawned involuntarily.

Brad laughed again. "I'll take the first shift, but I'd like a shower first. After I eat though."

A soft knock sounded at the door and Nikki approached with her pistol resting against her thigh. Robin was on duty in the hallway, but Nikki still opened the door just far enough to see before pulling it wider.

"We got a problem," Liam said softly, tucking his badge back in his pocket. He stepped to the side to allow Mel to enter the room. She wore Liam's jacket over her shoulders and the size of it made her look small and vulnerable. Her face was pale as she stepped into the room and leaned against the wall.

Nikki nodded to Robin before closing the door and looking at Mel. "What's going on?" she asked, her anxiety building.

"We need a first aid kit," Liam explained as he escorted Mel to the couch and took the jacket off her shoulders.

Her upper arm looked wet where the blood had soaked through the burgundy shirt.

Nikki gasped, crossing the room in two strides. "What the hell?" She looked at Liam. "Why is she here and not at a hospital?"

"I told him to bring me here." Mel raised her uninjured arm, touching Nikki's thigh to get her attention. "Nikki, it's just a flesh wound."

"Flesh wound, my ass," Nikki grumbled as she knelt between Mel's legs and began unbuttoning her shirt. She struggled to contain her fear and the irrational need she felt to protect Mel from everyone. Pushing Mel's shirt off her shoulder, she pulled the cuff to remove her left arm from the material. "Holy shit." She sat back on her heels. "Brad, bring me a couple towels."

Nikki fought to keep the emotion from her face as she examined the wound, placing a towel around Mel's arm to stop the blood flow. Nikki's eyes met Mel's and she was surprised at the flash of turmoil. Mel was clearly struggling too. There was a hint of pain, but mostly Nikki saw affection and then the cocky smile wiped everything else away. Nikki quickly looked away. For both their sakes, she knew Mel was going to try to break the tension in the room.

Mel looked up at the guys. "Flesh wound."

Nikki snorted.

Liam held up a baggie containing a bullet. "I pulled this from the wall behind her. It must have passed straight through her arm."

"See. Flesh wound," Mel stated again.

"You still need a doctor." Nikki stood to retrieve the few first aid supplies she carried in her bag.

"I can make that decision." The agents looked up to find Jan watching them from her bedroom doorway. "I had a few years of emergency room experience before I moved into politics." She crossed the room and knelt between Mel's legs as Nikki had done moments before. She unwrapped the towel and looked at the wound. "Nikki, can you please run water through the coffeepot and then get the red bag inside my suitcase?" Her voice was calm.

Nikki dropped the bag beside the senator and then returned to wait for the water to heat, staying back out of the way. Brad walked over to stand with her and squeezed her shoulder. She couldn't look at him. She was afraid if she leaned on him right now she might cry.

The senator spoke softly to Mel as she examined her arm. Mel shook her head vehemently and Jan stood to address the group. "I think we can get away without stitches since she doesn't want to go to the hospital." She opened her bag and began pulling gauze and tape from it.

Nikki carried the pot over and set it on the coffee table. She watched Mel's pale face and was surprised when she spoke to her. "Come over here."

Nikki slowly walked to the couch and sat down beside her.

"I'm okay." Mel laid her hand on Nikki's thigh.

Jan looked back and forth between them before smiling. "She's going to be fine. As soon as we get it cleaned out anyway." She dipped the towel in the hot water and pressed it to the open wound, making Mel grimace.

Nikki took her hand and Mel squeezed it hard as her wound was cleaned and then wrapped.

The senator stood. "I would like you to take some pain pills and go to sleep. What's the chance you'll listen to me?"

"She'll listen," Nikki answered for her.

Mel was silent, and Nikki's eyes grew large as she stared at her. Remembering the room full of people watching them, Nikki again fought to contain her emotions. She knew she needed to put some distance between them and she started to stand.

"Nikki, wait." Mel laid her hand on Nikki's leg, pulling her back down. "We have to go back out."

"No. You don't," Nikki stated, feeling exposed in the room full of people. She stood and began to pace. "You can't." Her blue eyes filled with tears as she turned them on Mel.

Mel looked at Liam. "We need twenty-four-hour surveillance on him." She lifted her arm and grimaced. "Especially now. I'm sure he knows he hit me and he'll be panicking."

Brad stepped forward. "I'll go with him."

Mel's head dropped and then she nodded. "I would appreciate that, Brad. I'll cover for you here."

Jan handed Mel a bottle of water and placed two tablets in her hand. "I will leave you to work out the details." She crossed to her bedroom and closed the door.

"You can cover for me tomorrow, Mel. Tonight you need to rest and sleep." Brad nodded at Nikki. "You get some sleep too. I'll fill Robin and Wayne in and they'll be watching from outside the door. I noticed earlier there's a detachment from the Bureau of Diplomatic Security sitting outside the hotel as well." He pulled on his jacket and nodded to Liam.

Liam took a step toward Mel and then stopped and Nikki watched him struggle with his concern for Mel. "I'll call Bowden and let her know what happened. I'm sure they'll send additional agents to help us continue surveillance."

Mel nodded, disappointment clear in her voice. "I'm fine, Liam. Well, I will be as soon as Nikki stops making me dizzy."

Nikki stopped pacing and leaned against the counter. She hadn't even realized she was moving. She watched Mel close her eyes and rest her head on the back of the couch.

"I'll check in with Josh too." Brad made a circle motion with his hand. "Of course, I'll leave all this out."

Brad followed Liam out of the room after bagging a couple of takeout containers from the coffee table to take with them.

CHAPTER TWENTY-SIX

Mel lifted her head from the back of the couch and looked at Nikki. "Come here." She patted the cushion beside her.

Nikki crossed the room and sat next to her, staring straight ahead.

"Are you mad at me?" Mel asked, touching her arm.

Nikki turned to face her. "No!" She lowered her voice to a whisper. "I'm not mad."

"I'm sorry I scared you."

"You didn't…" Nikki dropped her face into her hands and mumbled. "Who am I kidding? I was scared to death." She shrugged. "There was a lot of blood." She looked into Mel's face and then pulled her into her arms, relaxing against the back of the couch. Holding her tight against her body, she stroked her fingers through Mel's hair. Concentrating on Mel's breathing, Nikki felt her drift off to sleep. Her mind raged as it lectured her on all the reasons for not developing feelings for someone she worked with. In her heart, she knew it was too late. Mel was already a part of her. When she had seen the blood on Mel's arm, she had tried to tell herself it was just her arm, but the fear made her irrational and she wanted to lash out at someone.

Nikki didn't realize she was falling asleep, too, until a soft knock at the door brought her quickly awake and to her feet. Mel moaned but didn't open her eyes. Nikki pulled her pistol and opened the door enough to see Robin was alone in the hall. She motioned her inside. "What's up?"

"I wanted to ask you the same thing." Robin glanced at Mel's sleeping body. "She okay?"

"She will be." Nikki sighed, dropping into a chair at the kitchen table. "Everything okay outside?"

"Things are quiet. We have three agents in the hallway between the three senators' rooms and I don't think there are any other guests on this floor."

"That certainly makes things a little easier." Nikki walked over to Mel, sliding a pillow under her head and lifting her feet onto the couch before spreading a cotton throw across her body. Her gaze caught the pain pills still lying on the coffee table and she scooped them into her pocket. "Would you like something to eat?" She motioned at the still-open containers spread across the coffee table.

"No, I'm good. Wayne and I ordered room service when we returned earlier." She looked at Nikki's tired face. "You could sleep, you know?"

Nikki rolled her eyes. "I don't think that's going to happen for a while." She gave Robin an appreciative smile. "How about some coffee?"

Robin nodded and Nikki crossed to the automatic coffeepot, setting it to brew. She pulled cups from the cabinet and placed them on the table with creamer and sugar.

Searching for solid ground with small talk, Nikki broke the silence. "How long have you been with the Secret Service?"

"Almost eight years."

Nikki studied her face, realizing she was older than she had first thought.

Robin smiled. "Yes, I crossed the thirty-year line years ago." She picked up the steaming cup as Nikki returned the pot to the burner. "I only became a field agent about three years ago though."

"Why the switch?" Nikki poured sugar and creamer into her coffee and then grimaced at the taste.

Robin laughed. "The sugar and creamer won't keep you awake any more than the coffee. You should just drink it the way you like it."

Nikki stood and dumped the cup in the sink before filling her mug again. She took a long sip. "Better." She sat back down at the table. "Sorry, I'm a little out of sorts tonight. So, why the switch to field agent?"

"I was bored."

Nikki raised her eyebrows. "And have the last three years been less boring?"

"There have certainly been moments." She nodded at Mel. "Want to tell me what happened?"

"It has nothing to do with the senator," Nikki said quickly.

Robin nodded as if that explained everything and stood. "I should get back to my post." She held up the mug. "I'll take this with me."

Nikki gave her a smile. She was appreciative that Robin didn't push for details on Mel's shooting. "Thanks for the chat."

"Sure. I just wanted you to know Wayne or I will be outside all night. Call if you need anything."

"I'll let you guys know if the senator wants to get breakfast out before her flight. She didn't mention it tonight and I didn't think to ask."

"Wayne's going to relieve me in about four hours, but we'll both be back on duty by zero seven."

Nikki secured the door behind Robin and filled her mug with the coffee that remained in the pot before cleaning the glass carafe. She carried her coffee to the couch and sat down at Mel's feet. Setting her mug on the coffee table she untied Mel's boots and pulled them off her feet before removing her own boots. Picking her mug up, she pulled her legs under her and leaned back against the cushions, watching Mel sleep. It was hard to believe that twenty-four hours ago she was devouring every inch of that full, luscious body. Beneath the throw she could see the curves and she remembered each one of them. She slowed her breath to match the rise and fall of Mel's chest, trying to reconcile how much her feelings had changed over the last week. Desire alone was not new to her, but what scared her was the almost painful, passionate ache she felt for this woman. She was so strong and vibrant a few hours ago, and now she was pale and injured. Though Nikki knew her arm would heal, she couldn't get past the fear of what could have happened. Her world was changing so fast she couldn't feel solid ground beneath her, and now the realization of how fast she almost lost it all slammed into her.

Her phone vibrated and she shifted to pull it from her pocket. Brad's number displayed on the readout. "What's up?" she asked without a greeting.

"I just talked with Josh and he needs a courier pickup before we head back tomorrow."

"No shit." Nikki's head swam with the information. This is what Liam and Mel had been hoping for, but things had changed with Mel's injury.

"Liam talked with his boss, and they're going to send backup for them." He paused. "But they can't be here until about seventeen hundred hours tomorrow and the pickup is at fifteen hundred."

"So, Mel's going to have to do it." Nikki made it a statement rather than a question.

"Afraid so. Is she awake? Liam is asking."

"No, she's been asleep since you guys left. She didn't take the pain pills though, so I would imagine she'll wake up in a few hours."

"When she does, fill her in. We'll touch base with you guys in the morning, and you can meet up with us after you drop off the senator."

"Okay."

"Hey, Nik," Brad paused before continuing, "Robin has my number on speed dial so get some sleep. Liam and I are taking turns too. We'll need to be alert tomorrow."

"I hear you." Nikki clicked off the phone and tucked it back into her pocket. As long as it was tight against her body, she would wake up if it rang again. She slid lower on the couch and wrapped her legs around Mel's, pulling the bottom of the throw around them both. She wanted to sleep, but her mind kept turning over reasons why Daniel Abbott would shoot Mel. Clearly he felt pressure, but what was he hiding? And was he working alone?

CHAPTER TWENTY-SEVEN

Mel heard moaning. Someone was in pain and she needed to help them. Her eyes were glued shut and her body wouldn't respond to her commands.

"Mel, wake up." Nikki knelt beside her and stroked her head. "Wake up."

Mel moaned and the realization hit that she was the one in pain. Her arm ached when she tried to sit up.

Nikki slid an arm behind her and braced her into a sitting position. "I guess I don't need to ask how you're feeling." Nikki gently tucked Mel's hair behind her ear and kissed her cheek.

"I feel like crap and I have to go to the bathroom." Mel pushed herself to her feet and moaned again. "Good thing I don't need my left arm for this mission."

Nikki laughed, following close behind her. Mel stopped at the door and turned, putting a hand to Nikki's chest. "I can take it from here, cupcake."

Nikki rolled her eyes. "Did you really just call me cupcake?"

Mel closed the door in her face, but her laughter continued. When she opened the door, she rested against the frame. "Do you have any painkillers?"

Nikki pulled from her pocket the two pills the senator had given her earlier and Mel frowned. "Anything less intrusive?"

"Maybe but don't you think you should take these?"

"It doesn't hurt enough for me to be knocked out. I just need something to take the edge off."

"Oh, so that wasn't you who woke me moaning."

Mel stepped into Nikki's space, forcing her to take a step back. She repeated this until Nikki's back ran into the wall. Then she angled her body to protect her left arm and pushed her chest into Nikki's, holding her in place before kissing her hard. She broke the kiss and stared into Nikki's face. "I might have moaned, but it wasn't because my arm hurt."

Nikki pushed her backward and stepped away from the wall. "Right. And," she put a finger to Mel's chest, "you can't do that here." She tossed Mel a bottle of over-the-counter pain pills from her bag. "Since your arm doesn't hurt, see if you can open that bottle." She left the room as Mel struggled with the bottle. Nikki returned and took it from her, dumping two pills into Mel's palm before handing her an opened water bottle.

Mel downed the pills and then smiled. "Thanks, cupcake."

"I'm starting to think you had a head injury. Lose the damn 'cupcake' already."

Mel settled back onto the couch and sipped her water. "I vaguely remember you talking to Brad earlier. Did they find Abbott?"

Nikki slapped her forehead. "I forgot to ask. He called to tell me that Josh wants a courier pickup before we leave tomorrow."

"No way." Mel breathed out. "After tonight I really thought I'd blown it. If it is Josh, he's really stupid or he thinks he's still fooling everyone."

"I can't imagine he thinks you guys are in the dark." Nikki frowned, sitting down beside her. "Does he know you are Flagler Internal Investigation or does he think you are CIA like we did?

"I don't know. Weird thing is, we never identified ourselves and he never asked. Of course, Lewis knew the truth so he might have told him."

"Or maybe he didn't." Nikki shrugged. "We made the assumption you were CIA because of the mission, and then we never questioned it. Even after you showed up at Flagler. We were confused, but it didn't occur to me that you might not be who we thought you were."

Mel grinned. "I do like to keep you guessing." She closed her eyes and sighed. "When you came out on the porch all sweaty, that's when I knew I was in trouble."

"I knew in the bar when you kissed me. I couldn't think right for days. My head was all filled with you and your hard body." Nikki slid to the opposite end of the couch and leaned her head against the cushion.

Mel raised her eyebrows, questioning the distance between them.

"I can't be close to you, right now," Nikki stated. "In fact," she lifted her head from the couch, "you should sleep in the bedroom."

"I'd rather sleep here with you."

"Fine, but I'm setting my alarm for zero five thirty so I can shower before everyone starts moving around." She pulled her cell phone from her pocket and set the alarm before laying her head back down on the cushion.

Mel closed her eyes and slowed her breathing. The painkillers were starting to work. She could feel Nikki watching her and knew she was still worried. Her eyelids fluttered as she tried to open them. "Are you watching me?" Mel mumbled sleepily.

"No. Now go to sleep."

Mel could hear the smile in Nikki's voice and knew she had been right. "Good night, cupcake."

"Good night, Carter."

Mel smiled and let the lethargy she'd been fighting sweep over her.

CHAPTER TWENTY-EIGHT

Nikki woke five minutes before her alarm was set to go off. She slowly disentangled her legs from Mel's and crossed to the bedroom. Showering quickly, she dressed in a clean suit. She towel dried her hair and then ran her fingers through it. When she walked back into the living room, Mel was sitting with a cup of coffee balanced on her knee. Nikki fought the urge to drop her gaze to Mel's chest. She had pulled the burgundy shirt on her good arm and the bloody sleeve hung limp against her body. None of the buttons were fastened and the shirt hung open to reveal the black sports bra and a hard stomach.

Mel held up her cell phone. "Liam says everything's okay with them."

Nikki nodded as she handed Mel two pain pills from the bottle on the table. "I told Brad we'd give them a call after we drop the senator at the airport." She poured herself a mug of coffee and took a sip before combing through the cabinets. Under the sink she found a small trash bag and she used her fist to push a hole in the bottom of it. She slipped the trash bag onto

Mel's left arm and pulled it up until it covered the injury before tying it around her arm.

Mel smiled. "Thanks."

Nikki kissed her. "Go take a shower and then get back over here so we can brief everyone before we head to the airport."

"Be back in a few. By the way, I ordered a bunch of stuff from room service. See if you can save me something. I'm starving."

"Good idea. Thanks." Nikki checked the hallway before holding the door open for Mel to exit. She introduced Wayne to Mel and then watched her until she was safe inside her room. She held the door open and Wayne stepped in. Nikki pointed at the coffeepot and he nodded, quickly filling his cup before sitting at the table.

"Robin's in the shower," he said as she sat down across from him. "I understand there's been a slight change in plans."

"Yes, Mel was injured last night so she and Brad have switched positions."

"How bad is her injury?"

"It was a grazing shot so just a flesh wound. The senator fixed her up. Right arm still works fine and she's only taken over-the-counter painkillers."

"Thanks." Wayne nodded. "I appreciate being kept in the loop."

"It's hard to cross agencies. Can Mel return your car to the embassy and then wait with our vehicle while the three of us escort the senator to her flight?"

"I like that idea."

Nikki hoped Mel would see it that way too. She had no doubt in Mel's ability to do whatever came up, but since the car had to be returned anyway, it seemed the best plan in putting the senator's safety first.

The senator was the first to appear a few minutes later. "How is Agent Carter this morning?"

"Better. Thank you for patching her up last night."

"I thought I was having emergency room flashbacks." She smiled as she poured the remaining coffee into a mug and started a new pot. She looked at Nikki. "She was lucky. Why don't you guys wear vests?"

Nikki shrugged. "We do sometimes, but they were only doing surveillance last night."

"Surveillance can be brutal," Wayne cut in.

Nikki and Wayne both approached the door when room service knocked. Robin, Mel and Carrie came in ahead of the carts full of food. There were six plates of eggs and fruit as well as a variety of breads. Everyone ate quickly and with little conversation. Nikki was able to get Mel to the side and discussed the new plan with her. She was agreeable and claimed she didn't need any assistance with directions to the embassy. Wayne left and returned with a luggage cart. Once everyone's bags were loaded, Wayne and Mel took the bags to the parking garage and loaded them into the car. Wayne conducted a thorough check on both vehicles and Mel left for the embassy in his car. Wayne contacted Robin when he arrived in front of the lobby and she herded everyone out.

Robin sat beside Wayne as he drove, and Nikki scanned the iPad looking for the least congested streets to get them to Route One, which would take them to the airport. The senator was quiet and even Carrie didn't seem to have anything to say. Nikki was fairly sure Carrie was the only one who didn't know about Mel being shot, and it was probably best that she didn't. The senator had waved Mel into her room before she had left with Wayne, taking the opportunity to check her wound before they departed. She hadn't had a chance to ask Jan how it looked, but she had to trust that Mel would let her know if there was a problem. At least she hoped she would.

As they were pulling into the departure lane to check their bags, Mel texted that her cab had cleared the first airport checkpoint. By the time the luggage was unloaded from the car and tickets were obtained, Mel had arrived to take possession of the car and move it away from the terminal until Nikki returned. Nikki was able to locate the supervisor she had spoken with previously and obtained permission to accompany the senator to her gate again. Once there, Carrie and the senator sat immediately and began discussing the agenda for the day. Nikki sat close to them with her back to the wall and the ninety minutes passed quickly. The senator's voice was smooth as she rolled through her key points for the next meeting. Nikki had admired her dedication before she met her and, now that she knew a little more about the personality behind the professional, she liked her even more.

Robin and Wayne stood on opposite sides of the room. Their postures were relaxed but their eyes were vigilant. When the gate attendants began preparing the walkway for boarding, Nikki approached first Robin and then Wayne. She thanked each of them for their assistance before saying sincerely that she looked forward to working with them in the future. Wayne was professional and distant as he nodded his agreement. Robin glanced at her quickly before returning her gaze to the senator and surrounding area. "Take care of your friend," she said softly.

Nikki smiled. "That's not an easy task."

"I got that idea." Robin returned her smile as they approached the senator. "Ready to board, Senator?" Robin asked, all trace of her smile having disappeared and the stoic look that matched Wayne's having returned.

"Give me just a minute, please." Jan placed her hand on Nikki's arm, turning them away from the group. "If you can, check that wound again before you leave tonight."

Nikki's surprise at the senator's knowledge of their itinerary did not show on her face as she nodded her understanding. "Thank you for your assistance and your discretion."

Jan nodded. "Josh Houston is not my normal contact at Flagler," she stated. "This desire for additional protection was made to Josh at Agent Carter's request."

This time Nikki couldn't contain her surprise. "You knew Agent Carter before last night?"

Jan grinned. "How do you think I knew not to argue with her about going to the hospital?"

Nikki shook her head in disbelief. "Because you patched her up before?"

Jan winked at her. "I know many secrets about Agent Carter." She glanced at Wayne and he nodded that it was time for her to board. "Ask her about Germany." Jan smiled devilishly, "Or better yet, maybe I'll get the chance to tell you the story when we aren't on foreign soil."

Nikki was still shaking her head as she watched them board. She knew she wasn't Mel's first lover and she would never be jealous of past affairs, but she couldn't believe the senator had implied there might be a story there. Nikki pulled out her phone and texted Mel that she was headed back to the car. Putting aside all thoughts of Mel's past, she turned her attention to the afternoon ahead of them and sent a short text to Brad. He replied with their location and told her to call when she was in the car.

CHAPTER TWENTY-NINE

Nikki dropped into the seat beside Mel and sighed. "Time to shift gears." She pulled out her iPad and punched in the coordinates Brad had given her before dialing him on the car's Bluetooth.

"Greetings," Brad said cheerily.

Mel rolled her eyes at his chipper tone and Nikki smiled. She was used to Brad and happened to like his quirky ways.

"Our fine senator has boarded her plane safely and we are ready to focus on Daniel Abbott," Nikki responded.

Liam's voice was heard on the line as he began explaining where things stood. "We ordered him a pizza right after midnight. He wasn't happy, but he did answer the door so we could confirm his location."

"And since he refused the pizza, we got to eat it," Brad said happily.

Nikki could hear the laughter in Liam's voice as he continued. "This morning he left his apartment and came down to the street. He looked around for about ten minutes and then disappeared back upstairs."

"Yeah, it was weird," Brad chimed in again. "I wanted to order him another pizza since it appeared he was waiting for something."

"And you didn't want him to be disappointed?" Nikki asked.

"Right, and I was hungry."

"Do you need us to grab you guys something to eat, and coffee?" Mel asked.

"No, Liam finally gave in to my whining about thirty minutes ago so I should be good for another hour at least."

"Honestly, Nikki, how do you manage him on missions?" Liam chuckled.

"With lots of energy bars."

"Oh please no," Liam exclaimed. "Don't give him any sugar. The caffeine is bad enough."

Mel laughed and Nikki tried to talk as she joined her. "Do you want to trade partners?" She placed a hand on Mel's thigh. "I have something here I could trade."

"No, we're fine," Brad answered before Liam could and they could hear Liam laughing in the background. "Seriously though…Liam is about to take his first nap of the night and is already tucked into the backseat." Brad paused. "I see you guys. Go past us and park on the other side of the street."

Mel executed an illegal U-turn and pulled to a stop on the curb.

"Let's switch to earwigs," Brad suggested. Nikki pulled two cases from the glove box, handing one to Mel. She inserted her own earpiece and switched on her lapel microphone. "Testing." She heard Brad's voice in her ear.

"Loud and clear," Nikki said as Mel nodded her agreement.

"Liam has elected not to join us for the moment," Brad explained. "He thinks hearing voices in his head will interfere with his sleep."

"Yeah, I hate these things too," Mel complained. "That's why I transferred to internal investigation. I work alone so I only have to listen to myself."

Nikki and Brad laughed.

"I'm going silent for now, Mel, so you won't have to hear me in your head," Brad stated.

The silence stretched as Mel and Nikki got comfortable in their seats. Nikki motioned for Mel to turn off her microphone. They would still be able to hear Brad if he spoke, but he didn't need to hear their conversation.

"So," Nikki stretched out the single syllable word for several seconds. "You knew Jan Wyatt before yesterday?"

"Is that a question or a statement?" Mel asked, giving her a quick glance.

"Both, I guess." Nikki smiled. "I thought you might want to elaborate."

Mel wrinkled her face. "Nope."

Nikki laughed. "Oh, come on." Mel shook her head so Nikki continued. "She suggested I ask you about Germany."

Mel rubbed her face. "Yeah, she would suggest Germany."

"So." Nikki waited patiently.

"It was years ago, before I started with internal investigations. I was assigned to protect Dr. Wyatt for a week in Germany. She was attending a conference with several other doctors from various countries." Mel shifted in her seat, placing her hand on Nikki's knee. "And we slept together."

Nikki gave her a shocked look. "And that's the story?"

Mel laughed. "Okay, we didn't sleep together. I was just checking to see if you were still listening."

"Oh, I'm listening."

"Another US doctor had his sights on Jan. He had pursued her in the past when she was still married, and she was concerned he would be more of a problem now that she wasn't married anymore." Mel sighed. "And he was. After the first night we moved to a different floor, and I started sleeping on the couch."

"He got into the room?"

"Oh yes. That first night he talked the desk clerk into giving him a key, and he strolled right in. Luckily, she and I were sitting in the living room." She waved her hand around. "Just chatting. We hadn't gone to our separate bedrooms yet."

"Did you kick his ass?"

"No, I was very professional. At least I was at first. I escorted him out of the room and explained what would happen if he tried that stunt again. Two days later, he cornered her in between seminars. I was maintaining my distance, trying to be discreet, and it took me several seconds to arrive on the scene. He had his hand over her mouth and the other one under her shirt."

"Geez. Did you kick his ass then?"

"Oh yeah. Well, actually it was his nose I broke."

Nikki shook her head. "I am constantly amazed at how people behave."

"He filed a complaint saying she led him on and I acted irrationally, but we were able to produce statements from several people who had witnessed his behavior. Even the desk clerk that he had talked the key out of gave a statement."

"So, you and Jan are friends now?"

"I guess you could say that. It's not like we get together outside of work, but we call if we need something. I'll even do security for her if she asks." Mel glanced quickly at Nikki. "You're not jealous, are you?"

"Of course not. I know you have lots of women in your past. Just so I'm the only one in your present."

Mel smiled. "I think you're all I can handle."

Nikki typed on her iPad. "I could use some coffee. How about you?"

"Sure. There's a shop on the corner behind us."

Nikki nodded. "Yep, I see that." She slid out of the car and headed for the coffee shop.

CHAPTER THIRTY

Nikki returned and handed Mel one of the tall containers of black coffee she was carrying. After removing the lids, both inhaled, enjoying the aroma before taking sips.

"Tell me about your family," Mel said.

Nikki frowned at her. "You followed me to their house!" she said vehemently. "Besides, you read my file. Tell me about yours."

"Okay." Mel smiled at getting Nikki riled so easily and then her face grew serious. "My father was killed when I was fifteen, and my mother raised me and my seven-year-old sister alone. Mom lives in Tennessee, and my sister plays college football in the Atlantic Coast Conference."

Nikki's eyes widened. "I've heard of her. Tallahassee University, right?"

"That's her."

"Cool." Nikki hesitated, not sure if she should inquire about Mel's father or not.

"He was a career soldier killed in the line of duty." Mel answered without her asking.

"That's tough."

"For you as well," Mel said softly. "You were only ten when your parents died."

"Yeah, it's hard to remember them sometimes. I have a few memories, but they're mostly from pictures."

"But your foster parents were good to you?"

"They were. I struggled for a year or two after my parents were killed. I didn't want anyone in my life but, luckily, they were persistent, and I eventually moved in with them permanently."

"But you weren't adopted?"

"No."

"Why?" Mel pushed.

Nikki rubbed her face. She'd only had this discussion with a few people in her life. Bob and Sandra, of course, and then later the therapist at Flagler. She glanced at Mel and saw only compassion on her face. "At first I was afraid to love anything for fear it would be taken away, but later it just didn't feel necessary. They knew I loved them and they were my parents. An official decree didn't seem important."

"No siblings, right?"

Nikki was relieved at the change in topics. "Yep. I'm an only child."

"Spoiled rotten then?"

Nikki laughed. "Are you asking or telling?"

"I don't think I want to answer."

Brad's voice echoed through their headsets. "Hey, Nik. We should probably make a run back to the hotel and check out. I don't want to be moving around close to the pickup time."

Nikki looked at her watch. "I'm ready when you are."

"Okay then. Mel, let's swap."

"On my way." Mel picked up Nikki's hand and held it to her mouth. "Don't forget me before I get back to Florida."

"No chance."

Mel kissed her fingers before placing Nikki's hand back on her own leg. She reached into her jacket pocket and pulled out her hotel room key. "Take this and you can shower in my room."

Nikki nodded.

Brad pulled open Mel's door, and she slid out, punching him in the arm. "Take care of my girl." She didn't wait for a response but took off at a jog.

Brad slid in beside Nikki. "I'm ready for this mission to be over. How about you?"

"Yeah, my eyes are burning, and I feel like I have been up for days."

They drove the short distance back to the hotel in silence. Nikki grabbed her bag from Brad's room and crossed the hall. When she opened the door the silence consumed her. It felt like an ominous sign and Nikki couldn't help shivering. She placed her bag on the bed and turned on the shower. Stripping out of her suit, she placed it into the laundry bag and stepped into the shower. The water was cool, and Nikki wasted no time under the spray. She was happy to pull on her comfortable jeans and running shoes instead of a suit and heels. Noticing a travel-sized bottle of lavender body spray on the bathroom counter, Nikki sprayed a small amount on her wrist. The fragrance immediately engulfed her and images of Mel crashed in on her. The first time she had experienced the scent was in the bar the night Mel had kissed her. At the time, she hadn't made the connection with Mel, but now, seeing the bottle, she remembered all the times she had smelled it. She spritzed her neck and under her shirt before placing the bottle back on the counter.

Looking around the room to make sure she hadn't forgotten anything, she noticed Mel's burgundy shirt, dark with dried blood, hanging across the back of a chair. She crossed the room and gently touched the collar, trying not to think about how much worse Mel could have been injured. Clearing the morose thoughts from her head, she turned to leave and noticed a hotel notepad and pen lying on the desk. She picked up the pen as she subconsciously began to compose a heartfelt letter to Mel, but then laughed at herself. Not appropriate and there certainly wasn't time so she wrote two words, "Yours, Cupcake." She tucked the paper between the clean shirts in Mel's suitcase.

She grabbed her bag and returned to Brad's room. While Nikki checked out of the hotel, returning all the room keys except for Mel's, Brad stepped into the restaurant and placed a take-out order. After a security check on the sedan, they returned to the surveillance site. Back within range of their communication devices, they informed Mel and Liam that they had returned with food.

Almost as soon as they parked, Mel appeared at Nikki's door, stuck her head through the open window and passed their borrowed communication equipment to Nikki. She started to speak and then closed her eyes. Nikki watched her sniff the air and knew she was smelling the lavender body spray. Mel opened her eyes, smiled at Nikki and then looked at Brad. "Damn, you smell good, Agent Morton."

"Why thank you, Agent Carter." Brad grinned. "I've been told I clean up well."

Nikki rolled her eyes at both of them and looked at Mel, motioning toward the backseat. "Climb in."

Mel frowned at her. "The backseat, really?"

"Get in, Carter. I want to check your arm."

"I'm fi—" Mel started.

Nikki glared at her and Mel climbed silently into the backseat. Nikki climbed out and followed her, closing the door behind them.

She motioned with her hand for Mel to remove her shirt. "Don't make me do it for you."

"Isn't this uncomfortable?" Mel smiled as she met Brad's eyes in the rearview mirror.

He winked at her. "It's just getting good."

Nikki glared at him as she removed the old bandage and added more antiseptic. Taping a new bandage on, she helped Mel slide her arm back into the shirt. Mel sat back on the seat and buttoned her shirt. "You guys okay to hold down the fort here? We want to go check out the location where the package exchange will take place."

"No problem," Brad answered.

Nikki nodded as she passed Mel her hotel room key, grasping her hand in a quick squeeze before letting go.

Mel gave her a wink before returning to her conversation with Brad. "We'll run over there now and then come back for a while." She rubbed a hand over her face. "We'd like to follow Abbott, but there's always the chance he's not the person you're meeting."

"That's true," Brad grumbled.

Mel climbed out, taking a bag of food, and gave them a wave. Nikki slid out and back into the front seat. "Carter and I found a coffee shop on the corner. Interested?"

"Sure," Brad agreed. "Liam and I have been hitting that place since the first night. Not a very pleasant man running it, but they have a nice variety of drinks. Today, I feel like black coffee though."

"Be right back." Nikki closed the car door behind her.

Brad studied the green door leading to the apartment building housing Daniel Abbott before digging into the bag of food.

CHAPTER THIRTY-ONE

"I think if we park on the street we'll be able to see who enters the alley." Mel stared down the alley toward the brick wall blocking the end of the street.

"If it is Abbott, why'd he choose a dead-end alley with no escape route?" Liam questioned.

"I sure as hell don't know. He's been so nervous and now he's confident about getting in and out with us tailing him." Mel sighed. "What are we missing?"

"I wish I knew." Liam started walking toward the car. "Let's head back."

Mel followed him.

* * *

Nikki returned and passed a large cup to Brad. They sipped their coffee and ate their food in silence. Nikki's thoughts kept returning to Mel and Liam preparing to catch whoever they would be meeting. None of this situation seemed right to Nikki, especially Josh's part in the whole thing. She'd always liked Josh as an on-site leader. He was clear and concise with his orders and until all of this she had believed the missions had been successful.

Nikki's cell phone buzzed and she checked the readout. Punching the on button, she greeted Mel.

"What's up, Carter?"

"We're back."

"That didn't take long," Nikki commented with a puzzled look at Brad.

"No, there wasn't much to see. It's a dead-end alley."

"A dead-end alley," Nikki said aloud for Brad's benefit. "No escape route? That seems crazy."

"We thought so too. Maybe it's not Daniel," Mel contemplated.

"Maybe this is just a normal package pickup and it's not connected," Brad said to Nikki.

Nikki nodded and repeated his comment into the phone. "Maybe it's not connected to all of this."

"Maybe…" Mel's voice trailed off, clearly thinking about the possibility. "I guess we'll find out when we pick up the guy. It should be easy to tell if he's involved or not."

"Give us a call when you guys are clear and, if we need to, we can open the package," Nikki suggested. Brad raised his eyebrows and Nikki gave him a shrug. "We need to clear this whole situation up. I don't like not knowing who to trust, especially within our own organization."

Brad nodded his agreement.

"Okay," Mel answered. "We'll give you guys a call when we're clear here."

"Be careful," Nikki said softly.

"You guys too."

Nikki slid her phone back into her pocket and pulled out the iPad. Taking a sip of coffee, she looked at Brad. "Let's head on over there now. We have about forty-five minutes and I wouldn't mind being early."

Brad nodded and slipped the sedan into gear. Nikki gave Liam a mock salute as they passed. She tried to look at Mel too, but the dark windows blocked her. Liam, sitting in the driver's seat, was barely visible.

* * *

"Let's give him about thirty minutes. If he doesn't come out and start toward the pickup location, we'll head over there to nab us another potential suspect." Liam shoved the last bite of his sandwich into his mouth.

"Works for me." Mel sat silently for several seconds. "Did you touch base with Dayton at the embassy?"

"Yeah, he said to park in the garage. There's a room in the northeast corner we can use. No one should bother us since it's Shabbat and even the embassy is closed. He said he would give the marine guard a heads-up that we might be doing an interrogation there so we won't get hassled."

"Right, the Sabbath day. Most things are closed from sundown to sundown." Mel gathered their trash and stuffed it back in the bag. "I'm going to hit the coffee shop on the corner before it closes too. Want something?"

"A black coffee would be great. Thanks. Keep your phone handy and I'll call if I have movement."

"Roger that."

She walked briskly to the corner and entered the small shop. She took in more of the shop than she had been able to during her first visit when following Abbott. It appeared to be completely empty. Mel felt a twinge of discomfort at this. She remembered the man behind the counter and watched him as he again studied her closely. His face was blank when she placed their order, and he immediately turned his back, filling both cups with coffee before setting them on the counter in front of her. His eyes flicked back and forth from her to the cash register as he rang up her order and mumbled the total cost. She paid him and picked up the coffee cups to leave. Turning back, she attempted one last time to give him a smile but froze at the look of hatred in his eyes. He quickly turned away, clearly unnerved at having been caught. Mel hesitantly turned and left the shop. Her mind whirling at the oddity of his behavior, she returned to the car.

She passed Liam a cup. "No movement?"

"All is quiet," he said, removing the lid and taking a sip of the coffee. "Hmm…that's good." Noticing Mel's silence, he glanced at her. "Everything okay?"

She frowned. "Yeah, I guess so. Just had a weird encounter with the man in the coffee shop."

"The skinny guy behind the counter?"

"That's him. I'd swear he just gave me a death stare."

Liam laughed. "I noticed he was a bit standoffish when I was in there earlier." Liam held up his cup. "But his coffee is good. And he sells delicious croissants and muffins in the mornings."

Mel nodded as she took a sip of the steaming coffee. She had to admit the coffee was good. They drank in silence as they each watched the street around them. Mel's mind wandered across many topics, never settling on any specific one. She glanced at Liam when he dropped his half-full cup onto the floorboard of the car. "Liam?" she slurred as everything in front of her went blurry.

CHAPTER THIRTY-TWO

Brad backed the car into the alley and turned off the ignition. "I don't like this, but I'll ram him if we have to get out fast."

Nikki took a sip of her now cold coffee and grimaced. It felt like acid as it hit her stomach. Her nerves were on edge as she worried about Mel and Liam. She glanced around again as if she would be able to see them. Brad watched her for a second and looked back at the empty alley. "You probably won't be able to see them, Nik. I doubt they'll take him down until we leave."

"I know, but I have a bad feeling about all of this." Nikki glanced at her watch. "Five minutes." She took a drink of coffee and grimaced again. Opening her car door, she dumped the remaining coffee on the ground. "That stuff sucks when it's cold."

Brad's smile faded as a white van pulled into the alley. "Here we go."

"I see two people," Nikki said softly as the van pulled to a stop in front of them. As she and Brad climbed out of the sedan, she casually shrugged her shoulders, repositioning the pistol in her shoulder holster to make sure it was free of any restrictions in case she needed to pull it.

"You make contact and I'll cover you." Brad leaned against the car, looking relaxed. "Keep cool, Nik. Just another pickup. We do this all the time."

She nodded, never taking her eyes off the men in the vehicle. Their lips were moving and they seemed to be having an argument. After a few minutes, the driver rolled down his window and motioned her forward. Nikki approached slowly and from an angle to allow Brad an unobstructed view of the two men. The driver pulled a manila envelope from the dashboard and passed it out the window to her. She took the envelope and began retracing her path back to the car. Conversation wasn't necessary; she had seen all she needed to. The driver was Daniel Abbott. The passenger's face was familiar as well, even though she couldn't place him right away. Their heated conversation had resumed as she left, but she was unable to identify any of the words they spoke. She slid into the sedan and Brad joined her. Together they watched the white van back out of the alley and speed away.

Nikki took a deep breath as she tossed the manila envelope on top of her bag in the backseat. "It was Abbott." She looked around the alley. "I wonder where Liam and Carter are." She glanced at Brad. "Should I text them that he has another guy with him?"

Brad started the engine and eased out of the alley before answering her. "It wouldn't hurt."

Quickly, Nikki punched a message to Mel on her cell phone. She stared at the phone after hitting send as if a response would be instantaneous.

"I'm starving, but let's wait until we get through security at the airport before grabbing something. Time is short and I don't want to miss our flight."

Nikki didn't answer him at first but eventually nodded as what he had said registered. Within minutes they were back on HaYarkon Street and approaching the US Embassy. Brad stopped at the guard gate and asked the officer on duty to call them a cab. Once they were parked, Brad unlocked the trunk and they secured their weapons inside the lockbox. Nikki left a voice mail message for Ron Dayton letting him know the car was in spot ten and reminding him their gear was in the trunk. After seeing all the security checkpoints at the airport, Nikki now understood why it was less of a hassle for the embassy to pick up and return their weapons to the airport than to try to do it themselves. With their bags slung over their shoulders, they returned their identification and weapon permits to the officer on duty before climbing into the back of the cab.

At the airport, the driver dropped them at Departures, where their checked baggage was carefully screened before turning it over to the airline and picking up their tickets. The trip through immigration was quick, and they had thirty minutes before their plane would begin boarding.

"Do you see somewhere fast?" Brad asked as they passed through the food court.

"Burger Ranch?"

"That works for me."

They carried their food to the departure gate before consuming it. Finally seated on the plane, Nikki dropped her head back against the headrest and closed her eyes. She slept fitfully during the four-and-a-half-hour flight to Paris, her thoughts jumbled and filled with gunshots. When the pilot announced they were about to land, she opened her eyes and sat up. Her head was fuzzy and her eyes still burned from lack of sleep.

"Did you get any sleep?" Nikki asked.

Brad groaned. "Barely."

"At least we'll be back in the States by midnight and we can sleep in a bed for a couple of hours before our flight to New Orleans Saturday morning."

"I will dream about that during this eight-hour flight."

With only an hour layover in Paris, they barely had time to grab food and arrive at the gate before boarding the plane to D.C. Nikki watched Brad consume his third pastry as she glanced at her cell phone again. She had sent Mel two more texts and still had received no response.

Brad shoved the last bite of the pastry into his mouth before patting her leg. "I'm sure they're fine." He held up the bag of food. "Are you sure you don't want another one?"

She wrinkled her nose. "No thank you. I don't think I'll be able to eat again for a while. At least not until I adjust back to our time zone."

Brad grinned. "We should get barbecue on the way back to the office tomorrow."

Nikki grimaced. No food, and definitely not barbecue, sounded good right at the moment. Her stomach churned as she agonized over where Mel could be and what she might be doing. The plane would be taking off soon, and she would have to turn off her cell phone until they landed. She dialed Mel's number from memory and glanced out the window while she waited for it to ring. It went to voice mail on the first ring. Nikki frowned. "Her phone is turned off."

"That's odd." Brad frowned too. "That's their only form of communication."

"The backup team arrived hours ago, so why would she turn off her phone?" Nikki sighed. "I guess she might be back in her room catching some sleep, but if she was, why didn't she respond to my earlier texts?"

"I'm sure you'll have a response from her when we land. Did you leave her a voice mail?"

"No." Nikki dialed her number again. When the voice mail answered this time, she left a short message. "Carter, call me when you get this. We're taking off from Paris now and should be in D.C. in about eight hours. Call me, please." Nikki punched the disconnect button and powered down her phone before sliding it into her pocket. She settled back into the seat and replayed the night she spent with Mel, remembering how it felt to press her body against Mel's back as she slept. She had felt safe and comfortable. She wanted that feeling again. She wanted Mel again.

CHAPTER THIRTY-THREE

A door slammed somewhere above her and Mel lifted her head, licking her cracked lips. Her stomach roiled at the metallic taste of blood mixed with dirt. She tried to see into the darkness surrounding her, but it was too thick. Her arms and legs were bent behind her and tingled with numbness when she tried to move them. She moaned from the pain of shifting as she realized they were tied together.

"Mel?" Liam's voice called softly.

"Liam!" Her voice cracked, and she swallowed hard, pushing away the edge of panic. She squeezed her eyes shut and tried to take a calming breath. She was not in Afghanistan. Donala would *not* be coming to torture her. She was in…Israel? With Liam and…*Nikki! Please don't let Nikki be here too.* "Is there anyone else…Nikki…Brad?"

"No, it's just us."

Mel said a silent prayer for Nikki's safety. "Where are we?"

"In a basement, I think. Are your arms and legs tied together too?"

"Yep."

"Slide toward me and let's see if we can undo the connecting rope. Mine doesn't feel very tight."

She started to inch toward him, but the shooting pain in her ribs made her stop moving. "I think my ribs were hit by a freight train," she groaned.

Liam closed the remaining distance between them and maneuvered around her until they were back to back. He began working on the rope connecting her arms and legs. "I haven't been awake long, but I heard two men arguing just now. One was angry because the other one had been kicking us while we were unconscious. I wasn't sure if you were down here with me or not." Liam grunted, giving a tug on the rope. "They didn't do a very good job tying you. These knots are fairly loose."

Liam concentrated on the knots, saying no more but giving an occasional quiet groan as he shifted position.

"Are you hurt too?" she asked gently when he shifted yet again.

"Bumps and bruises. No broken bones."

Mel thought about the men Liam had heard talking earlier. "Did the men sound familiar?" Mel asked.

"Not to me, but maybe you'll recognize Abbott since you listened to all those phone recordings." Liam grunted again. "Got it. Now you can at least sit up."

She moved slowly, rolling her legs in front of her until she was sitting. Her head swam and she fought the urge to vomit. She sat very still until the feeling passed, then slid her hands under her butt, pulling her thighs into her chest. Her shoulders throbbed with the strain, but eventually she was able to stretch her arms under her feet and pull her tied hands in front of her body. She gently touched her face, probing the sore spots to check for damage. She moaned when her fingers touched her eyelid. "I don't think I'll need eye shadow for a while."

"That's a positive note," Liam said with no humor.

Mel squirmed closer to him until she could reach the ropes connecting his arms and legs. She ran her fingers up the rope until she felt the knots and began working them back and forth.

Minutes turned to more than an hour before she had success. It took Liam longer to work his hands under his body and get them in front of him. Mel heard him grunt as he pushed himself into a standing position.

"Wow, that feels good." Liam groaned as he stretched his body. He sat down facing her. "Now for the other knots."

Mel began working at them, but they were tighter and closer to his skin without any play between the knots. "These aren't going to be as easy, Liam."

"I know, but it's our only way out of here."

Mel heard the anxiety in his voice, and she hesitated before questioning him. "What did you hear them say?"

Liam was silent in the darkness, and she bumped his arm with her hand. "Liam?"

"They're not sure what to do with us."

Mel continued to work the knots while she thought about their situation. "How'd we end up here?"

"I've been thinking about that too," Liam said. "I think the coffee guy drugged us."

"Whoa. What?" Mel asked surprised.

"I remember drinking the coffee and then seeing Abbott come out of his apartment building. I was trying to tell you, but I couldn't form the words. It's like my body wouldn't respond and that's the last thing I remember."

"Yeah," Mel finally agreed. "I remember coming back to the car with the coffee." She paused for a minute. "He gave me the death stare."

"I think he was the one beating us. The other guy is the one upset about what they're going to do with us. He said everything is all screwed up now."

"So it really was the death stare." Mel contemplated this knowledge. "What does he want to do with us?"

Liam hesitated. "Get rid of us."

"Then I guess we better get ready to defend ourselves." Mel pulled harder on the knot.

CHAPTER THIRTY-FOUR

Nikki crawled into the cool sheets and reached out to set the alarm clock. She was asleep before Brad came out of the bathroom. The alarm went off while the sky was still dark and Nikki had to remind herself where she was before rolling out of the bed and stumbling to the bathroom. As soon as the steam from the shower cleared her head, her first thoughts were of Mel. She hurriedly finished and dressed so she could check her phone for messages. She sighed when she saw there were none.

Brad rolled over and looked at her. "Still no call from her?"

"No call and no text. Something is wrong, Brad."

"I'd like to reassure you, but I'm starting to agree." He got to his feet. "Let me shower and then we can talk about this."

Nikki stuffed her dirty clothes into her bag and heard the manila envelope crinkle in the outer pocket. She pulled it out and sat down on the edge of the bed. She had told Mel they would open the package if she needed them to. Now Mel needed them to. Nikki had never considered opening a package after she had picked it up. Her job was only to transport, never to open or ask questions. However, this situation was different. Mel and Liam's lives could be in danger, and whatever was in the envelope could hold some information. She was still sitting on the bed holding the sealed envelope when Brad opened the bathroom door.

"I was thinking the same thing. Open it." He sat down on his bed across from her.

She gently ran her finger under the flap, pushing through the sticky glue. Reaching inside, she withdrew four black-and-white pictures. The first two must have been snapped hurriedly from inside the coffee shop. They might be too blurry to other eyes, but Nikki could easily identify Mel's stride in the grainy shot. The last two photos, taken from somewhere in front of the car, were sharper and clearly showed Mel and Liam sitting in their surveillance sedan on the street outside Daniel Abbott's apartment. Nikki looked at them and then passed them to Brad.

"He must be asking Josh to identify them," Nikki suggested. Brad nodded.

When he didn't comment, Nikki continued. "We can't give these to Josh. Not if we believe he's involved."

"Come on, Nik. Josh has to know what the score is after all the surveillance on us last week."

"Maybe, but he doesn't know they were in Israel too."

"Okay, then." Brad agreed. "What if we give him the two fuzzy ones of Carter? We can hold on to the clear ones for now."

Nikki nodded. "I'd feel better about that." She rubbed her face. "We don't even know what's going on over there right now. Something is keeping them from contacting us."

Brad was silent for a few minutes. "I tried Liam when we arrived in D.C. His phone is off too." He looked at her and then stood. "We can't do anything until we get back to Flagler. Besides we don't know if anything is wrong. We aren't in the same loop as Mel and Liam and we don't know where their case might have led them. Let's try not to worry until we know there's something to worry about." He picked up his bag and she followed him out the door.

* * *

Nikki was withdrawn on the flight and Brad didn't try to coax her out. She tried to envision what she would do when she arrived at Flagler. Part of her wanted to get back on a plane and return to Israel, with or without permission from Flagler. She worried at the problem as they arrived in New Orleans, throughout the jumper flight back to Pensacola, and as she and Brad retrieved their car for the drive to Flagler. Nikki sat silently in the passenger seat as he cleared them through security and back into Flagler's parking lot.

Apparently Josh had asked security to notify him of their arrival, and he met them at the front door. "Package?" he said as a greeting.

Nikki said nothing as she pulled the manila envelope from her bag and handed it to him.

"I'll meet you in the debriefing room," he said as he turned and walked away.

Nikki's gaze followed him until he turned the corner at the end of the hall. She looked at Brad and he shook his head. Following Josh down the hall, they dropped their bags in the empty office and went straight to the debriefing room. Lewis was waiting when they entered, and they each took a seat across from him. "I know you guys are ready to get home. We'll get started as soon as Josh gets here."

Josh walked in and Nikki noticed he no longer carried the manila envelope. She glanced at Brad and he raised his eyebrows. Nikki spoke first. She wanted to see if Lewis was aware they had made a package pickup, so she told the entire mission from start to finish, leaving that part out. Josh's head remained bent over his laptop. Nikki waited for Lewis to question her, but when he finally looked up from his own typing he only asked Brad if he had anything to add. Nikki avoided looking at Brad so it wouldn't look like they had something to hide. Brad shook his head no and they were both dismissed.

"Wow," Nikki said as they stepped into the hallway.

"So, apparently, Lewis didn't know about the package," Brad said softly.

"It seems that way." Nikki led the way into their office and sat down at her desk. "Let's do your report first and then you can get out of here."

"Are we going to include the package pickup?"

Nikki nodded. "Of course. Josh would expect us to record it."

"Okay. Here goes." Nikki typed while Brad talked, and then she saved his report and printed him a copy.

Brad retrieved his copy from the printer and returned to her desk. "What are you going to do?"

"I don't know yet." Nikki smiled at him. "Don't worry."

"Well, I am worried. Not just about you either." He turned to leave and then looked back at her. "I won't go to sleep when I get home so I'll be able to sleep tonight. Call me if you need something or if you hear from them."

Nikki nodded and then motioned for him to leave. She began typing, and the words flowed quickly, especially since she left out all the parts involving Mel and Liam. She finished her report and saved the document. After emailing herself a copy, she sat staring into space. She needed to find out what was going on and she didn't know who to ask. As far as she knew, Mr. Flagler was the only one in this building who knew Mel and Liam were in Israel and it didn't make sense he could be the leak. Why would he ruin his own company? She couldn't go home without information about Mel. If talking to the head of Flagler Security was a mistake, then she would have to face the consequences later. Right now he was her only source of information.

She stood up and moved quickly into the hall, nearly colliding with the other woman who had been shadowing her. "What...where...why are you here?"

"I had a meeting," the woman said hesitantly. "I'm Angela, by the way."

Nikki placed her hand on Angela's arm, moving them out of the hallway and back inside the empty office. Nikki looked her in the eye. "Have you heard from Carter?"

"I can't talk about an ongoing investigation." Angela's expression was stone-cold.

"I don't want to talk about the investigation. I just want to know if they're okay." She glared at Angela. "Tell me what's going on."

"Look, I know you are a good agent and I respect you, but I don't have the authority to disclose any information to you."

"Then take me to someone who does," Nikki demanded.

"That's not going to happen."

Nikki turned to walk away and then spun back to Angela. "She was shot. Do you know that?" Angela's face showed surprise, and then it became unreadable again. "What?" Nikki asked. "I'm not supposed to know that?"

Angela started to speak and then shook her head. "Their mission is confidential."

Nikki fumed. "He was watching her. I have pictures."

Surprise crossed Angela's face again as the frustration and fear echoed in Nikki's voice.

"Her phone is turned off. Just tell me she's okay."

Angela looked around the empty room. "She *will* be okay."

"What the hell does that mean?"

Angela looked away from her glare.

"Shit! You don't know where she is either, do you?" Nikki dropped into the closest chair and put her head in her hands. "This is so fucked up!"

Angela sat beside her. "What pictures do you have?"

"Josh sent us to pick up a package before we left Israel, and it contained pictures of Mel and Liam on surveillance."

"And you have them?"

"We gave Josh the fuzzy ones and kept the ones he'd be able to identify them with quickly."

Angela stood. "Let's go."

"Where?"

"Just come with me, okay." Her tone had softened. "You want to know what's going on. Right?"

Nikki followed Angela to the parking lot and tossed her bag into the backseat of the red Charger when Angela unlocked its doors.

"Show me the pictures," Angela said when they were both in the car with the doors shut.

Nikki pulled the two pictures from her bag and handed them to Angela.

Angela took a deep breath and picked up her phone. After a minute, she began to talk, and Nikki listened to her side of the conversation. "I'm coming in with Mitchell." She paused as she listened to the voice on the other end. "Yes, she has information we need." Angela put the car in gear and exited the parking lot as she listened. "No, I don't see any other choice."

She hung up the phone and glanced at Nikki. "You're right. We don't know where Mel and Liam are."

"Shit."

"The last time we heard from them was Friday morning. We did know Mel had been shot and that they were thinking about taking down your contact after the package pickup."

"That was the plan when we talked to them about an hour before, but we didn't see them there. We just hoped they were out of sight." Nikki sighed. "Carter had said she would call when they were secure in case they needed to know what was in the package. I texted her several times but got no response, and when I called her phone it went straight to voice mail."

Angela nodded. "I'll let Mrs. Bowden tell you what we've done so far."

"She's in charge of the mission for you guys?"

"Yes."

"And you think she's going to read me in?"

"Yes." Angela looked at her. "But if she doesn't, I will."

Nikki nodded and sat back in the seat.

CHAPTER THIRTY-FIVE

A door slammed causing Mel and Liam to freeze. Angry voices speaking Hebrew filled the silence.

Mel touched Liam's arm and leaned close. She closed her eyes and concentrated on translating and identifying the voices. The men stomped around above their heads before exiting back out the door and slamming it behind them.

"I'm fairly sure that was Daniel Abbott," Mel stated. "Were they talking about food?"

"Yes, the one you think is Daniel wants to give us food and water. It appears we've been held for over twenty-four hours now."

"Well, that explains my hunger and the need for a bathroom."

"Yeah, as much as I would like food, I would like to have my hands free more."

Mel nodded even though he couldn't see her. They needed to get their hands and feet free so they could defend themselves.

* * *

Nikki was surprised when Angela pulled to a stop in front of what appeared to be an abandoned warehouse on Parker Street. The roll-up door rumbled loudly as it raised to allow them access. Angela pulled into the first available spot and Nikki followed her quietly as she went inside. She couldn't believe this office was a part of Flagler. It was something out of a futuristic movie. Nikki had been in the operations room at Flagler a few times, but it was half the size of this room. There were at least ten large-screen computers, and three life-sized screens filled the opposite corner of the room. A fiftyish, tall, thin woman stood beside the only other person in the room. Her long, dirty-blond hair was pulled back in a ponytail accentuating the attractive features of her face. She was dressed in a gray pantsuit and she leaned over the technician's shoulder while he typed on the keyboard. Both of them watched the monitor in front of them.

The woman looked up as they approached. She appraised Nikki but said nothing and Nikki felt the intensity of her stare. Angela stepped forward and spoke first. "Mrs. Bowden." She gestured toward Nikki. "Meet Agent Nicole Mitchell."

Nikki reached out her hand, and Bowden hesitated a second before she responded in kind. Her grip was firm, but the look on her face made it clear she was not quick to trust an outsider. She stepped away from the monitor and headed for the coffeemaker. Nikki glanced at Angela and then followed her across the room, trailed by Angela. Bowden's stride was long, and she had a touch of what Nikki would call a swagger despite her feminine appearance. In fact, Nikki thought, she looked like an older version of Mel. Feeling an instant bond with her, she decided to ignore her initial hostility. If Mel trusted this woman, she needed to as well. Bowden poured a mug of coffee and handed it to Nikki.

"Thank you." Nikki inhaled the aroma before taking a sip.

"You looked like you could use a cup." She glanced at Angela. "You?"

"Yes, thank you."

Bowden poured two more mugs and handed one to Angela before picking up her own. She took a seat at the small table beside the break area. She glanced at Angela and then at Nikki. "You have something for me to see?"

Nikki glanced at Angela and then pulled the photos out of her bag. Bowden adjusted the glasses on the end of her nose and closely examined the pictures before glancing up at them. She removed her glasses and tossed them on the table, her scowl taking in Angela and Nikki. "Where did these come from?"

"They were in the package Brad and I picked up before leaving Tel Aviv," Nikki said hesitantly. She was in the presence of a supervisor within Flagler ranks, and she knew they had broken a lot of rules by opening the envelope. Though she was a little ashamed that her actions did not follow protocol, she also was ready to defend them. Mel was missing, and she would make it clear nothing would stand in her way. "Agents were missing," Nikki stated.

Bowden appraised her and Nikki again felt the intensity of her stare. She eventually nodded and returned her eyes to the photographs. "And you recognize this location?"

"Yes, it's outside Daniel Abbott's apartment." Nikki looked at Bowden and then Angela, searching for a sign of recognition to the name. Neither acknowledged, so Nikki continued. "The other two photos in the envelope were of Agent Carter standing on the same street outside a coffee shop. They were fuzzy and it'll be hard for anyone to identify her."

"But you could?" Bowden again made eye contact searching Nikki's face.

"Yes." Nikki could have said more. She could have explained how she identified Mel's button-down shirt or the soft curves of her hips that melted into the hard-muscled thighs or the cocky stance that looked so natural on Mel. She didn't say any of these things. She waited for Bowden to ask her next question.

Bowden took a sip of her coffee as she held Nikki's eyes with her own. Whatever she was searching for, she seemed to find and set her mug on the table with a thump. "Okay, then. Tell me everything that you know."

Nikki frowned. "I will, but first I'd like to know what's being done to find them."

After a minute, Bowden finally nodded. "By the time our second team had boots on the ground, we knew something was wrong. Both Agent Russo and Agent Carter had turned off their phones. We immediately split the team, and two went to the package site and two went to the hotel to sweep their room."

Nikki glanced away as she remembered the note she had left for Mel. Relieved she hadn't signed her name, she covered her movement with a drink from the mug.

Bowden watched her closely. "I'm guessing we're going to find your prints all over the room?"

Nikki nodded and then added. "Brad's too."

Bowden leaned back in her chair, and it was clear to Nikki she had reached her own conclusion. "And the note on hotel stationery was from you?"

Nikki blushed involuntarily. She wouldn't, no, she couldn't deny she was involved with Mel. She stared back into Bowden's eyes before answering. "Yes."

"Well, that'll save us some time then." She looked across the room at the technician. "Hey, Todd, scratch the analysis of the note."

"Roger that," he called back.

Bowden looked back at Nikki. "Is there anything else we need to know right now?" Nikki shook her head. "Okay. So, we have a program set up to ping their phones every thirty seconds. No luck so far. The data from their computers has been sent back to us, and we're combing through it." She sighed and, for the first time, Nikki saw the stress in her eyes. "At this time we have nothing."

"You're aware they were tailing Daniel Abbott?" Nikki asked, focusing on Bowden but watching Angela's reactions from the corner of her eye.

Bowden gave a small nod. "We sent a team to pick him up, but he wasn't at home so they're sitting on his apartment. The embassy car was still parked on the street."

Nikki exploded to her feet. "Then that's where they were taken from. They didn't even go to the package pickup." As she said the words, their meaning slammed into her and she dropped back into her chair. "It's true then. They have been taken hostage," she said slowly.

"We've come to the same conclusion, Nikki." Angela spoke for the first time.

Nikki rubbed her face. "Why didn't you just tell me that?" She felt the fear grab her as she looked at Angela.

"Agent Mitchell." Bowden called Nikki's attention back to her. "We needed to see if you reached the same conclusion. You were on the ground with them and we weren't sure if something might have changed their position. Now maybe you'll tell us everything you know."

Nikki nodded and began replaying everything from the time they had followed Liam and Mel back to the hotel on Thursday. She saw Bowden frown when she said Brad went with Liam for surveillance, but she kept talking. She didn't need to justify their participation, especially now, when they were the last ones to have contact with the two missing agents. Nikki sat up as she remembered the data Liam had found in Daniel's apartment.

"He has another cell phone. One Carter didn't know about."

Bowden frowned. "Who has another cell phone?"

Nikki looked around. "You have Agent Carter's data from her laptop?"

Angela nodded and crossed the room, returning with a laptop and a data stick. She handed both to Nikki without looking at Bowden for approval. Nikki inserted the data stick and began looking through Mel's files. She found the pictures Liam had sent of the cell phone bill and enlarged them on the screen. "Daniel Abbott has a second cell phone. The bill shows an incoming call from Mr. Flagler's office."

Bowden read the cell phone number off the screen to Todd, and he began typing. "Big screen, Todd." Todd hit a few buttons and his computer screen was mirrored on one of the big screens in the corner of the room. Bowden, followed by Nikki and Angela, crossed the room to stand in front of it.

"It's on right now," Todd said excitedly. "Searching…got it. He's at the coffee shop on his street."

Nikki frowned. "What's he up to?"

"Maybe he's watching the new surveillance team," Angela suggested.

"And having a latte?" Nikki grumbled.

Bowden turned back to Todd. "See who else has been calling that number. I'm going to call and have the team pick him up."

Nikki looked at Angela and then crossed back to the table. "I'm going to keep looking through Carter's data."

"I'll get Liam's data and join you." Angela tried to give her a reassuring smile. "We'll find them."

CHAPTER THIRTY-SIX

Mel stuck the tips of her fingers in her mouth. They were raw where the blisters had ruptured. "Almost there," she mumbled, her fingers still in her mouth. "Just give me a minute."

Liam stood and stretched before sitting back down in front of her. Ignoring the pain shooting through her fingers, Mel pulled on the knots with renewed vigor, tugging the ropes back and forth. "I've got them," she finally said as she unwound the remaining ropes.

Liam rubbed his wrists. "Let me see yours."

"Hold on." Mel wrapped the rope around one of his wrists and then wrapped the rope that held his feet and hands together around the other wrist. "Now if they come back before we're completely untied, you can put your hands behind your back and hold your feet. It'll look like you're still tied if they don't look too closely."

"Good idea." He began working on the knots at her wrists.

Mel swallowed hard and tried not to think about water or food. She tried to calculate how much time had passed, but without her watch or cell phone, she had no idea.

"How long do you think we've been down here?"

"I'm not sure. We know we were unconscious for most of the first twenty-four hours at least."

"So it must be the middle of the night now." Mel stretched her legs out to the side and tried to ignore the pain that rippled through her ribs.

Liam heard her small intake of breath and paused. "Ribs?"

"Yep. They surprise me every time I move." Mel paused for a second, looking around her. "It's so dark. I wonder if this is a bomb shelter."

"I thought so too." Liam tugged on the knots at her wrist. "He didn't wrap yours as tight as mine. It shouldn't take long to get these off."

Mel felt the tug and pull as Liam worked on the knots holding her hands together. She moved her thumb and gently touched the ruptured blisters on the tips of her fingers. Not for the first time since she had woken up, she thought about Nikki and how she would be taking her disappearance. She remembered the panicked look on her face when she had seen the bullet wound and wondered if anyone from her team would give Nikki information. Remembering Nikki's rage when they'd first started tailing her, Mel felt sorry for anyone who might stand in her way.

She felt the pressure release as Liam pulled the remaining ropes off her wrists. She gave each one an involuntary rub before holding them back out for Liam to put the fake knots back on each one.

They each pulled their knees into their chests and began working on the ropes holding their feet together. It didn't take long until they were free and both immediately stood stretching. "You don't think…" Mel trotted quietly up the stairs and tested the locked doorknob. "Well, it was worth a try." She came back down the stairs and started walking around the room until she found a wall. Tracing her fingers across the cold brick she circled the room. "Guess it is a bunker."

"Yeah," Liam answered. "Not a single ray of light."

"I don't think the stairs are wide enough to try and kick the door down."

Before Liam could answer they heard movement above them. A door slammed and footsteps crossed the floor.

* * *

Angela set a cup of fresh coffee beside Nikki before dropping into the chair across from her. Nikki nodded her thanks but continued to search through the data Mel had compiled on Daniel Abbott.

"So," Angela said casually. "You and Carter, huh?"

Nikki leaned around her computer screen to see Angela's face. She couldn't help but smile when she saw Angela grinning. "Yeah. I guess so." Nikki hesitated. Would Mel say they were together? She felt weird talking about them being together when she didn't even know where Mel was. "I mean we haven't talked about it or anything." Nikki struggled with the appropriate words. "Besides, we were a little busy with her getting shot and all."

"Right. I wasn't trying to put you on the spot, Nikki. I just wanted to make sure I had it correct before I stepped on someone's feet."

"Well, you should talk with Carter first. I can't really speak for her," Nikki stammered. Would Mel be interested in Angela? Her entire body roared with jealousy as she thought of anyone other than her touching Mel. "I don't really know who she's interested in so you should wait and talk with her." Nikki looked up at Angela and stopped talking.

"Wow." Angela gave her a slow smile. "That was an interesting speech, but I was actually thinking of asking out you, not Carter."

"Oh." Nikki's face flushed but she recovered quickly. "I can speak for myself then." She winked at Angela. "I'm flattered, but someone else has my attention right now."

Angela laughed. "She's a lucky woman."

"No, I am," Nikki said softly as she closed the open file and selected a new one. Mel's disappearance was never far from her mind, but being here with Mel's co-workers made her a little curious. She leaned around the monitors again and looked at Angela. "How long have you known Carter?"

"I met her the first time a couple of years ago, but this is the first time we actually worked together." She grinned. "Carter is a bit of a legend in our office. She always works alone and is a bulldog until her case is closed. This is the first time that I recall her working with a team."

"So, basically she doesn't play well with others?" Nikki asked.

"No, no, she gets along well with everyone, but she prefers to do her own research and follow her own leads."

"So she has trust issues?"

Angela laughed, but then her face grew serious. "She might but she has good reasons for it."

Nikki frowned. She wanted to ask, but she knew this was a story she didn't want to hear from anyone but Mel. She looked up to see Angela staring at her.

"This isn't the first time she's been captured," Angela said, lowering her voice.

Nikki wasn't sure if this was supposed to make her feel better or worse. She held her breath, but words wouldn't come and she was glad when Angela returned her attention to reviewing files. Nikki let out her breath and concentrated on the screen in front of her. She was surprised to see an hour had passed when Angela stood. "More coffee?"

Nikki nodded, but before Angela could step away Nikki pointed at the screen. "Look here." Angela walked around the table and slid into the chair beside her. Nikki read aloud. "Daniel Abbott's father and little sister were killed by a sniper." She calculated in her head. "Twenty years ago next month." She frowned. "And then his mother killed herself a year later."

"Where's that information coming from?" Angela asked.

Nikki scanned the computer. "An Israeli newspaper archive. But look, Carter wrote a note on it."

Angela read the note aloud. "Three brothers?"

"Yes, three brothers." Nikki closed her eyes. "Maybe Daniel Abbott has two brothers. Maybe one of them was with him at the package pickup yesterday."

Angela stood up. "Todd, can you dig into Daniel Abbott's family?"

"Sure." He nodded as his fingers flew across the keyboard.

Nikki touched Angela's arm. "I want to confront Josh."

Angela frowned.

"It's time. We need to know where he stands and what he knows."

"You can talk to Bowden about it," Angela suggested.

"Talk to me about what?"

Nikki looked up as Bowden approached them. "I want to confront Josh. Show him the evidence and see what he has to say."

"I guess you can do that since he should be arriving here any minute." She looked at Angela. "Stay with her. From this point forward, she's your responsibility. I don't want her going off half-cocked."

Angela didn't seem happy, but she nodded and motioned Nikki back to her seat at the table. She poured two fresh mugs of coffee and set one in front of Nikki before sitting down across from her. Nikki's phone rang and she looked at the ID screen. "It's Brad."

"You can't tell him where you are," Angela stated and motioned for her to pick up the call.

"Hey, Brad."

"Do you know anything new?" Brad asked.

"I'm working on it. Nothing new yet though."

He sighed. "Are you at Flagler? I want to come in and help you. I can't stand sitting here doing nothing."

"No, I'm not at Flagler. I'm with Carter's team. I'll let you know when we have something."

Brad hesitated. "Okay, but call if I can help."

Nikki stood and stepped away from Angela. "If I return to Israel, you'll go with me?"

"Without permission?"

"With or without," Nikki stated firmly.

"Yes," Brad answered without delay. "Call me."

Nikki disconnected the call. She knew she could count on Brad, but she hoped it wouldn't come to them traveling without permission. She looked up as the elevator doors opened. Josh, escorted by two Flagler agents, passed through the room before heading down the hallway. Nikki looked at Angela, and she stood as Bowden approached Todd. She patted him on the shoulder as she passed him. "Just keep working on it, Todd." She looked at Angela and Nikki. "We missed him."

"Abbott?" Angela asked.

"Yep. When the team went to the coffee shop they said not only was Abbott not there but the shop was closed."

"What?" Nikki calculated the time in her head. "It's not even midnight over there."

"Yes." Bowden agreed. "And the sign on the door said they were open until midnight every day but Friday."

Nikki slapped her hand to her forehead and dropped into the closest chair. "Oh wow. I knew he looked familiar."

"Who looked familiar?" Angela asked and even Todd looked up from his computer monitor.

"The cranky man behind the counter in the coffee shop was the passenger in the van when we made the pickup."

Bowden touched her shoulder. "Are you sure?"

Nikki nodded and looked at Todd. "Find out who owns that coffee shop and how they're connected to Daniel Abbott."

Todd looked at Bowden, and she nodded her agreement to the request. "Let's go talk to Mr. Houston."

CHAPTER THIRTY-SEVEN

The door at the top of the stairs opened and Mel and Liam scurried into their false captive positions. The light from the upstairs room silhouetted the three men coming down the stairs. "We should just let them die," one of the men said in broken English.

"Then our work will have been for nothing," the third man said in perfect English. He motioned the other two men forward with the pistol in his hand. "Just give them the food and we'll figure out what step to take next."

Mel looked up into the face of the man from the coffee shop as he dropped a bag in front of her. She felt the impact of his boot in her stomach as the pain soared through her ribs. She sucked in a breath and fought to maintain consciousness.

Liam roared to his feet and charged the man with the pistol, pushing him to the floor. Mel tried to stand and fight with him, but the world was spinning as she staggered to her feet. She punched the coffee-shop man in the face, and he stepped back holding his jaw. Before she could move closer to swing again, he pulled a pistol from his jacket pocket and fired a shot.

Mel quickly stepped back into the shadows and was thankful the wall was there to hold her upright. Out of his line of sight, she circled around behind him. The beam of the flashlight caught her as she kicked her leg in an arc and the flashlight clattered across the room. The pain in her side exploded and she fell against the wall, trying to prepare for her next strike.

"Everyone stop," Daniel Abbott demanded, clicking the hammer on the pistol in his hand. He motioned to the man fighting with Liam. "Tie them up again and let's get out of here."

"Gladly." The man stood and picked up his pistol from the floor, bringing it down hard on top of Liam's head.

Mel's stomach roiled at the sound, and she dropped beside Liam. His eyelids fluttered before closing completely. The men grabbed Mel and secured her arms and legs before tying them together again. She tried not to moan as they grasped her bullet wound before pushing her stomach and face into the dirt.

Liam did not make any sounds as they tied him up and then stomped back up the stairs. Mel heard the door slam as they left the house. She inched her way closer to Liam, the ropes cutting into her wrists with each movement. Ignoring the pain, she slid behind Liam and started working on the ropes holding his hands and feet together.

Within minutes, her fingers were bleeding. She leaned her head against Liam's shoulder. The knots were tighter this time and she probably wouldn't be able to untie them. It had taken every ounce of her strength to stand and fight. Her vision was blurred and every breath caused a stab of severe pain. She had no idea how long they had been down here without food and water. Her head ached and she fought to remain conscious.

She had tried to avoid thinking about Nikki, but now she didn't have Liam's voice to distract her. Nikki was stubborn and Mel knew she would try to track them down. She only hoped Nikki hadn't realized they were missing until she had left Israel. Mel couldn't allow herself to even think Nikki might be out there now tracking these guys on the streets of Tel Aviv. For her own sanity, she had to believe Nikki was safe and back in the States. If she was able to reach out to someone on Mel's team, maybe they would keep her out of trouble. Bowden's team never worked with other departments, but Nikki could be persuasive when she was properly motivated. Mel sighed. Unfortunately, Nikki might not be able to locate someone from Mel's team.

She thought about the last time she had seen Nikki and how she had smiled when they parted. She thought about how soft her hair was to the touch and how she smelled. How her body looked and felt when she was aroused. When she thought about never being able to touch her again, her heart ached. She immediately sat up. This was not the end. She would find a way out of here. She had been in worse situations. Afghanistan was worse, but these guys didn't work for Donala. She took a deep breath, letting it out slowly, and forced herself to think clearly. Remembering the flashlight, she pushed herself onto her knees and began slowly crawling across the floor. Unable to hold her balance with her arms behind her back, she toppled forward and landed with her face in the dirt. She was thirsty and desperately needed a bathroom, but first she had to get these ropes off again.

* * *

Nikki watched through the glass as Bowden banged on the table again. "You are not answering me honestly, Josh. We already know you have had contact with them. You can't deny that, so just tell us who they are."

"I don't know what you're talking about," Josh stated firmly.

Bowden stood and motioned through the mirror for Nikki and Angela to come in. She'd decided, it seemed, that it was time to let Josh see the damage he had caused up close. Nikki entered first, hesitating in the doorway. She appraised Josh with stony eyes before sitting down across from him. Bowden and Angela leaned against the wall out of his line of sight.

"I respected you, Josh. I followed every order you gave me without question."

He started to speak and she held up a hand. "I'm sure you didn't mean to get involved with them, but now you are. And you might be the only link we have to Agent Carter and Agent Russo. Tell me who they are, Josh."

"I don't know."

Nikki fought to control her temper. Unless she planned to beat it out of him, and she knew it might come to that, she needed to keep calm. "Okay, you don't know who they are. Tell me how you get in touch with them then."

"I—"

"Josh," Nikki cut him off, "think before you speak. They've already killed at least one person and now you hold the lives of two agents in your hands."

"I—"

"Josh," Nikki cut him off again. "I trusted you with my safety, and now I find out you continually put me and my team in harm's way."

"Not really, Nikki. It was all harmless," Josh defended himself.

"Was Tehran harmless, Josh?" Nikki rose to her feet, causing Bowden to place a hand on Angela's arm to keep her from interfering.

"Tehran?"

"Almost a year ago, you sent Brad and me to Tehran to bring home a package. Then you changed your mind and we left it at a bus depot."

Josh nodded. "Yeah, I remember." He shrugged. "So?"

"So?" Nikki banged her hands on the table. "Are you going to tell me that package wasn't a bomb?"

Angela looked at Bowden in surprise.

Josh's face went pale. "I didn't know. I mean...that's not what they said." His voice was stronger now. "I asked them and they denied it."

"Tell me what you did, Josh." Nikki leaned down into his face. "Tell me now!"

"They only wanted a small amount of information. They already had details, so I wasn't giving them that much more."

"You didn't wonder how they got the information they had."

Josh shrugged. "It seemed harmless."

Nikki wanted to scream. "There's that word again, Josh. Harmless. Nothing about this was or is harmless. Are they holding the agents?"

"I don't know."

"But they sent you pictures, right? What were you supposed to do with the pictures?"

"They just wanted me to identify the people in them and to know if they worked for Flagler."

"And did you?" Nikki asked vehemently.

"They haven't called for the information yet, and besides, the picture was too grainy. I was unable to make a positive identification."

Slowly Nikki registered what Josh said. "They haven't called you?"

"No."

"Is that how you make contact with them?"

Nikki tensed as he reached into his pocket. She felt defenseless without her pistol. Josh pulled out a cell phone and tossed it on the table. Angela grabbed the phone and left the room.

"You never call them? What if you need to deliver information?"

"No, they call me with the request and then call me back to get the information."

Nikki glanced at Bowden. "There's someone else at the Pensacola office involved." She looked back at Josh. "Someone who has been calling Daniel Abbott from our office and Mr. Flagler's."

Josh's eye's widened. "They used Mr. Flagler's office? Even I don't have access to it."

"Just harmless. Right, Josh." Nikki stormed out of the room with Bowden following her.

* * *

Mel tightly gripped the small piece of metal, now covered in her blood, sliding it back and forth on the ropes that held Liam. She estimated it had been an hour or more since the men had left and Liam had been knocked unconscious. The small piece of metal which she had found in the spot where the flashlight had broken worked almost as a knife. She slid her fingers between Liam and the rope to protect him from being cut. The ropes holding Liam's feet and arms together had been severed and she was now working on the bindings around his hands.

Liam groaned and Mel sawed faster. "Liam." She nudged his body with her shoulder. He groaned again. "Liam," she said urgently.

"What?" he croaked.

"How's your head?" she asked with relief.

"On fire."

"Just lay still. I almost have your hands free."

He lay silently from several minutes while she sawed at the ropes. "I'm sorry, Mel," he said softly.

"Liam?"

"When I saw him kick you, I couldn't stand it. I should have waited until we could do a more coordinated attack."

"It is okay, Liam. We'll get these ropes off again and then we'll surprise them."

"What are you cutting with?"

"A piece of metal from the broken flashlight."

"Sweet. What about the food they had brought us? Did they take it back with them?"

"No. Just a second." She pushed the metal through the rope slicing into her hand again. "There, your arms are free."

Liam groaned and slowly sat up. "My turn." Sliding the piece of metal from her hand he began sawing at her ropes. His process was faster since his arms were free and he was able to put tension on the ropes.

CHAPTER THIRTY-EIGHT

Angela slid into the chair next to her, placing a deli sandwich and a bottle of water in front of her.

"Thanks," Nikki said, glancing at her watch. She couldn't stop her mind from calculating the time in Israel. It was already Sunday morning there. She had been thinking for hours that she needed to return to Israel. She needed to be closer to Mel. Time was passing too fast; she had been held for more than thirty-six hours already. She couldn't stop herself from thinking about what kind of situation they might be facing now. She shook her head and rubbed her hand over her face. Glancing at Angela she asked. "Has Todd found anything?"

"He hasn't been able to tie the coffee-shop owner to Daniel Abbott yet."

"But we know his name now?"

Angela rolled her eyes. "We have a name, but it doesn't have any past records. It's like it only appeared about five years ago."

Nikki frowned. She looked around the room and noticed more people had arrived. Almost every computer had a technician in front of it, and each was typing frantically. Angela followed her gaze. "Everyone has been called in now. I don't think anyone figured out how serious this was at first. We all thought it was one man working alone to make Flagler look bad."

Nikki remembered Mel saying Mr. Flagler's reputation was being attacked internationally. Mel. Mel waited in Israel for her to find her. She needed to return. "I want to go back to Israel." Nikki looked at Angela. "Do you think Bowden will approve it?"

Angela touched her arm as she stood. "I can ask."

Nikki nodded. She stared at the sandwich Angela had placed in front of her. The thought of food made her stomach queasy, but she opened the bottle of water and took a sip.

Angela touched her shoulder as she sat back down beside her. She nodded toward the elevator, and Nikki looked up as Mr. Flagler walked into the room. He stopped to talk with Bowden, and together they approached the table where Nikki and Angela sat.

He sat down across from them. Nikki stared into his bloodshot eyes. He had sent Liam and Mel to Israel and now their lives could be on the line. The stress and worry Nikki felt was reflected back at her from his face. He gave her a gentle smile. "How are you doing, Agent Mitchell?"

"I've been better, sir."

Bowden introduced Angela, and he shook her hand. He glanced at the three of them. "I was hoping you ladies could give me a summary of where things stand now."

Bowden and Angela ran through the technical details and Nikki walked through all of the events of the last several days. Nikki glanced at him when she finished. "Sir, Agent Carter believed this attack wasn't directed at Flagler, but at you personally."

He nodded. "I've been exploring that possibility myself." He pulled a data stick from his pocket and passed it to Nikki. "That's all of the missions I handled personally. Starting in the beginning when I was boots on the ground for each one we accepted."

Nikki inserted the data stick into her computer and loaded it through the Flagler search engine. She began typing, and Angela leaned over her shoulder for a better view. Nikki glanced at her and then at the keyboard before quickly typing two words.

"Middle East?" Angela nodded. "Okay. It's a place to start."

Nikki frowned. "Yeah, but that's too many to read through. We need to narrow it down even more."

"Since kills aren't recorded, try sniper missions," Angela suggested.

Nikki entered the request focusing on the computer screen as they all waited for the search results. "One hundred and fifty."

Angela groaned. "That's still too many. We don't have time to read them all."

Nikki glanced at Mr. Flagler. "Sir, do you remember a mission in Tel Aviv about twenty years ago. A man and his daughter were killed."

"Twenty years ago?" He was silent for a few minutes. "I did work as a sniper back then." He frowned at her. "Do you think this is because of someone I killed? I didn't kill any kids."

Nikki entered a date range based on the newspaper article Mel had saved on her laptop. While the computer searched, she pulled up the article and turned the computer around allowing Mr. Flagler and Bowden to read it. They both looked up at her when they finished and Mr. Flagler spoke first. His face was flushed and he spoke softly. "It was me, but I didn't know his daughter was on his lap. I remember his name." He shook his head. "Hell, he was making a bomb with her sitting right there. That's so crazy."

"This was Daniel Abbott's father and little sister," Nikki said, turning the laptop back around. The search engine had retrieved five files, and Nikki opened each file until she located the one marked Tel Aviv. She read the report for the incident with Angela leaning over her shoulder. Then they turned the laptop around for Mr. Flagler and Bowden to read it as well.

Mr. Flagler nodded. "I had forgotten the details, but reading my case report brings them back. Denny Cohen was suspected of being the bomb maker behind several civilian targets. We went in to conduct surveillance but found him in the act of making a bomb. If we had had thermal imaging, I would have been able to see two heat signals. I'm sorry the little girl was killed, but her father killed and injured a lot of innocent people."

"That's it," Nikki said, looking at Angela. "So, if we assume the coffee-shop man is one of Daniel's brothers, then maybe the other brother is using the same last name, even if it's not their real names."

Angela nodded and walked over to Todd. She spoke to him for several minutes while he asked questions and then began typing. Angela returned to the table. "I'm going to check on the cell phone Josh gave us and see if the technicians have pulled anything from it."

Mr. Flagler stood. "I'm going to talk with Josh and see if he can give us any more information."

Nikki waited until she was alone with Bowden before speaking. "I assume someone is running checks on everyone who works at the Pensacola office again."

Bowden nodded.

"We know someone there was calling Daniel Abbott. And maybe that someone is the third brother." Nikki took a deep breath before looking Bowden in the eye. "I want to go back to Israel. We're getting close, and I want to be there to help in the search."

Before she could respond, a technician Nikki had not met arrived at the table. Bowden nodded her okay for the technician to speak in front of Nikki.

"Agent Russo was correct. Daniel Abbott has another residence in Tel Aviv. It's a house on the edge of town."

"Send a team to search it." Bowden said immediately. The technician nodded and hurried away. "Let's get the details and then I'll consider allowing you to return."

Nikki nodded. She knew she would return, and, for the first time in her life, it didn't matter if she had her boss's approval or not. Mel needed her and she would not let her down.

Bowden read the determination on Nikki's face and she spoke again. "Do not do anything stupid, Agent Mitchell. You're under my command now, and I'll make the decision when it's time."

Nikki nodded again, but they both knew when the time came she was going with or without permission.

"Mrs. Bowden," Todd called from his workstation.

"What did you find?" She walked toward him with Nikki on her heels.

"Coming up on the big screen now." Todd continued to type. "There's a janitor at the Pensacola office who has only been there for a little over a year."

"That time period fits," Nikki added unnecessarily.

"He has a computer science degree from the University of Jordan. The agent who did his background grilled him about being overqualified for a janitor job, and he gave a sob story about needing to send money home and no one would hire him in his field because he was from the Middle East."

"What's his name?" Nikki asked.

Todd frowned. "Well, that's the weird part. He is employed as Warren Levee, but when I track him back to Israel he comes up as Warren Levy." Todd pointed to the big screen. "See the two different spellings."

Nikki stepped closer to Todd. "Can you compare facial recognition for the coffee-shop owner with all Israeli individuals with the last name Levy?" She sat down at the workstation beside Todd. "Is it okay if I use this computer?"

Todd nodded, already absorbed in tracking her request.

Bowden stepped behind her. "What are you thinking, Agent Mitchell?"

Nikki spoke while she typed. "Angela said the coffee-shop owner had no background older than five years so we know he had a different name. Maybe Todd can find his real name." She looked at Bowden and shrugged. "I want to see what Daniel Abbott's mother's surname was before she married Denny Cohen."

"I was tracking the brothers earlier, and Abbott is the foster family name that adopted them after their parents died," Todd explained as he typed. "Oh, wait. Here's something. Akim and Warren Abbott were killed five years ago in a car accident."

Nikki took a deep breath. "So Daniel Abbott's brothers were killed and then came back to life as Akim and Warren Levy."

"They didn't bury them too deep but just enough to pass first glance," Bowden murmured.

"And we have a match." Todd displayed Akim Levy's driver's license photograph on the big screen.

"That's him," Nikki said. "That's the man from the coffee shop and the one in the van at the package pickup." She turned to Todd. "What about Warren Levy? Can we send someone to pick him up?"

Todd typed for a minute. "He hasn't shown up for work the last three days, and his cell phone is pinging in the Middle East. That would be Israel, to be exact." He continued to talk while his fingers flew across the keyboard. "He's on the move."

"Todd, are we sure we have all the residences for Daniel Abbott now?" Bowden asked.

"Yes, he has two. The apartment and a house on the edge of Tel Aviv."

"Okay. Then let's see what property the two Mr. Levys have in their names."

"On it," Todd advised without looking up.

"Yep," Nikki said excitedly, reading from the computer screen in front of her. "Pamela Levy married Denny Cohen and gave birth to three boys and one girl." She looked at Bowden. "It's only a matter of time until we have our hands on one of these three guys, and then we'll have a location to where they're being held." She stood. "I need to be there."

Bowden leaned against the computer console and stared at the ground before making eye contact with Nikki. "Against my better judgment, I'm going to let you go. Give me an hour to coordinate things. Angela will take you home to shower and pack. I'll call her with the details." She turned and walked away.

Nikki breathed a sigh of relief and looked at Todd.

He smiled. "Not many people get their way with her. You must have said something right."

Nikki nodded, afraid to speak. She didn't want to say or do anything to change Bowden's mind. In her head, she calculated the time it would take them to get back to Tel Aviv. Flying time alone would take fourteen hours. She wondered how fast the tactical team already in place would be able to coordinate. She took a deep breath. First they had to get their hands on one of the three guys to find out the location Mel was being held.

Angela returned giving Nikki a smile. "Ready?"

"Yep."

Nikki followed Angela to the elevator and they returned to the parking garage. As soon as their seat belts were secured, Angela gunned the Charger's engine and the tires squealed as she maneuvered around the tight corners getting them back out on Parker Street.

Nikki leaned her head against the back of the seat rest. "Guess I don't have to give you directions."

Angela chuckled. "I think I can find it." The silence stretched between them. "Can I come in this time?"

Nikki laughed and some of the stress released from her body. She would have enjoyed a hard workout tonight, but getting on that flight was the most important thing in her mind right now. Her body would be keyed up until she was looking at Mel again, and there wasn't anything she could do about it.

Angela turned into her driveway and Nikki dug her keys from her bag before throwing the strap over her shoulder. She unlocked the front door, leaving it open for Angela to follow. "There's bottled water in the kitchen and not much else. Help yourself to anything you can find."

Angela nodded and Nikki took the stairs two at a time. She opened her bag and dumped everything onto the floor of her bedroom. The suits would need the dry cleaners so she would have to separate things later. She stuffed clean jeans, several shirts and undergarments into the bag before stripping off everything she was wearing and tossing it into the growing pile of dirty clothes. The shower was refreshing, and she stood for a few moments letting the warm water beat down on her tired muscles. Dressed and carrying her freshly packed bag, she returned downstairs to find Angela browsing her bookshelves.

"Ready?" Nikki asked.

"Sure." Angela headed for the door. She waited until they were back in the car before relaying details to Nikki. "I have a ready bag in the trunk, so we're headed straight for the airport. A Flagler jet has been fueled and is waiting for us. With one refueling stop, we should arrive by fifteen hundred tomorrow."

"That's about what I had calculated. That's almost midnight Israeli time. Do we have any new information?"

"Daniel Abbott's house was empty. Warren's phone is on, and Todd is trying to locate him. I'm not sure why the difficulty, but it's something about a bouncing signal."

Nikki nodded.

"It looks like the other two have turned their phones off. Probably picked up burner phones. We'll get another update when we get closer. Hopefully they'll have an address by then and be preparing to make a grab."

"Yeah, hopefully," Nikki said softly before laying her head against the back of the seat.

CHAPTER THIRTY-NINE

The jet was idling on the tarmac when they arrived at the airport. Nikki followed Angela up the stairs and tried not to stare at the elegantly decorated private jet. The seats were white leather and placed here and there throughout the cabin. Angela stepped to the side and motioned for her to pick any location she wanted so Nikki chose a double seat about midway back on the left. She liked that it faced the cockpit instead of the rear or one of the sides. She tossed her bag on the seat beside her and reclined in it. Resting her head against the soft leather, she tried to settle her racing pulse. She closed her eyes to organize her thoughts. The last week had been a whirlwind.

Angela reviewed data on her laptop and left Nikki to rest. About five hours into the flight, Angela sat up straighter and the squeak of the leather chair caused Nikki to open her eyes.

"Is there something new?"

Angela nodded. "Akim has a house in Jordan and tech traced Warren's cell phone there. A two-man team has been dispatched to get a visual."

Nikki nodded. "When are they going in?"

"Before daybreak tomorrow morning. The tactical team is still waiting for eyes on the ground to confirm their presence."

"I want to be there when they go in. Can you get us to Jordan?"

"I'll work on it."

Nikki nodded again and turned her gaze to the darkness outside her window. Her head hurt as she thought about Mel and Liam being held captive for almost forty-eight hours now. She closed her eyes and said a silent prayer that they were okay. It wouldn't be long now until she would know their status. For the first time since they had boarded the plane, Nikki dozed off. She awakened as Angela secured the cabin door.

"We're refueled and ready to depart." She placed a bag on the chair beside Nikki. "Eat."

Nikki opened the bag and removed a muffin. She broke off a small piece and stuck it in her mouth before taking a drink of water. "Thanks."

Angela opened her own bag and they ate in silence. Nikki chewed each bite thoughtfully before washing it down with water. Her mouth was dry, and she couldn't taste the muffin. Halfway through, she dropped the remaining portion back inside the bag and laid it aside.

"What's bothering you?" Angela asked after watching her for several minutes.

"I don't understand why they would transport them all the way to Jordan when Daniel has a house in Tel Aviv. The risk seems too great."

"Maybe they felt the risk of keeping them in Tel Aviv was too great."

Nikki sighed. "What's their end game?"

Angela nodded. "That's been bothering me too. What were they trying to accomplish when they captured them?"

"Before Carter got shot, they were playing their surveillance really close. Maybe he was just trying to get them off his tail."

"And now that he has them?"

Nikki shook her head. "I can't think about that." Several seconds of silence stretched between them. Nikki sat up straighter. "I have to believe they're trying to escape."

"I like that thought."

Nikki rested her head against the seat again and closed her eyes. In four hours they would arrive in Tel Aviv and she would need to be focused. There was nothing she could do between now and then but mentally prepare.

* * *

Mel attempted to swallow again. Liam had poured a small amount of water into her mouth earlier when it was clear it would take him longer than he thought to release her hands from the ropes. They had shared a croissant and her mouth felt like it was filled with cotton. She longed to down the entire bottle sitting at her feet. The four croissants and two bottles of water that had been left for them wouldn't last very long. The urge to go to the bathroom had increased and lessened several times over the hours. It was increasing again and she tried to hold still so Liam could saw at the ropes. Her muscles were numb and no longer ached from the inactivity as they had in the beginning.

"Almost, Mel," Liam said hopefully. He pulled hard with each hand and she felt the play increase. He yanked again and the ropes broke, releasing her hands.

She rubbed her wrists. They didn't hurt nearly as badly as her fingers, where the blood had finally dried in her cuts. She stood. "I'm sorry, Liam, but I have to do this."

He stood, too. "I know what you're going to say and I'll dig us a hole." He used the wall to find his way into the farthest corner. When he finished, Mel followed the sound of his voice, shuffling slowly. She used the corner to help balance herself and managed to alleviate the pressure on her bladder before filling in the hole.

Shuffling back to where Liam sat, she collapsed down beside him and opened the water bottle. Taking baby sips to curb her thirst and prevent her downing the entire bottle, she alternated with small bites of a croissant. Beside her Liam worked silently on the ropes wrapped around his legs. She searched the floor until she found all the pieces of the broken flashlight. Her fingers played with each piece as she examined it. Now that their hands were free she started working on the next plan. "How are your lock-picking skills?"

"Did you find something we could use as a pick?" he asked hopefully.

"Not yet, but there has to be something in this flashlight."

Liam held up the piece he was working with. "Maybe I can break off a strip of this piece."

"We'll give it a shot when our legs are free." She rubbed her face and it tingled. "Dammit. I think they tampered with the water."

"Sorry, I forgot to mention that. My head is so fuzzy. Just sip and maybe we can avoid getting too much of it at one time."

CHAPTER FORTY

Nikki and Angela were off the plane as soon as it touched down. They entered the main terminal and cleared customs quickly before renting a car. Angela gave Nikki the address where the tactical team was preparing and Nikki pulled up directions on her iPad. As they raced through the crowded streets, it was hard to tell it was almost midnight. People of all ages lined the streets waiting for the most popular clubs to open.

"Makes New York City look lame, doesn't it?" Angela asked as they watched a raucous group of partiers pass by their car.

"Another city that never sleeps."

"I've been to other cities in Israel but never Tel Aviv. I've heard the beach is beautiful."

"It is." Nikki was glad for the idle conversation. It took her mind away from the delay in getting to their destination.

Angela accelerated through the intersection. "Much more welcoming to English-speaking tourists than I expected."

"It's definitely more westernized than most cities in the Middle East."

They drifted back into silence as the speed of traffic increased. The lights of the city dropped behind them and soon the white stone of their destination stood above them. They were cleared to access the building by an armed young man holding a clipboard.

Angela asked for Tom Sperry, and they were directed to a tall, dark-haired man in black tactical clothing. Seeing them arrive, Tom motioned them over to the table where he stood alone looking at the plans for a house.

Introductions were made and Nikki stepped up to the table. "Is this Akim's house in Jordan?"

"It is." Tom pointed to the plans. "Here's the front and this is the main road for approach. Unfortunately, there is no nearby road to access the back so we plan to bring men in on foot through the neighbors' backyards." He glanced at both of them. "I understand that you guys want to be present when we go in?"

Both women nodded.

"The tactical team had to cross the bridge before it closed two hours ago so they have already departed. I knew you guys wouldn't be here in time, so I've chartered a flight for us that will depart in about three hours. You can crash here until then. We have showers and a few cots set up."

"Any news back from the surveillance team?" Angela asked.

Tom nodded. "There are lights on inside the house, and heat sensors pick up at least two individuals moving around inside."

"We'll follow you to the airport and return our rental car."

"Sounds fine," Tom agreed. "I'll be around if you need anything before then. We should have another briefing update in about two hours." He pointed out the showers before disappearing down the hallway.

Angela looked at Nikki standing silently beside her. Her displeasure evident on her face. "What's going on, Nikki?"

"I just can't wrap my head around the distance. To move them that far takes coordination. They wouldn't have passports to clear the checkpoints, so they would have to pay someone off. That would take planning."

"Okay, then tell me what you think?"

Nikki looked at her watch. "We have over two hours before we need to be back here. Let's go check out Abbott's house."

"I checked the tactical team's logs after you mentioned that on the plane, and they didn't find anything when they cleared his house earlier today. That's why they focused on Akim's house, and besides, Warren's cell phone was tracked to Jordan."

Nikki shrugged. "It would make me feel better. You can stay here if you want."

Angela's eyes grew wide. "Bowden would kill me if I let you out of my sight."

Nikki laughed. "Let's go then."

Angela drove and Nikki directed her after downloading Abbott's address from the Flagler database. The house was dark when they arrived, and Nikki stared at it in the silence. Slowly she released the door and slid out of the seat.

"Damn it, Mitchell. Where do you think you're going?"

"You didn't think I meant we would just stare at the house for two hours, did you? I'm going in."

"No!"

"I'm not having a discussion with you about this, Angela." She closed her door and started walking toward the house.

Angela climbed out and followed her. "I *really* don't like this."

"Fine. Just be quiet."

Nikki picked the lock and pushed the door open. Taking her small mag light from her pocket, she involuntarily reached for her absent pistol. Remembering her pistol was still secured in the lockbox from their first trip to Israel, she cursed herself for not asking Angela for another weapon. She flashed her light toward Angela and was pleased to see her holding a pistol. At least one of them was armed.

They searched every room before returning to the kitchen entryway. Nikki sighed. "I was sure they would be here. Thank you for checking it with me."

"No problem." Angela walked toward the door. "Can we go now?"

"Sure." Nikki followed her onto the porch before stopping.

"What now?" Angela's unhappiness was reflected in her voice.

"Bomb shelter," Nikki said excitedly. "Doesn't every house have to have a bomb shelter?"

"Only ones built after nineteen fifty-one."

Nikki didn't hear her answer because she had already returned inside the house. The beam of her flashlight circled the room. She glanced at Angela when she stepped back inside. "Where would it be?"

"Probably access would be in one of the main rooms. Let's return to the car and I'll get the house plans. If it has one, then we'll come back in."

Nikki ignored her, flipping on the overhead light and continuing to search the room. Her pulse raced. She was close and she knew it. The room shouldn't be hidden. It would need to allow easy access for the residents in case the air-raid siren went off. Finally, her hands found a crease in the wall not readily visible to the eye. She ran her hands around it and located the latch hidden behind a full coatrack. The door pulled open and the light from the kitchen flooded the darkness.

"Carter?" Nikki said softly as she slowly descended the steps. Her flashlight moving across the dirt floor before focusing on two bodies. "Angela!"

Nikki knelt beside Mel, shining the light into her face. Blood caked the edges of her mouth and her right eye was swollen shut.

"Light," Mel moaned. "Turn the damn thing off!"

"Sorry." Nikki switched the light off and dropped it beside her before helping Mel into a sitting position.

Angela was beside her checking Liam, and Nikki could hear him groaning as she moved him. Nikki ran her hands over Mel's body checking for other injuries while she talked softly to her. Mel groaned and shifted away from Nikki's touch when her fingers found the damaged ribs. "Stop!" Mel growled.

"I'm only trying to see how badly you're hurt."

"I'm fine. Just untie my feet and let's get out of here."

"I couldn't agree more," Liam grumbled beside her.

Nikki pulled a knife from her pocket and cut the ropes holding Mel's legs before helping her to stand. She handed her knife to Angela and she cut Liam's bindings. Mel slowly took one step at a time, leaning heavily on Nikki. At the top, Angela propped Liam against the wall and cleared the kitchen before they headed to the car. Nikki helped Mel into the backseat. Her heart ached with the desire to climb in behind her, but Angela would need help with directions and Nikki needed to focus on getting them somewhere safe. Liam dropped into the backseat and Nikki pushed the door shut. She slid into the front seat as Angela started the car and they pulled away from the house.

"Where to?" Angela asked.

"Hospital?" Nikki began typing on the iPad bringing up directions.

"No!" Liam and Mel said together.

Nikki turned in her seat to look at them as Angela pulled to the curb. Their faces were pale and clearly they were dehydrated, but they had walked out on their own.

Angela picked up her phone and dialed. "Mrs. Bowden." Everyone was silent while she spoke. "We got them. Mitchell was right." She paused. "Yes. I believe that's necessary. Okay. Thanks."

She glanced at Nikki. "Back to the Sheraton."

Nikki pulled up directions and got them moving before she spoke. "Drop me at the door and I'll get us a suite. You guys can wait in the garage and I'll come get you."

"A room has already been reserved and someone is waiting for us," Angela said softly. "Just get us to the hotel."

Angela parked in the garage, and they helped Liam and Mel out. Taking the freight elevator to the nineteenth floor, Angela led the way to the first door on the left. She knocked softly and the door opened immediately. Leaving the door open for them, Wayne stepped into the hall and assisted Angela with Liam.

"Put one in each bedroom," Senator Jan Wyatt directed.

At first Nikki was surprised to see Jan, but a feeling of relief quickly washed over her. She should have known Jan would be waiting for them. Nikki didn't stop to talk, giving her a nod in greeting before following her orders.

Mel collapsed onto the bed and squinted up at Nikki. "Thanks for finding us."

Nikki gently touched her bruised jawbone and forced the tears from her eyes. "I'm sorry it wasn't sooner."

"Out. Everyone out," Jan said forcibly. "I need to do a quick check on both of them and get some fluids moving." She pulled items from her red bag as she talked. Straightening up, she pointed at the door. "Out."

Nikki hesitated, looking at Mel, who nodded. "I'm fine."

Crossing to the door, Nikki took a last glance back, and Mel said again, "I'm fine. Really."

As she closed the door Nikki heard Jan say, "You're not going to convince me of that, Melissa, so hush." She turned to find Robin holding a mug of coffee and gladly took it from her. She collapsed into a chair and leaned her head back against the cushion. "When did you guys get back?" Nikki asked, opening her eyes and looking at Robin.

"About three hours ago." She sat down across from Nikki with her own mug. "Senator Wyatt gave us the details this morning when she told us we would be returning to Tel Aviv. She was adamant that she be close enough to offer assistance should she be needed. We even swung by the hospital when we arrived in Tel Aviv so she could pick up some supplies."

"An hour or so ago, we found out they might be being held in Jordan and she freaked," Wayne said as he sat beside Robin. "We were going to be on the chartered flight with you guys in a couple of hours."

"Someone called her about ten minutes ago to tell us you had them and were on your way here," Robin finished for him. "They look pretty rough."

Nikki nodded but couldn't speak. In her mind she could see Mel's battered face, and she jumped to her feet when Jan opened the bedroom door.

She scanned the room and focused directly on Nikki. "I gave her a sedative so leave her alone." She headed for the second bedroom. "I'll do a more thorough check once I get Liam started on fluids."

Nikki waited until Jan entered the room holding her second patient and then crossed to the bedroom she had just left. Opening its door slowly, she stepped into the room and closed the door behind her.

Mel opened her non-swollen eye and patted the bed beside her. Nikki took a seat and gently caressed her hand, avoiding the cuts and rope burns. Words wouldn't come and something inside her head screamed.

"Look at me, Mitchell."

Nikki slowly raised her head.

"I'm going to be fine." Her eyelid fluttered as the drugs began to work their way through her body. She lifted her hand, but it fell back into Nikki's.

Nikki collapsed her fingers around it, resisting the urge to pull Mel's bruised body into her arms. She wanted to hold her tightly until this horrible nightmare went away. Instead, she sat silently.

The bedroom door opened. "I see you listen as well as your partner." Jan stepped into the room.

Nikki stood, Mel's hand still grasped in her own.

"Give me about ten more minutes and then you can come back in. Just to sit with her, though. No talking."

Nikki nodded, laying Mel's hand on the bed. Her eyes never leaving Mel, she backed to the door and stepped out. She didn't want to leave the room, but she knew Jan needed to ascertain if there were any life-threatening injuries. She felt no jealousy leaving Mel in Jan's hands. It was clear Jan cared deeply for Mel and would take good care of her.

* * *

She met Jan at the door of the bedroom as soon as she stepped out. Jan smiled. "Sit. I need coffee." She refilled Nikki's mug before sitting beside her with her own mug. Wayne and Robin were back outside on their security detail and Angela had gone to the desk to get them another room. Alone in the silence,

Jan appraised her. "She'll be fine. They both will." She sighed. "Mel's body is a little more bruised than Liam's, but his head took quite a thumping. I think they've both been drugged so it'll take a while for that to work through their system. Mel has several cracked ribs and a lot of bruises. I'm worried most about internal injuries, though, so I'll monitor both of them closely for the rest of the night. If everything goes well, tomorrow morning we'll put them on a plane back to the States."

"That's fast."

"I know but they need medical evaluation that I can't provide here."

"Are you traveling with us?"

"Yes, I've canceled the rest of my trip. Mel and I have been friends for over ten years." She gave Nikki a smile. "And we've never been more than friends."

"Thanks." Nikki smiled back.

"Go sit with her as long as you want, but try to get some sleep too. I'll catnap on the couch so I can keep an eye on both of them."

CHAPTER FORTY-ONE

Nikki's eyes popped open as Mel's fingers twisted in her hair. The morning sun was beginning to peek through the clouds and her neck hurt from the weird position she had slept in, but she was happy to see that Mel was awake.

Nikki sat up and grinned down at her. "How are you feeling?"

"Oh," she groaned. "Almost human."

"When Jan checked on you about an hour ago, she said your vitals were great. I expect she'll be ready to move you in the next couple of hours."

"I'm ready to be at home so I won't argue with her."

"I'm ready too."

Mel's eyes drifted closed, and Nikki pulled the hand she had cradled in hers against her cheek. For the first time since she realized Mel was being held, she thought about what this woman meant to her. No matter how many times she told herself romance wasn't going to be in her life, she couldn't stop the flutter in her chest when she looked at her. Even now, with her right eye swollen shut and her bruised jawbone, she was beautiful. Nikki kissed her damaged fingers and laid the hand back on the bed. She folded her arms beside Mel and rested her head on her forearms. She didn't think sleep would come again, but her eyes burned so she closed them for a moment.

* * *

Jan placed a hand on Nikki's shoulder. "Hey, sleeping beauty," she joked.

Nikki sat up and tilted her head back and forth to work out the kinks. She looked into Mel's clear eyes and then at Jan. "Is it time to go home?"

"It is." Jan smiled. "The hotel has agreed to loan us two wheelchairs and we'll use them to get these guys out to the cars. Everyone has been advised that we are ready to move out."

"I'll be ready in five." Nikki touched Mel's leg as she walked around the bed and grabbed her pack. She carried it into the bathroom to brush her teeth and hair. She stripped, rolling her dirty clothes into a ball and stuffing them into her bag. She pulled on clean jeans and a T-shirt over her sports bra and briefs. A shower would feel good, but she could wait until she got home. It was more important to get Mel and Liam back into the care of a US hospital.

She returned to the bedroom to find it empty. In the main room, Mel and Liam sat side by side in wheelchairs, both grumbling and complaining about how they would prefer to walk. Jan ignored them as she unhooked their IVs for transport. Nikki swung her bag over her shoulder and put her hands on the back of Mel's wheelchair. She ran her fingers through Mel's hair and gently rubbed the back of her neck.

Mel twisted her neck to look back at her. "You remember what happened the last time you rubbed my neck, right?" she whispered.

A faint blush quickly covered Nikki's face and she stilled her fingers. "I think you're safe until you heal."

"I may be, but are you?"

Nikki shook her head. "Please be still so we can get you to the plane."

Mel laughed. "Whatever you say, cupcake."

Nikki gave the chair a push to follow Jan out the door. "Let's see if we can find a stairwell to push you down."

Nikki's comment carried down the hall and Jan turned to look at her. Mel laughed again and Nikki shook her head. "What can I say? She's a troublemaker."

"Don't I know," Jan stated as she followed Robin down the hall. Wayne pushed Liam behind them and Angela brought up the rear.

When they exited the elevator into the garage, Wayne and Nikki parked the two wheelchairs to the side and asked everyone to wait. Angela tossed Nikki the car keys and she followed Wayne to the other side of the parking garage where Wayne opened the trunk to access the gear to check the vehicles. Together they cleared both vehicles and picked up the others, still waiting beside the elevators. When Mel and Liam were each tucked into the backseat of a car, Robin and Angela returned the wheelchairs and checked everyone out of their rooms. They came back with bottles of water and pastries for everyone. Exhausted from the trip to the car, Mel leaned against Nikki as soon as she settled into the backseat beside her. By the time the car was moving, her eyes were closed and Nikki could hear steady breaths as she slept.

The ride to the airport was quiet with only light traffic. Rush hour had been over for at least an hour and Nikki internally calculated the time back in Pensacola, realizing it was only a couple of hours past midnight there. She had been in Tel Aviv for barely twelve hours. By this evening, she would be back at her house and tucking Mel into her bed. She knew that was crazy, that Mel would probably have to be kept at the hospital for a couple more days. Nikki would stay with her until she was released. As far as she knew, Mel lived in Tallahassee and didn't have a place to stay in Pensacola. She touched Jan's shoulder over the seat. "Are we flying back in to Pensacola?"

Jan twisted in the seat to look at her. "Yes. It was Mr. Flagler's request. Why do you ask?"

"I was just wondering since Carter's from Tallahassee I thought maybe we were taking them there."

Jan nodded her understanding. "I think Liam is from Tennessee."

"Oh, I didn't know."

"My understanding is the internal folks usually work alone, but if they do team them up, they do it with agents from another office."

"That must be a lonely job," Nikki said softly, more to herself than anyone else in the car.

Jan nodded and turned back around in her seat. "I would think so too, but Mel seems to enjoy it."

Wayne pulled the car onto the tarmac and right to the stairs of their plane. Nikki gently woke Mel, and with help from the others, she managed to get her settled on the plane. Liam and Mel were stretched across several seats and Jan began hooking up IVs again. Nikki settled at Mel's head and she slid up until her head rested in Nikki's lap. "That okay?" she mumbled.

Nikki stroked her hair and the places her face wasn't bruised. "Of course. Go back to sleep."

After the plane took off, Jan settled into the seat beside Nikki. "I gave them both something to help them sleep. I think the flight will go easier if they aren't waking up every time we land and take off."

Nikki nodded. She was grateful to Jan for keeping her informed. It felt so unusual not to have all the details and be working whatever the mission was in her head. Right now she could only think about Mel and how she had wrecked her life. Everything had been so orderly before. She understood now why she hadn't had any real relationships. It wasn't because she didn't want one; it was because having someone else in your life took away your control. She glanced down at Mel sleeping in her lap. She could give her control, would do so willingly. She couldn't help thinking that she just might like it. They both might.

CHAPTER FORTY-TWO

The Flagler private jet landed in Pensacola early Monday evening and local paramedics boarded the plane with stretchers to carry Mel and Liam to the waiting ambulances. Jan gave directions and Nikki tried to assist and stay out of the way, whichever was needed. She followed Mel's stretcher as it exited the plane, intending to ride to the hospital in the ambulance. She would catch a taxi back to Flagler later to pick up her SUV. Waiting at the doors of the ambulance, however, was a younger and taller version of Mel. Her sister? Shoulder-length chestnut hair and deep brown eyes appraised Nikki as they approached, taking in the sight of Nikki's hand laying on Mel's arm. Before either could speak, a woman appeared from behind the doors of the ambulance and ran to the stretcher. Nikki stepped back as she approached.

"Oh, my baby," she crooned as she touched Mel's arm above her bandaged hand.

"I'm fine, Mom," Mel mumbled.

The younger version of Mel pulled their mother back from the stretcher so the paramedics could lift it inside the ambulance. The woman sobbed and clung to Jan when she approached. Jan spoke softly to both of them and they nodded before getting into a nearby car. Nikki glanced around her, not sure where to go. Mel had her family; she didn't need her hanging around after all.

"Agent Mitchell?" a male voice called to her.

She turned to see a man wearing a suit approaching her. "I'm Joey. Mrs. Bowden sent me to pick you up. You need to debrief."

Nikki glanced at the ambulance and then back at the man.

"Agent Mitchell?"

"Yes, right. I'm ready." Nikki's eyes followed the ambulance as it began to move away from them.

"Nikki?"

The soft feminine voice pulled Nikki's gaze back and she focused on Angela standing beside the man.

"Let's get this over with." Nikki began striding toward the black SUV that had been parked behind the ambulance, and Angela and Joey had to lengthen their stride to catch up with her. She climbed into the backseat, and Angela sat up front making small talk with Joey as they traveled through town. When they arrived at Parker Street, Angela led the way to a closed office with a keypad on the door. She punched in her code and then pushed the door open. Mr. Flagler and Bowden sat inside, drinking coffee and chatting while they waited. Both looked rested and much more relaxed than the last time Nikki had seen them. It was hard to believe that almost forty-eight hours had passed since she had left this office not knowing where Mel was or how they would get her back.

Angela poured them each a cup of coffee and guided Nikki to a seat across the table from their superiors.

Mr. Flagler smiled at them both. "Excellent job, ladies."

"Not exactly what we sent you to do," Bowden added, "but I can't say we are upset with the outcome."

Nikki sipped her coffee and politely answered their questions, filling in any blanks Angela left out, until they had told the entire story. She was starting to feel confined and she needed to get out of this office soon. Her emotions were bubbling to the surface, and she didn't know how much longer she would be able to hold them in. Finally, Mr. Flagler stood and Nikki took that as a sign she could ask to leave.

"I can give you a ride," Angela offered as they stepped into the hallway.

"No thanks," Nikki said as she hurried toward the exit, taking the stairs at a frantic pace. She pushed through the steel door onto the street and blindly headed toward the sounds of traffic. She walked for several blocks before she realized she wasn't sure where she was, so she flagged down a taxi to take her back to Flagler.

At the security entrance, she paid the cab and walked to her car. Tossing her bag across the seat, she slid behind the wheel. She sat for a second to process, realizing it was the first time she had been alone in over a week. Texting Barbara, she asked if she could pick up the girls tonight and received an immediate positive response. She drove straight there and opened the gate to the backyard. She didn't want to be rude, but she wasn't in the mood to chat so she avoided the front door. The girls whimpered and cried when they saw her, and she quickly herded them into the car.

She moved like a zombie around her house. Food was expected so she boiled pasta, choosing to skip the acidic tomato sauce from a jar. She tried to eat a few pieces but they seemed to catch in her throat. Her stomach roiling, she dumped the rest of the plate into the trash can before heading upstairs to the shower. Turning on only the hot water at first, she allowed the bathroom to fill with steam before stepping into the scalding water. Her body didn't feel connected to her mind and she just wanted to feel something. Her mind wandered with sleep and exhaustion while she bathed, often stopping to lean against the shower wall. Her hair still wet, she sat down on the couch and called both dogs up with her. One snuggled into each side of her and she stroked their soft fur. She might have cried if she had the energy but all she could feel now was numbness. She wanted to be with Mel, but she wasn't sure she was needed or even wanted.

CHAPTER FORTY-THREE

Nikki couldn't remember falling asleep, but when she awoke her neck ached from resting on the back of the couch. She pushed to her feet and immediately the dogs sat up too. She needed to see Mel. She needed to see her now. Her head fuzzy from sleep, she pulled on jeans and a T-shirt before sliding her bare feet into running shoes. Seeing her for a second was all she needed. She only needed to make sure she was okay. The dogs were eager to follow her even though it was still dark outside. When she started the car and saw the clock on the dash, she couldn't believe she had been asleep for almost ten hours. No wonder she was so groggy.

She parked the car at the hospital, leaving the windows down partway for the dogs. She didn't like to leave them in the car, but the early morning was cool and they were happy to be with her rather than left at the house.

She realized when she entered the hospital and saw the empty reception desk that she might not be welcome this early in the day. Rachel worked dayshift, but Nikki didn't know if she was on duty today or not, so she pulled out her cell phone and dialed her number.

"Hello," Rachel mumbled.

"Rachel. It's Nikki."

"What's wrong, Nikki?" Rachel's voice was filled with concern, and Nikki could hear the movement of her sitting up in bed.

"I'm sorry to bother you so early. I need to know the room number of a…uh…a friend. She was brought into the hospital yesterday."

"Oh. Okay." Rachel paused for a moment and Nikki could hear more rustling. "What's her name?"

"Mel…Melissa Carter."

"It will take me a few minutes and then I'll call you back."

"Thank you, Rachel." Nikki pushed the button to disconnect the call and dropped onto a plastic chair in the waiting room. She couldn't believe she hadn't thought of this before she drove to the hospital but, really, it didn't matter. She needed to see Mel, and if Rachel couldn't help she would wander the halls until she found her.

Within five minutes Rachel called her back with the room number, and Nikki jogged to the elevator. When she reached the room, she took a deep breath and tried to calm her nerves. She squared her shoulders and turned toward the door. It was time to be honest about her feelings. She needed to tell Mel how she felt before she lost her again. She placed her palm against the door and was pushing it open when her eyes made contact again with the intense stare of Mel's little sister. Nikki hesitated, surveying the rest of the room. Mel's mother was there too, sleeping in a recliner beside the bed. Nikki took a step backward.

She had what she came for. She had needed to see for herself that Mel was still okay and clearly she was. She would wait until Mel was better before she talked to her. She needed time to heal before Nikki pummeled her with feelings and emotions. She turned and fled, taking the stairs two at a time. Back in the car, she drove to the beach. The sun had come up while she was in the hospital and the glare of it reflected off the water. The dogs swam before running up and down the beach chasing the seagulls into the air. Nikki walked behind them, but the longer she walked the faster she moved until she was jogging. Even with ten hours of sleep, her body was exhausted and her eyes felt raw. She ran on autopilot until her legs began to rebel from muscle fatigue, and she turned, heading back toward the Ford.

When she was within sight of her car, she collapsed onto the beach. Bending her legs, she placed her forehead on her knees and cried. She was always the strong one, the independent one. "No, you can't stay overnight." "No, you have to leave now." "No, I don't want you." Now she felt as if she were being held captive by her emotions.

She brushed angrily at the tears on her face. She needed time away from Mel, that's all. Her life would return to normal then.

Yeah, that's all she needed: time away from the first thing in her life that had pulled at her in years. Her vision blurred again from the tears. She couldn't remember the last time that she had cried uncontrollably. Struggling to regain some control, she lifted her head and watched and listened as each wave crashed onto the shore. Mesmerized by the rhythm that wasn't a pattern, she finally felt her body relax and her pulse slow.

The dogs realized she wasn't walking anymore and returned to lay beside her. One on each side, they sandwiched her with their bodies, sharing their warmth and comfort. Nikki rested her head back down on her knees and allowed her eyes to close. They burned from the tears and the salt in the air.

* * *

"Nikki." Brad shook her shoulder.

She lifted her head and looked at him. Her mind still hazy, she focused on his face and tried to smile reassuringly.

"What are you doing, Nik?" he asked softly, stooping down in front of her.

"Stop pestering her, Brad."

Brad looked up at his wife and frowned. "I'm not pestering her. I'm concerned."

Marianne spread a blanket across Nikki's shoulders and handed her a bottle of water. She gave her husband's shoulder a pat before sitting down beside him in the sand.

Nikki thought she should offer an explanation, and she tried to form words with her dry mouth. "I went for a run."

Marianne smiled reassuringly for her to continue.

Nikki opened the bottle of water and drank half of it before speaking. "I guess I fell asleep." Finally realizing where she was, she gave a panicked look around for the dogs. Finding them frolicking in the surf, she relaxed and leaned back, resting her hands on the ground beside her.

Marianne's eyes searched her face, but she made no comment on her appearance. Nikki's face felt stiff from the dried tears, and she was thankful for the silence until her gaze focused on Brad.

Brad studied her for several seconds, but lacking Marianne's tact he couldn't stop himself from asking. "Were you crying?"

No matter the situation, Nikki was not going to have a conversation about her emotions with Brad. He had never seen her show any kind of weakness, and she wasn't about to let that start now. She stood and Brad and Marianne did as well.

Nikki could hear the struggle in Brad's voice as he took solace in stating the facts as he knew them. "I talked with Lewis. He said you found them and that they're going to be okay."

Nikki nodded.

"He said all three of the men are in custody now and that they'll stand trial for kidnapping and maybe murder." Brad's eyes searched her face.

Nikki didn't know they had been caught. She hadn't even thought about asking any questions after her debriefing. She gave a relieved sigh. "That's good news."

Brad continued to ramble, repeating what he had been told. "Apparently, they were trying to lure Mr. Flagler to Tel Aviv so they could kill him on the anniversary of their sister's death. When Mel and Liam got in their way, they thought the kidnapping would expedite their plan. Abbott claims he was about to release them." He shrugged. "He also claims that they aren't responsible for the murder of Mel's snitch in Argentina."

Marianne put her arm around Nikki's shoulder, steering her away from Brad and back toward the parking lot. "We left the boys with their grandmother so we have some time to kill." She gave Brad a warning look before hesitantly suggesting, "Why don't you drive home in her car? The dogs will be more comfortable with you."

He nodded, happy to have an opportunity to continue his talk with Nikki without his wife interrupting.

Nikki thought about protesting but decided there wasn't any need. She handed her car keys to Brad and opened the rear door for the dogs before sliding into the passenger seat. She downed the remaining water and tossed the bottle onto the floorboard of her car.

Brad wasted no time once they were seated inside the car. "What's going on, Nik?"

"It was a bit of a roller-coaster ride and I'm trying to regroup from it all." She glanced at him. "I'm okay."

"What happened over there?"

"Angela and I were briefed by the team leader, but it didn't seem right to me."

Brad spared her a quick frown before returning his attention back to the road.

"How much do you know?" she asked him.

"I know we had a rogue janitor working at Flagler who was making phone calls from all over the building, even in secure areas."

"Right, that was Warren Levy. The third brother was the coffee-shop owner, Akim Levy."

"Oh, I remember him. It's weird how we were in there so many times, and now we find out he was involved."

"Really involved. We believe he drugged Mel and Liam."

"No way!" Brad exclaimed. "I wondered how they had captured them."

Nikki rubbed her face, finally waking up enough to clear the crusted tear streaks from her cheeks. "Anyway, the tactical team had tracked Warren's cell phone to Akim's house in Jordan, and after searching Daniel's apartment and house in Tel Aviv, they were adamant that's where they were being held." Nikki sighed as she remembered the uneasy feeling she had when she thought about Mel being taken to Jordan. "Transporting them all the way to Jordan seemed really risky to me with the checkpoints they would have to make it through."

"I would have agreed with you. It would be much easier to keep them in Tel Aviv."

"So I convinced Angela, my chaperone, to check out Abbott's house again. That location simply made more sense to me. After we had searched with no luck, it hit me that every house had to have a shelter so we started looking for access."

"That's really awesome, Nik. I'm so glad you guys found them but," he paused for a moment before continuing, "they were beaten?"

Nikki thought about Mel's battered face, and her stomach clenched again. "Yeah." Nikki was thankful they had arrived at her house and she didn't have to say anymore.

By the time they unloaded the dogs and got into the house, Marianne had arrived with breakfast. They unpacked the eggs, bacon and biscuits while Nikki pulled plates from the cabinet. Without thinking, she filled her plate, but when she sat down to eat her stomach churned. She took a couple of small bites of scrambled eggs before sitting back from the table. She met Marianne's eyes and received a smile. She smiled back, appreciative of their kind gesture. Marianne had never tried to intrude in anything she and Brad did and she never hinted at any kind of jealousy. Nikki knew teams that had trouble with their closeness and she was thankful for Marianne's attitude.

Nikki studied her plate before looking up to find Marianne still watching her. She smiled but narrowed her eyes preparing for the flurry questions.

"So tell me about this woman?" Marianne said with a grin.

Brad laughed. "I thought we weren't grilling her."

"We brought her home and fed her. Now she can tell us everything." She gave Nikki an evil smile.

Nikki shrugged. "Brad can tell you about her."

"Oh, he gave me his version already. Now I want yours."

"Yeah, she's hot," Brad injected.

Nikki threw her napkin across the table at Brad.

"Well, she is," he defended himself.

Nikki shrugged. "I can't argue with that."

The silence stretched between them as Marianne tried to read both of their faces. Finally, she spoke softly. "She's hurt? Brad says they're going to be okay, right?"

"Right." Nikki did her best to block the immediate reflex her body felt each time she remembered Mel's discolored face. "Dehydrated and a lot of bruising, but nothing that will be permanent."

"Except for the emotional trauma," Marianne said.

Nikki stared at the table as the silence stretched between them again.

Marianne continued. "But you guys hooked up, right? So where do you stand now?"

Nikki shrugged. This was the one question she was afraid to ask herself and she wasn't sure how to answer it.

"Yeah, so why aren't you at the hospital?" Brad asked.

"Her mother and sister are with her," Nikki said as if that explained her absence.

"Okay." Brad enunciated each syllable slowly.

Nikki shrugged. "They didn't need me hanging around too." She hoped she didn't sound as needy to them as she did to herself.

"You like her, right?" Brad asked, getting right to the point.

"I like her." Nikki smiled. It felt good to admit it. She did like her. She liked her a lot.

"Well, that's great!" Brad slapped her shoulder. "Let's head over there and check on them then."

Nikki nodded. She didn't want to admit it but she liked that idea. She could check on them, see Mel, and it wouldn't be awkward because Brad would be with her.

"If it's okay with you, Nikki, I'll hang out here with the dogs until you guys return," Marianne asked.

CHAPTER FORTY-FOUR

Nikki climbed into the passenger side of Brad's car and buckled her seat belt. Her hair was still wet from the shower that Marianne had insisted she take, but she felt relaxed and more in control. Comforted by Brad's presence, she leaned her head against the back of the seat and closed her eyes. She could feel Brad's eyes on her occasionally but was thankful for his silence. They walked side by side across the parking lot and into the hospital. Brad remained silent, with only a questioning raise of his eyebrows as they passed the reception desk without asking for directions. Nikki exited the elevator and stopped outside the door, glancing into the room through the small window. Mel was asleep, but her sister remained vigilant at the foot of her bed. Nikki stepped back to allow Brad to enter first. Before he could open the door, it burst open.

"Wait!" Mel's sister said as she pulled open the door and collided with Brad. "Oomph."

"Sorry." Brad placed a hand on her arm as they both righted themselves.

"Yeah, sorry." Her gaze focused on Nikki. "I thought you were leaving again and I wanted to catch you. You're Nikki, right?"

Nikki took a deep breath before stepping forward and offering her hand. "Nikki Mitchell." She nodded at Brad. "My partner, Brad Morton."

"Shea Carter." She shook their hands before her focus returned to Nikki. "She's been asking for you."

Nikki couldn't stop the smile that spread across her face, and her breath caught as Mel called from inside the room.

"Get in here, Mitchell."

Nikki pushed past Shea and crossed the room in two strides. Her gaze focused on the bruised face before raking down the body covered by the light sheet. She couldn't see any signs of other physical injury, and her eyes returned to her face, meeting Mel's stare.

"Your face is a beautiful kaleidoscope of colors, Agent Carter." Brad stepped to the other side of the bed and looked down at Mel.

Mel grinned up at him. "You say the sweetest things, Agent Morton."

Shea handed her sister a plastic cup of water and then took a seat in the corner, leaving the agents to talk.

"Have you been debriefed?" Brad asked.

Mel shook her head. "I thought maybe that's what you guys were here for."

"Nope, strictly a social call." He smiled at Nikki. "But since we're here, I could call in and see if we can take care of that for you."

Mel nodded at him before returning her gaze to Nikki. She nodded at the chair on her right side and Nikki moved around the bed. Brad squeezed her arm as they passed and he headed for the door.

"I'll step outside to call in. Be right back."

* * *

Nikki pulled the chair next to the bed and sat down with her elbows resting beside Mel.

"Thanks for coming," Mel said, placing her hand on top of Nikki's.

"I checked on you earlier this morning," Nikki said, clearly struggling for control.

"I'm okay. Really," Mel said, trying to reassure her.

Nikki nodded, unable to find the words she wanted to say.

Mel took a deep breath as she wound her fingers through Nikki's. "I missed you."

Nikki nodded again as the welling tears started to fall. Mel pulled her hand from Nikki's and cradled her face. Using her thumb, she stroked the tears away. "I tried not to think about you when we were locked up. I hoped you weren't even aware that we were missing."

Nikki's eyes widened. "I knew something was wrong before we even boarded the plane. You said you'd call when you were clear."

"And I would have."

Nikki leaned her face into Mel's hand. "That's why I had to get back to Israel and find you."

"Thanks for that, by the way."

"I wasn't ready to let you go yet." Nikki grasped Mel's hand with both of hers and squeezed. "Your boss wasn't real keen on me helping with the search."

Mel raised her eyebrows and took a sip of water, meeting her sister's eyes for the first time. She could tell Shea was surprised at her show of emotion but she didn't care. If she had her way Nikki would be around for a long time and Mel wasn't about to let her reputation keep her from letting Nikki know how much she cared.

Brad stepped back into the room. "Mrs. Bowden is coming to debrief you and Liam. She should be here any minute."

Nikki stood and joined Brad, her eyes never leaving Mel's. "We should leave then."

"You'll come back, right? I'm going to be ready to leave by noon."

Nikki glanced at Shea.

"I'll be leaving within the hour," she said. "I have to get back to Tallahassee."

Looking around the room, Nikki realized for the first time that Mel's mother wasn't there. "And where's your mom?"

"She left this morning." Shea rolled her eyes. "She had a meeting this afternoon that she couldn't miss."

Mel shrugged. "So, can I get a ride?"

"Yes, I'll come back with my car after we visit Liam." Nikki smiled broadly.

"Later, Agent Carter," Brad said as he pushed Nikki out the door. He glanced back from the door. "I'm really glad you're okay."

Mel was still smiling as the door closed behind them.

"That's quite a catch, big sister." Shea leaned back in her chair, stretching her long legs out in front of her. "You know what you're doing, I hope?"

Mel narrowed her eyes. "I know exactly what I'm doing."

"Are you in love with her? She's certainly in love with you."

Mel rubbed her face before looking back at Shea. "Yes, I think I am."

"Wow. Big, tough Agent Carter is softening. Are we about to share our emotions, sis?"

Mel pulled the pillow from behind her head and threw it at Shea. Shea stood and was preparing to whip it back at her, when the door opened and a woman in a dark suit strode into the room.

Mel pushed the button to raise her bed until she was in a sitting position. "Mrs. Bowden, meet my little sister, Shea."

Bowden glanced at the pillow in Shea's hand and smiled before reaching her hand out to shake. "Nice to see Agent Carter's spirit is holding up."

Shea placed the pillow behind Mel's head and fluffed it before kissing her cheek. "I'll call you for details later," she whispered into her cheek. Grabbing her bag, she headed for the door. "Take care of yourself, sis."

"Thanks for coming, Shea. Drive carefully." She turned to Bowden. "Let's get started. I want to get out of here."

CHAPTER FORTY-FIVE

Three days later

"Stop."

"What?"

"Do not come in here if you plan on fluffing my pillow, checking my bandages or doing anything else to make me more comfortable."

Nikki stood in the doorway, watching Mel make her demands. She loved the look of Mel reclined in her favorite chair with both dogs on the floor beside her. Her hair was still damp from a recent shower and one leg stuck out from under the blanket covering her. The bruises on her face were starting to turn a healing color of yellow and she didn't moan every time she shifted in the chair. Mel had done nothing but sleep and eat for three days, and Nikki had done nothing but watch her. She wanted to talk, to hold her and to make love to her, but she knew they both needed time to recover.

"What if I'm only here to see if you need anything?"

"Nothing has changed in the ten minutes since you were last in here. I'm fine. I have a blanket, a drink, a snack and the television remote. What more could a girl want?"

Nikki gave her a devilish smile. "Ask me that in a couple more days and I'll have an answer for you."

Mel stood, dropping the blanket and the remote to the floor. "Why wait?"

Nikki took a step backward. "No, no, no." She put both hands up in front of her. "No. You need to heal."

"Are you kidding me? That's why you have been keeping your distance? I'm not some fragile china doll." She grasped Nikki's hand, pulling her toward the guest bedroom.

"Mel, wait." Nikki pulled back on her arm, stopping their movement. "I don't think this is a good idea. You're still hurt."

Mel turned to face her and narrowed her eyes. "I have slept in the guest bedroom and refrained from touching you for the last three days because I thought you needed time." She took a step closer. "Only to find out it was because you thought I was too injured to make love to you." She took a step closer and pushed Nikki's back against the wall.

Nikki shivered as Mel placed a hand on either side of her head and pressed the full length of her body into her. Mel's voice was soft and she moved her lips within inches of Nikki's ear. "I want you." She placed a lingering kiss directly below Nikki's ear. "Now." Her lips worked their way down Nikki's neck. "Cupcake."

"Don't call me…"

Nikki's words faded as Mel's mouth covered hers, deepening her kiss until their tongues came together. Nikki felt a gap between them as Mel's hands came off the wall and cupped each one of her breasts beneath her T-shirt. Her body responded immediately to the caress as the fabric slid over them. She wanted Mel naked and in her bed. She pushed off the wall and spun them toward the stairs, gently running her hand across Mel's stomach, sensitive to her bruised ribs.

"Bedroom, cupcake?" Nikki asked into Mel's ear.

Mel pulled her head back so she could look at Nikki. "Hey, cupcake." She frowned. "That's my line."

Nikki kissed her hard, deepening the kiss and leaving Mel gasping for air when she pulled away. "Bedroom, cupcake?" Nikki asked again.

Opening her eyes, Mel captured her gaze. "Oh, yeah."

Bella Books, Inc.

Women. Books. Even Better Together.

P.O. Box 10543
Tallahassee, FL 32302

Phone: 800-729-4992
www.bellabooks.com